# In the Heir

# ALSO BY RUTH CARDELLO

## LONE STAR BURN

*Taken, Not Spurred*

*Tycoon Takedown*

*Taken Home*

*Taking Charge*

## THE LEGACY COLLECTION

*Maid for the Billionaire*

*For Love or Legacy*

*Bedding the Billionaire*

*Saving the Sheikh*

*Rise of the Billionaire*

*Breaching the Billionaire: Alethea's Redemption*

*Recipe for Love* (Holiday Novella)

*A Corisi Christmas* (Holiday Novella)

## THE ANDRADES

*Come Away with Me*

*Home to Me*

*Maximum Risk*

*Somewhere Along the Way*

*Loving Gigi*

# THE BARRINGTONS BILLIONAIRE SERIES

*Always Mine*

*Stolen Kisses*

*Trade It All*

*Let It Burn*

# TRILLIONAIRES

*Taken by a Trillionaire*

# TEMPTATION SERIES

*Twelve Days of Temptation*

*Be My Temptation*

# *In the* Heir

## RUTH CARDELLO

Montlake
Romance

Published by Montlake Romance, Seattle

www.apub.com

Amazon, the Amazon logo, and Montlake Romance are trademarks of Amazon.com, Inc., or its affiliates.

ISBN-13: 9781503943018
ISBN-10: 1503943011

Cover design by Eileen Carey

Printed in the United States of America

*This book is dedicated to my nephew, Joe, and his fabulous children: Judy and Jack. At the end of the day, family is what matters most. I am grateful to have been blessed with you in my life. For the good times, the tough times, the memorable vacations, and the lazy days by the pool—I thank you. —Aunt Ruthie*

# *Westerly*

## *Family Tree*

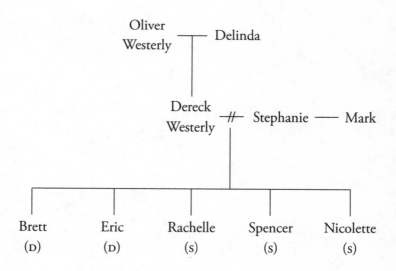

Oliver Westerly ─┬─ Delinda

Dereck Westerly ─╫─ Stephanie ─── Mark

| Brett | Eric | Rachelle | Spencer | Nicolette |
|---|---|---|---|---|
| (D) | (D) | (S) | (S) | (S) |

(D): stays with Dereck after the divorce

(S): stays with Stephanie after the divorce

# Prologue

Delinda Westerly steadied herself by gripping the back of an eighteenth-century Chippendale chair in her sunroom. Her pristine terraced gardens had become a playground for a herd of children currently racing about with the antique stone chess pieces her husband had added to the grassy area above the garden.

"There you are," said Alessandro Andrade from the doorway behind her.

Delinda turned slowly to face him. "Yes, here I am."

She hadn't meant to reveal her disappointment in those few words.

With a concerned expression on his face, Alessandro walked toward her, but stopped when he saw the children lining up the chess pieces on the garden wall. He knocked on a glass pane, though none of the children seemed to hear.

"Let them be," Delinda commanded softly. "Oliver had those pieces made for Dereck when he was ten. He would love to see them still being played with." She smiled sadly. "Only one of them is broken, and I believe it was from the day you and your brothers were using the pawns as lawn darts."

Alessandro chuckled. "I'll confess my guilt now, since I'm reasonably certain the statute of limitations is less than fifty years."

"Fifty years, it seems impossible for time to have flown by that quickly. It's been over thirty since I lost Oliver, but somehow it still feels like yesterday."

Alessandro placed his hand on hers. "He was a good man."

With a simple nod, Delinda agreed and sighed.

Alessandro searched her face. "Are you tired, Dee? I shouldn't have brought everyone today. It's too much, isn't it?"

Clasping her hands in front of her, Delinda said, "I'm not on death's doorstep. Not yet, anyway. Although sometimes I wonder why I'm the one who is still here."

"Don't even think such a thing. Every moment we have is a gift. You are a gift—to all of us."

Delinda pressed her lips together briefly before saying, "That's kind of you to say. I know your mother asked you to watch over me and you have. I still miss her. She was a beautiful woman with a big heart. And her laugh—you couldn't help but laugh along when you heard it. I always envied her ability to be so free, so openly loving. She taught you and your brothers to be the same. When I see her great-grandchildren running through my garden, I feel her smiling."

Alessandro cleared his throat and, with emotion, said, "I'm here because you're family."

"You've always been generous with that term, but my *family* couldn't be bothered with something as insignificant as my eightieth birthday." She stopped and brought a shaking hand to her white curls. "I'm sorry, Alessandro. You don't know what a comfort it's been to have you and Victor come by today."

"Where is Dereck?" Alessandro asked harshly.

Delinda waved a hand in the air dismissively. "He said he would be here. I'm sure he forgot. He'll apologize tomorrow."

"Did you invite your grandchildren?"

"Brett had an important meeting he couldn't miss. He sent flowers. Or his secretary did. Eric is in Europe filming his next movie."

She blinked back a sudden wave of emotion. "I sent an invitation to the others, but Stephanie poisoned them against me long ago. I didn't expect them to come." She walked to the windows that overlooked the garden where the children were playing. "There was a time when my grandchildren were the ones making a mess of my gardens. How did I lose them? How did I lose *all* of them?"

Alessandro came to her side. He sounded as if he were about to say something, then stopped. He cleared his throat again. "Did you invite Stephanie?"

"No," Delinda said curtly. "If I never see that woman again, it will be too soon."

"Twenty years, Dee. They've been divorced for twenty years. It's time for you to—"

"When she left my son, it nearly destroyed him. I knew from the moment I met her that she was trouble, but Dereck wouldn't listen to me. If he had—"

"You wouldn't have Brett, Eric, Rachelle, Spencer, or Nicolette."

Spinning angrily toward Alessandro, Delinda said, "I don't have them. Don't you see? She took them away from me. Turned them against me."

"I don't believe that."

"They're not here, are they? Not one of them."

Alessandro's tone was gentle yet firm as he said, "I remember my mother saying if you want a rose garden, don't plant weeds."

Delinda had wanted confirmation that the state her life was in was not of her making. "I don't know if I like what you're suggesting."

Alessandro led Delinda to sit in one of the chairs before taking a seat across from her. "You've never kept your feelings about your son's wife a secret."

"Ex-wife."

With a sigh, Alessandro continued, "She's the mother of your grandchildren. They love her. If you want them in your life, you need to let go of the past."

"You don't know what she did."

"I don't care, Dee. That's the point. People make mistakes. Whatever happened between Dereck and Stephanie was their business, and it happened long enough ago that you can't continue using that as an excuse for why you don't have a relationship with your grandchildren."

"So this is my fault?" Delinda asked with a gasp.

Alessandro raised and lowered a shoulder unapologetically. "You're planting weeds, Dee. Nothing will change while you do."

Delinda slumped a little. "Weeds? You make it sound easy. I wouldn't know where to start." She shook her head sadly for a moment before remembering something. "You reunited with your brother's children. How did you do it?"

Slapping a hand on his knee, Alessandro smiled. "Maddy claims responsibility for that." He shrugged again. "I didn't approve of her meddling, but it worked, so who am I to argue with her methods?"

Despite how bleak Delinda felt, she chuckled at the thought of Alessandro's precocious daughter, Maddy. The girl had a spirited and mischievous nature. With a smile, she asked, "What did your daughter do?"

"She and her friends played matchmaker with each of my brother's children. Her theory was that love heals all wounds."

"And it worked?" Delinda leaned forward. "Could it with my family?"

"I don't know," Alessandro said hesitantly.

With a shake of her head, Delinda sighed. "Of course it couldn't. How ridiculous to even entertain the idea. Sorry. My eighty-year-old brain must be getting feeble." She hugged her arms around herself. "My family is shattered, Alessandro. It's not just their relationship with me that's broken. Brett hides in his office. Eric hides overseas. Neither is close to his younger siblings anymore. When Stephanie turned her back on our money, she turned her back on half of her children and split the family. Even if they never come back to me, I pray they find each other."

A knock on the already-open door announced the arrival of Alessandro's brother, Victor. With an easy smile, he asked, "Is the birthday girl ready for cake? I'm asking because the children are planning a coup if they don't get some soon."

Alessandro beckoned Victor to join them. "You're just in time. Delinda needs our help."

Instantly serious, Victor took a seat beside Alessandro and studied Delinda. "Is everything all right?"

Before she had a chance to answer, Alessandro said, "How would you rate your matchmaking skills?" He briefly outlined what they'd discussed. "Do you think we could do this without Maddy?"

With a confident shrug, Victor said, "I'm Italian. Who knows more about love?"

Delinda sat straighter. "Alessandro, do you really think my grandchildren marrying could heal my family?"

Alessandro leaned forward and took her hand in his. "We'll give it a try, but there is something you must do first."

"Anything," Delinda promised.

"You must forgive Stephanie and move forward."

After a pause, Delinda asked with a pained smile, "You couldn't ask for something more simple, like a kidney?"

# Chapter One

"No matter what he says, remember he's no better than we are."

Alisha Coventry looked across the limo at Spencer Westerly, her best friend's younger brother, and her heart broke for him. He sounded nervous even though she knew he'd hate that it showed. The Spencer she'd grown up with had reigned over their high school. Captain of the football team. Top of his class. Confidence personified . . . until a week ago.

Alisha hated seeing him so unsure of himself. With his thick head of blond hair, serious brown eyes, and tall, athletic build, he'd never been short of female admirers. He should have been conceited, but his mother had raised him better than that. He was a good man, and shouldn't feel as though his accomplishments were somehow *less* than other family members'.

His start-up company, WorkChat, might one day make him a household name. All it needed was an additional infusion of capital to reach its potential.

Which was why Alisha had agreed to marry him. That, and she'd learned how important it was to Spencer's pride that he succeed in business; if she could help that by ensuring the injection of cash, all the better. She reached out and gave his hand a supportive squeeze.

"You're damn right he's not. Your brother was given everything. So his name is on a skyscraper, so what? That doesn't mean he accomplished anything. You're building your company from nothing. Don't let him intimidate you."

"That's his goal, you know. It's why Brett sent the limo and wanted to meet in Boston. He doesn't want me to forget how important he is or why he was the one our father handed the company to." Spencer raised their linked hands and turned them so the diamond on her left finger was before them. "Now that we're here, I feel bad about dragging you into this. Are you sure you're up to pretending this is real? It sounded like a good idea when Rachelle suggested it, but I'll admit I didn't think about how it would be for you when I agreed."

"Don't worry about me. The whole idea of mandating marriage is archaic, and holding your inheritance in front of you like a carrot bothers me. It's manipulative. And wrong. I don't mind lying at all in the face of that."

Spencer raised an eyebrow. "And your friends?"

Alisha shrugged. "They didn't ask too many questions. I'm twenty-eight and you're gorgeous. And before you ask, I didn't lie to them. I simply didn't tell them the whole truth. Six months from now no one will even be shocked when we divorce. Marriages don't last anymore."

The limo pulled up in front of a tall office building in the financial district of Boston. "That's depressing, but if our families are any indication, it's accurate."

"Exactly."

"I want to tell my grandmother I don't need her money, but it would make a difference to how quickly I can get WorkChat off the ground. You should take something for helping me. At least let me pay your college loans."

"I didn't agree to marry you for the money," Alisha said softly.

"Why *did* you agree?" he asked, watching her expression.

Alisha considered his question. She'd survived her childhood and found happiness by living in the present instead of looking back. Although she still missed her mother, losing her to a stroke had actually been a relief, because she could now cut her father out of her life. Completely.

For reasons Alisha had never understood, her mother had taken her father back time and time again. Her mother would conveniently forget he had a temper when he drank, and that he'd unleashed it more than once on Alisha and her mother. She'd let him back into their lives long enough for him to go through whatever money they'd saved. Even then it would take an escalation of violence that required police intervention for her mother to throw him out again. Alisha had learned early to hide her bruises and lie to social workers. She understood what it meant to feel powerless, to believe she didn't deserve better.

No one would ever make her feel powerless again.

*And I'll never sit back and watch while someone else is made to feel that way.* "Isn't that what friends do? Help when they're needed?" she answered.

He looked concerned. "I shouldn't let you do this for me. Brett really is an asshole. He's a carbon copy of my father. Plus, if you survive today, we still have to present you to my grandmother. Did I mention that she asked us to her home for lunch on Sunday? The invitation included my mother. If that's not a recipe for disaster, I don't know what is."

Alisha tightened her hand on Spencer's. Family should be a person's strength, but sadly, that was no more the case with him than it had been for her. None of that scared her, though. A familiar fear nipped at her heels, but she refused to be afraid anymore.

*If my father came after me today, he'd have a fight on his hands.*
*Come for me and you'd better kill me.*
*If you don't, when I get up, and I will get up, I'm coming for you.*

Alisha let out a long breath. Thoughts like that were why she focused on the present and what she had to be grateful for. Spencer's home had been a peaceful one. His mother hadn't believed in raising her voice and his stepfather could have won an award for the gentlest man on the planet. Their home had made sense, and that was a big part of why Alisha had spent so much time there. Rachelle, Spencer, and Nicolette felt like her siblings. In her heart, they were, and she'd do anything for them. To lighten the mood, Alisha gave Spencer a shoulder check. "Don't worry. I can take care of myself. Your overblown ego of a brother doesn't intimidate me."

"Because you've never met him."

"Stop it. You're not going to make me nervous. There's only one thing that scares me, and that's the first day of school each year. Separating twenty-five children from their parents, sometimes for the first time in their lives, scares the hell out of me. I have one chance to make a good impression on someone who may be clinging to my leg and wiping snot on the hem of my skirt while screaming for his or her mother. That's when I pray for strength and guidance. This? It's a piece of cake." Just as she hoped, her words brought a smile to Spencer's face.

He slid out of the car and held a hand for Alisha to take. "Then come on, future Mrs. Westerly. Let's go face the dragon."


"Stop there." Brett slammed a hand down on his desk as his temper flared in response to an unwelcome announcement from Dennis Lockhart, the European market director for Westerly Corp. "We had an agreement. They will hold up their end."

Dennis said, "Daten Jetzt is claiming a change in European Union policies negates our current contract."

"We need to stay on the inside track in Germany or that market will go to shit."

"I wish I had better news for you, but we've hit a wall."

Brett swore. Dennis wasn't one to give up, which meant the situation was serious. "I'll look into it and call you back." After hanging up, Brett stood, ran his hand through his thick black hair in frustration, and shrugged off his dark-gray Kiton suit jacket.

Failure wasn't an option. It never had been.

Westerlys don't lose.

He impatiently made calls to everyone from the German minister for economics and technology to the German ambassador to the United States. He called in favors, threatened, and pushed through every roadblock until he had both the information and the ammunition needed. Then he called the CEO in question and laid out exactly what his company would lose if it didn't honor the initial deal. Within minutes he had confirmation that all would go as originally planned.

Satisfied, Brett hung up and flexed. *That, Dennis, is how to win.*

"Mr. Westerly?" his secretary's impeccably calm voice floated through the intercom. Gina Carlise was computer-like perfection in human form. If the woman had a life outside the office, Brett didn't know about it, and that was how he preferred it.

"Gina."

"Your brother is here."

"Send him in."

"He's not alone."

Brett frowned. He didn't like surprises, and the past week had been full of them. "Send *them* in." If he'd realized that missing his grandmother's birthday party would upset her the way it did, he would have gone. Of all his family members, he was the closest to his grandmother.

His interaction with the rest of his family was primarily special-occasion texts and e-mail updates. There wasn't time to get together beyond that, not if one wanted to achieve his level of success. He'd long ago given up trying to explain that to his siblings. They'd embraced the middle-class lifestyle his mother had dragged her youngest three children down to. As far as he could see, they were happy to settle for scraping by. They refused to accept money from their father, and every attempt Brett made to help them had been perceived as an insult.

Which hadn't stopped Brett from smoothing the way for them when he could. As his father had done, Brett made sure the family was taken care of even if it meant doing so behind the scenes. If they applied for a scholarship, they got it. A loan? The bank approved them. *Not that they knew that.* They'd never understood why Brett had chosen to live with his father rather than with his mother when she left the family home. His only regret? Not being able to watch over his younger siblings. They had taken it as a sign that he didn't care. Neither Rachelle, Spencer, nor Nicolette knew he employed people whose only job was to make sure his family got what they needed without ever knowing it was from him. It was better that way.

However, a week ago, his grandmother's lawyer had delivered her insane offer to dole out inheritances early to any of her grandchildren who married a person of her approval, *and* invited her, along with the rest of their siblings, to the wedding. Even as he'd read the ultimatum that if they were not married at the time of her death, their inheritance would be donated to a designated list of charities, he'd dismissed it as ridiculous. His lawyers were already looking into the legality of such a stipulation. It would never hold up in court. He hadn't been concerned until he'd heard that Spencer had gotten engaged, an impulsive act that necessitated direct intervention.

The door of his office opened, and Spencer walked in, dressed in a polo shirt and jeans with an equally casually dressed blonde on his arm. Brett sensed hesitation in his brother's entrance and sighed impatiently. "Come in, Spencer."

The woman at his side appeared to give his brother a nudge forward. She was pretty in a wholesome, milk-commercial kind of way, and full-figured. He wasn't surprised to see she wore little makeup. Definitely his brother's style.

*So that's Alisha Coventry.* He'd heard her name over the years and recognized her from photos with his sister. As his brother's conveniently announced fiancée, she wouldn't want to hear anything he was about to say. "We need to talk, Spencer. Gina, why don't you take my brother's friend to get some coffee in the café?"

Spencer straightened to his full height and pulled the blonde closer to his side. "That's not necessary. Whatever you have to say to me, you can say in front of Alisha."

Brett looked past his brother to his secretary. "Gina."

His secretary stepped forward and addressed his brother's security blanket. "I'd love to show you the café if you'd like to join me."

The blonde smiled politely at his secretary, then turned steely blue eyes to Brett. "Thank you, but I'd prefer to stay here."

There was a quiet confidence in her voice that had Brett looking her over again. She wore her hair in a wild, angelic style, but she returned his gaze without blinking. His brother could do worse than to choose a woman with a spine. "This is a family matter."

Spencer glanced down at Alisha, then looked back at Brett and said, "Alisha is family, or she will be very soon. We're getting married."

"That's what we need to discuss."

Gina excused herself discreetly and closed the door behind her as she left.

Alisha gave Spencer's arm a supportive squeeze. Not just any angel, a guardian one at that. Brett felt an unwelcome flash of attraction to her. He shook his head. She lacked the sophistication of the women he generally went for.

*And she's Spencer's.*

Spencer squared his shoulders. "Like I said, there's nothing you could say to me that you can't say in front of Alisha."

With a growl of frustration, Brett said, "Does she know about the clause?"

Alisha's chin rose proudly. "Of course I do."

Brett admired her spunk, but focused on what was important. He met his youngest brother's eyes. "You don't have to do this. I already have lawyers looking into our grandmother's mental competence."

Spencer shook his head in disgust. "You're serious? That's low, even for you."

A flush warmed Brett's cheeks as his temper rose. "She's obviously not in her right mind, and you're a fool if you marry someone just because she said you should."

Alisha's eyes widened. "Wow, you're exactly the way Spencer described you."

Spencer shook his head at her. Brett didn't like the message he witnessed them exchange. They were aligned against him, even though his brother said, "Don't."

The warm smile she gave Spencer sent a stabbing dark feeling through Brett that he wasn't sure how to interpret. When Alisha's eyes met his again, Brett liked the cold anger he saw in them even less. "I'm sorry. That was *rude* of me." Her stress of the word *rude* sounded like an accusation of its own.

Spencer's arm went around her waist. "If that's all you have to say, Brett, you've wasted your time and mine. Alisha and I are getting married. I don't need your help."

Brett sighed loudly. "We'll see what you say a week from now when Grandmother retracts the offer. Just don't do anything hasty." He ran a hand through his hair.

"Like elope?" Spencer asked as if he were considering it a dare he might accept. He looked down at his fiancée. "What do you say, Alisha? Vegas?"

Alisha shrugged. "Sure."

"Don't be an idiot. You don't have to do this."

Stepping away from Alisha, Spencer went nose to nose with Brett. "No, what I don't have to do is listen to anything else you have to say.

I have to invite you to the wedding, but you don't have to come." He turned, led Alisha out of the room, and slammed the door behind them.

Brett stood next to his desk, trying to shake off the storm of emotion raging within him. How did every conversation with Spencer end in a standoff?

His office door flew open as Alisha burst back through. With an audacity that took him completely off guard, she poked a finger into his chest and said, "You should be ashamed of yourself. You couldn't say one nice thing to your brother? If there is a fool in this room, it's you. Spencer is one hundred times the man you are, but you're too full of yourself to see it. Are you really trying to prove your grandmother is incompetent? What kind of monster are you?"

Unwelcome desire flooded through him. He caught her hand in his. "You know nothing about me."

There was a flash of something that looked a hell of a lot like passion in her eyes before she looked away. She tugged her hand free. "Don't ever touch me."

"Then keep your pretty little hands to yourself," he said gruffly.

"Alisha," Spencer said from the doorway. He rushed to her side. "I thought you were going to the bathroom."

She glared up at Brett again. "I was, but I couldn't help myself. I'm done now."

Her passionate defense of his brother was hotter than hell. Brett's life was full of women who played by his rules. In general, they were tediously predictable. Alisha certainly wasn't that.

Brett wondered what else she did in the heat of the moment. He stepped away from her and fought his automatic response to her. Noticing the sad expression on Spencer's face was enough to kill his boner. *What the hell am I thinking?*

He watched his brother lead Alisha out of his office for the second time and fought the urge to call her back. *Shit.*

Her words rang in his head: *"What kind of monster are you?"*

*Apparently, the kind who wants to fuck my brother's fiancée.*

Brett let out the breath he'd been holding in without realizing it. He wasn't an impulsive man when it came to women. He certainly wasn't the type that would ever consider anyone who belonged to someone else.

Still, he couldn't get the image of her charging up to him out of his head. There had been a fire in her eyes that he'd found exciting despite how clearly off-limits she was. He didn't want to think about how kissable she'd looked with her cheeks flushed in anger or the bounce of her gorgeous breasts as she'd walked off in a huff.

He closed the door to his office, told Gina to hold his calls, and made himself a scotch on the rocks. Only after he'd downed the double shot did he allow himself to remember how good Alisha's hand had felt in his. He inhaled and remembered the scent of her as she challenged him: sweet flowers and a kick of spice.

He hated how easily she'd made him want her.

Worse, there had been an answering hunger in her. He'd seen it in her eyes. *That's trouble I don't need. I should put her out of my head, but I need to know exactly what type of woman she is.*

*So I can help Spencer.*

Putting his glass down, he returned to his desk and called his secretary. "Gina, get me a full background check on Alisha Coventry." He didn't say more. He knew he didn't have to. Gina was that good.

A few hours later, he was reading through a digital file on Alisha. Police reports about domestic abuse. Modest career. Long association with his family.

*Does Spencer love her?*

*Why is she marrying Spencer? Does she see him as a meal ticket? I'm not an expert on love, but my gut tells me that woman is not in love. She couldn't look at me the way she did and be serious about my brother.*

*Or maybe women are all the same.*

Nothing would ever erase Brett's memory of hiding behind a chair while his father and mother fought for the last time. The proud Dereck Westerly had been reduced to a pleading, tearful man, promising to do anything if his wife would stay. He said he'd forgive her infidelity. He would forgive her anything, if she would only stay. It was the only time Brett ever saw weakness in his father, and Brett's love for his mother had withered that day. She'd dismissed his father and said she was leaving with the children. She claimed she needed to build a life away from him to be happy.

*Happy?*

What the fuck was that? Stephanie Westerly had deserted her marriage, broken up her family, to be *happy*. His father, on the other hand, had proved how life should be. Focused. Driven. Successful. Pursuing happiness had caused his youngest brother to believe he had to appease an old lady by marrying in haste. *That will never be me. I don't need anyone at my side.*

Maintaining the financial security of the family. Ambition. Affluence. That was what mattered. Life wasn't about being *happy*.

# Chapter Two

Scrubbing her hands in the classroom sink, Alisha tried unsuccessfully to remove the orange paint from beneath one of her nails. *What a week.* By five thirty the atmosphere was peaceful. From the moment her first student arrived in the morning until the last one was handed off to a parent, the day flew by. There was always a shoe to tie, a nose to wipe, or a frustrated little one to guide toward success. Keeping twenty-five kindergarten students not only productive but also inspired was not easy, yet it was satisfying.

Alisha had known she wanted to be a teacher from as far back as she could remember, and early childhood was what she'd chosen to focus on. The little ones came in as babies and, if she did her job correctly, left as confident students. Every school year ended with a sigh of relief and a short period of mourning because each class found a way into her heart.

This year would be even more of a roller coaster since she and Spencer were getting married. Possibly very soon, if their conversation on the way home the night before was anything to go by. She'd originally expressed a preference to have the ceremony in a month when school let out for the summer, but after meeting Brett, she completely understood why Spencer would want to do it sooner. The whole pretense would be done faster, Spencer could get his money, and life would go back to normal.

Alisha turned off the water, dried her hands, and gathered what she needed to take home. *What an arrogant asshole. No wonder his siblings want nothing to do with him.*

She made a disgusted sound as she remembered how he'd spoken to Spencer. During the ride home she'd asked Spencer why he bothered to go see him.

Spencer had shrugged and said, "A part of me always hopes it'll be different. It never is. He's a clone of Dad."

Alisha shuddered at that thought. If that was true, it wasn't hard to see why Stephanie Westerly had left her husband. People thought money bought happiness, but Stephanie was proof it didn't. She'd walked away from a life of luxury and leisure and had chosen to raise her children on her nurse's salary. Her second husband, Mark, had shared her simple philosophy and they'd made their home a happy one.

Stephanie loved her children. And Mark had been the father none of them had ever had. He'd never been too busy to talk. He even attended every one of Alisha's soccer games and sat with his stepchildren while they did their homework.

His illness, then death, eight years earlier had left a hole in their lives, but Alisha liked to think he lived on in all of them. Whenever Alisha was confused, she asked herself what Mark would have done.

*He wouldn't have told Brett off. He would have found something about him to like.*

*But I'm only human.*

*Sorry, Mark. It had to be said.* As Alisha tossed her bags into her blue Honda Civic, she admitted something to herself that she'd spent the prior night denying. *It felt good, too.*

*Really good.*

She paused before starting up her car as her thoughts wandered back to the man who caused her fitful night of sleep. She'd woken unable to remember the details of her dream but bothered that he appeared in it.

He was undeniably an attractive man. Tall and dark-haired, with incredible blue eyes. Add wealth into the mix and Alisha doubted many women turned him down. That wasn't what had stuck with Alisha, though.

No, it was his presence. Male confidence. Power. A hint of danger.

*My type only in movies and books. In reality, a nice man is a more practical choice every time.*

Her phone rang, interrupting her inner dialogue. She answered via her hands-free Bluetooth setup in the car. "Hello?"

"Are you just leaving now?" Rachelle asked.

"I had to clean up. We painted the papier-mâché covers for Mother's Day books today."

"The ones that are also picture frames? How did they come out?"

"Like something only mothers could love, but I get so many nice letters about them each year that I keep making them."

"Are you still meeting me at the gym at seven?"

"Absolutely. I just need to run home, eat something, and change."

"Yoga?"

Alisha groaned. Having a skinny best friend was sometimes a physical challenge. Rachelle loved to twist herself up into a variety of poses Alisha's body didn't fold into. Not that she was fat, but Alisha wasn't delicately built, either. She could run a marathon—in theory. Some people were blessed with fast metabolisms. Alisha was either gaining or losing weight every day of her life. She did her best, though, to eat healthily and exercise often. Summer was approaching and although she would never feel comfortable in a bikini, she would at least be bathing-suit ready. "Sure. Maybe meditation will help."

"Bad day?" Rachelle asked, instantly concerned. She was a first grade teacher, so she could empathize, and Alisha missed the days when they taught at the same school.

There was no way Alisha was going to admit to Rachelle that she was disappointed in herself for being attracted to Rachelle's oldest brother. "Just a long one."

"Let's hop on the treadmill after yoga. You can tell me all about last night. Spencer didn't want to talk about it."

*I don't blame him. I'm not going to say too much about it, either.* "Sounds perfect. See you at the gym."

"Great. See you there."

A few minutes later Alisha pulled into the driveway of the two-bedroom home she'd bought for herself. From the flowers she'd planted along the path, to the shutters she'd bought at a yard sale and refinished, she loved every inch of it. It was hers. She could have moved to Boston as many people did after college, but she'd chosen to stay in the suburbs. Why load herself up with more debt just to be living in Boston? And it wasn't in her heart. She'd always been impressed with the simplicity of Stephanie and Mark's life and knew she wanted something similar for herself. Her home was simple and beautiful. She liked to think it represented the life she'd made for herself.

Alisha changed into yoga pants and a fitted black tank top. The thinner she got, the more colorful her gym outfits became, but for now she was still in her winter-weight dark attire. She made a salad and ate while reading over the journals of the children who hadn't met with her that day, then quickly wrote notes on each and added smiley stickers to those who had completed work.

After stuffing her rolled-up mat, a towel, and water into a bag, she raced out the door and came to a skidding stop when she saw Brett leaning against a silver sports car parked behind her Honda Civic.

With his charcoal suit and dark glasses, he looked out of place in the driveway. Alisha's breath caught in her throat as he pushed off the car and straightened. She didn't appreciate the way her body warmed as he approached her. "If you're looking for Spencer, he's not here."

"I know."

Alisha almost took a step back, but she forced herself to stand her ground. He came to a stop a foot from her. Close enough to set Alisha's heart beating wildly in her chest with an odd mix of nerves and excitement. He was really better-looking than any man had the right to be. "I'm not sure what you think we have to say to each other."

He removed his glasses. There they were, those blue eyes she found impossible to look away from. She told herself she was imagining it, but she could have sworn there was sadness in them. Did his gruff exterior protect a man who'd experienced pain? In terms of worldly possessions and all things sought after, he had everything. But something had torn through him.

As one long moment dragged into two, she became sure he'd come to apologize and was having difficulty choosing his words. He probably felt horrible about the first impression he'd given her. She nodded at him in encouragement.

"How much would it take for you to not marry my brother? Fifty thousand? A hundred thousand? Name your price."

Alisha gasped as his words sank in. *I did not see that coming.* "You should go."

He leaned into her space. "Two hundred."

*You're getting less attractive the more you speak.* "Sorry to disappoint you, but not everyone can be bought. There isn't an amount you could offer that would be enough."

"I don't believe you," he said matter-of-factly.

"It doesn't matter if you believe me. It's the truth."

"Everyone has a price."

"Then *you* know the wrong people."

He seemed to weigh her claim for a moment before saying, "You don't love Spencer."

"Wrong again." She did, even if it wasn't in a romantic way. He was the little brother she'd never been fortunate to actually have.

Brett straightened and frowned. "You were dating someone else until two weeks ago."

As far as Alisha knew, Brett didn't talk to Rachelle often, and she couldn't imagine that her dating life was a topic of discussion when they did speak. "How do you know that?" Alisha decided it didn't matter. Instead of waiting for an answer, she waved a hand at him and demanded, "Why are you so determined to sabotage your brother?"

His head snapped back. "I'm not."

"He needs the money for his company."

"My father would give him a loan. I've offered to invest in his company. He doesn't have to marry you—" Brett was smart enough to stop there.

Had Alisha actually been dreaming of living happily ever after with Spencer, she would have been hurt by Brett's stance. She took a deep, calming breath. Regardless of what a jackass he was, this was Rachelle's brother. She remembered what Spencer had said about always hoping things would go better. She owed so much of the happiness she'd found to the Westerlys' welcome. *They taught me what a healthy family life could be like. Is this my chance to pay it forward?* She called upon her kindergarten-teacher patience and said, "Coming here was wrong. Offering me money to leave Spencer is insulting and hurtful. If you love your brother at all, don't do this. Leave now. I'll pretend none of this happened, and you should try to support your brother in a way that leaves him with his pride intact."

Brett's face tightened with emotion. Alisha braced herself for what was likely going to be an even more offensive comeback, and considering he'd already implied her loyalty could be bought, that was saying something. He brought a hand up and instinctively Alisha flinched before she realized he was merely replacing his sunglasses. He paused and his eyes snapped to hers. No longer angry with her, he appeared to be angry *for* her.

*How can that be possible? He doesn't know about my past. No one knows all of it.* She pushed back a twinge of shame and tensed defensively.

When he finally spoke, it was in a deep, gravelly voice. "I would never hurt you."

Alisha didn't have a ready answer for that. She didn't want to think the past had any hold over her anymore. She looked away and adjusted her bag on her shoulder. "Please just go. I'm already late to meet Rachelle at the gym."

He nodded, replaced his sunglasses, and without saying another word climbed back into his sports car and drove off. When he was out of sight, Alisha finally got into her own car and started it. She then seemed to lose momentum and simply sat there.

*What was that?*

*Did he honestly think I'd take the money?*

She remembered how he'd looked as he stood over her, still very much the arrogant man she'd met the day before, but with an underlying sadness that made her wish she knew how to help him connect with Spencer.

*I don't understand you, Mr. Angry Westerly.*

She backed out of the driveway and pulled into traffic, unable to dislodge him from her thoughts. She had driven several blocks before she realized she was headed in the opposite direction from the gym. She used a side road to turn around and sighed. *But if it's any consolation, I understand myself even less.*


Brett returned to his office and worked through the night. When the morning light fell across his desk, he stood and stretched.

*I shouldn't have gone to Alisha's house. She was right about that.*

*But I had to know if money was her motivation.*

Brett pushed out of his chair, moving to look out his office window as his mind filled with images of Alisha. *My brother's fiancée.* He grimaced. *That's what she is.*

*Vetting her integrity didn't change that.*

Things would have been a hell of a lot easier if she'd taken his money. He would have instantly lost all respect for her. Instead, he found himself in the rare position of envying his youngest brother. No one had ever stood in defense of Brett, had her loyalty tested and then passed that test, or even claimed to love him.

Not the way Alisha had stood up for Spencer.

The women in Brett's life were realistic. They understood that relationships, regardless of how heated they became in the bedroom, were nothing more than mutually beneficial associations with a healthy side of sex. *Friends with benefits* was too generous a description for his last several lovers. They'd been beautiful and passionate, but loyal? He doubted many of the men he knew were married to women who would stay with them if their finances took a dip.

That's how women were. They put their own needs first. A man could only be hurt by them if he forgot that. *And I never will.*

It was difficult to reconcile his views on women with his impression of Alisha. She wasn't materialistic. Both her home and vehicle were well cared for but not pretentious. She was protective of Spencer even when it put her in what could have been volatile situations. He frowned as he remembered her flinch. It confirmed what Child Protective Services had suspected but had been unable to prove—her father had extended his abuse of her mother to her. The idea of hurting a woman was so foreign to Brett that he could hardly wrap his head around it. His parents' divorce had been emotional for all involved, but even during the worst of it his father had never raised a hand to his wife or children.

That Alisha had survived such a childhood and had remained strong was remarkable.

Brett put a sticky note on Gina's computer keyboard, instructing her to locate Alisha's father. If he was still alive, Brett would make sure he never hurt Alisha again. How Brett achieved that would depend on the willingness of the other man to disappear.

"I figured you'd be here," his father said as he walked into the office. Brett turned, unsurprised to see him in a suit. Neither the early morning hour nor the fact that he was retired had softened Dereck

Westerly's edge. "Did the German contract come through? I heard you hit complications."

Brett motioned for his father to sit in one of the chairs in front of his desk and took the seat across from him. "I did, but it's all ironed out now."

"You look like shit."

Rubbing a hand across the stubble on his chin, Brett said, "Long night."

His father nodded. "I've had my share of those. Need any advice?"

Brett shook his head. His father was referring to work-related issues. As a child, even though Brett had chosen to stay with his father, he hadn't known him well until he'd started working with him at the family company. Men as successful as his father hired nannies and tutors. He'd never had time to meet with any of Brett's teachers or watch one of his football games. Later, he hadn't gone to visit colleges or help Brett choose his first apartment. Business was where they'd connected. "I'm good."

His father crossed one ankle over the other. "You should have told me you weren't going to your grandmother's birthday party."

"Would you have gone?" Brett challenged. He didn't expect his father to answer his question, and he didn't.

"She's upset no one went. That's why she came up with the crazy idea of having all of you marry. She's getting more erratic as she gets older. I can't believe Spencer was foolish enough to get engaged because of this. Does he actually think he'll get his inheritance early? The document won't hold up in court. My mother is obviously not competent to manage her own estate anymore."

Even though Brett had said almost exactly the same thing two days earlier, he didn't like it when his father said it. It lacked compassion and loyalty. He could almost hear Alisha labeling it as hurtful. What was the alternative, though? Sitting back and watching his own inheritance be given away to charity? There was no chance in hell he was going to marry anytime soon.

*I don't need it anyway.*

*But Spencer does.*

"Does it matter, Dad? It doesn't affect you directly. Marriage might be good for Spencer."

His father sat forward in his seat. "Have you been drinking?"

Brett folded his arms across his chest. "I won't block him on this."

Surging to his feet, his father looked down at him. "Marriage isn't good for anyone. Name one person you know who is fucking happy after a year of marriage. One." When a name didn't immediately come to Brett, his father raged on. "See? No one. It's a contract designed for failure. Till death do you part? Death doesn't come as quickly as it used to, Son."

*Wow.*

Brett had spent most of his life looking up to his father, emulating him. Listening to him was like looking in the mirror most of the time, but for once, Brett didn't like what he saw. His father had had a long, successful career. His legacy would endure through the company, and he had enough money to live the rest of his life however he chose.

*Yet, he's here. In a suit. Alone and bitter.* Seeing his father in this less than flattering light was disconcerting. It also prompted the question: *Will that be me in twenty years?*

"What was your father like?" Brett asked aloud, surprising even himself with the question.

"My *father?*"

They were entering uncharted territory, but Brett wanted to know. He'd heard of him through his mother, but never brought him up with his own father. *I don't believe we're nothing more than the product of how our parents shaped us. Where did it go wrong for you, Dad?* "He founded this company, so I know you had one."

A flash of pain shone in Dereck's eyes. "There is nothing to know about him."

"Nothing?"

His father's jaw tightened visibly as he sat back down. "He was a weak man. A selfish coward who may have started this company, but also nearly ran it into the ground."

The emotion in his father's voice was unexpected. It increased Brett's curiosity. "Grandmother seems to miss him."

"Because she didn't know him . . . the real him."

"But you did?"

"I stepped into his shoes, didn't I? You learn a lot about a man when you do that."

*Yes, you do.* Taking over Westerly Corp. was teaching Brett as much about his father as it was about himself. "He died of a heart attack, didn't he?"

"He died of heart medication complications."

It was an ambiguous response that Brett wouldn't have questioned in the past, but his father had called his grandfather a coward. "He overdosed?"

His father stood and ran a hand through his now-white hair. "You're the one person who might benefit from the truth. When I took over, I discovered my father had been borrowing money from the company for a long time, but he'd finally reached a point where it was due. He wasn't man enough to face what he'd done, so he checked out for good. The weight of it fell on me. The cover-up. Everything. I negotiated deals I would have had a moral issue with had I not been so close to losing everything—compromising myself so your grandmother could stay in her big house. I'm not proud of what I did back then, but I would do it again because it ensured you would never be in that position. And I hope I raised you to understand that the welfare of the family should always trump your self-interest."

*You did, but I never understood why until now.* "He died the year I was born?"

"Yes."

Brett stood. "Did you ever tell Mom how he died?"

If his father had an Achilles' heel, it was his ex-wife. She was another topic normally off-limits. "The doctors said it was accidental. What your grandfather did was a stain on our family history that no one needed to know about. Least of all your mother or grandmother. They would have thought it was their fault. That they could have saved him somehow. His death was better remembered as an accident."

The weight of what his father had carried by himself made what had happened to him afterward even more tragic. "That couldn't have been easy, and then Mom cheated on you."

His father's face blanched. "Where did you hear that?"

"I was in the living room when you fought over it. I was twelve and curious, but not fast enough to get out."

"You never said anything."

"Because you never did. You seemed to want people to think you had cheated on her. I never understood why. I still don't."

His father walked to the door of the office before he said another word. "Your mother is a wonderful woman. I was a horrible husband. She deserved better than what I gave her. Your mother wouldn't have cheated if I had remained the man she'd married." He closed the door and the discussion as he left.

Brett sat back down at his desk, but it was a long time before he started working again.

# Chapter Three

"This is your grandmother's house?" Alisha asked Rachelle, as her jaw dropped in shock. The building rose up above its ocean backdrop like a mansion in an old movie. Its stone facade, as impressive in length as in height, boasted more windows than Alisha could count at a first glance. How many bedrooms would a place like that have? Alisha could only imagine. "Why did you mooch half my lunch through high school?"

Rachelle looked much less impressed by the building, but she chuckled. "Because my mother was a health food nut who didn't believe in sugar. And you had Twinkies."

"Something I knew you'd thank me for one day," Stephanie said cheerfully from behind her daughter as she stepped out of the car. "I'm still waiting."

Spencer joined them with his youngest sister, Nicolette, by his side. "Am I the only one who would rather be dragged across cut glass and then doused in lemon juice than go inside?"

Despite the delicate sundress she wore, Nicolette raised her arms in a pose that a weight lifter might use to show off her muscles. "Alone we are weak against the evil queen, but together we are strong."

Stephanie shook her head at her youngest. "Your grandmother is not evil. She's just . . . particular."

Nicolette made a face. "Five bucks says I'm the first one she insults. It might be Rachelle, though, who needs to put on weight." Her tone mimicked her grandmother's. "Spencer, when are you going to get a real job?"

"Stop, Nicolette," her mother chastised gently.

Rachelle chimed in, "Mom, are you sure you want to come in? Didn't she say you were not welcome in her home?"

With a sigh, Stephanie looked up at the large wooden entrance. "That was a long time ago. She's eighty, and no matter what she says, she's family. Plus, she means well. Try to translate everything she says to, 'I care about your well-being.'"

Nicolette put an arm around her mother. "I'll be fine unless she says something rude to you."

Spencer nodded in agreement. "It's a deal breaker for me as well. Inheritance or no inheritance."

Alisha lagged behind the group.

Stephanie turned and looked from her son to Alisha. "Are you two really in love? Tell me you're not engaged because of that ridiculous letter you all received from her lawyer."

For a moment Spencer's expression resembled a deer caught in the headlights of his mother's gaze. Alisha slid beneath his arm and smiled brightly. "Of course it got him to pop the question, but I've loved Spencer for as long as I can remember." That was true. They'd gone on vacations together, fought and made up a hundred times over. She was grateful every day that he, along with the rest of the Westerlys, was part of her life.

Stephanie smiled, but there was concern in her eyes. "Alisha, you've always felt like one of my daughters. I can't imagine a better wife for Spencer, but I want to make sure the two of you are doing this for the right reasons. Money doesn't make life easier. It comes with its own problems."

Spencer hugged Alisha to his side. "We know what we're doing, Mom."

As she carefully watched her son's expression, Stephanie asked, "You love her?"

Spencer nodded.

Nicolette chuckled. "Talk about awkward if he said no."

Rachelle joined in. "I never imagined you two together, but now that I see it—it works."

Alisha tensed. She didn't mind lying to their grandmother or hedging the truth around the rest of them, but Rachelle seemed to have forgotten that it had been her who had originally suggested they marry. Alisha had laughed it off at first, then considered it more seriously when Spencer had shared how his company needed the capital. She was tempted to take Rachelle aside, shake her, and remind her that none of this was real. It was like a play, and she was only saying the rehearsed lines.

There were no sparks between her and Spencer, and she wondered how the others couldn't see that. If he kissed her, she doubted it would feel any different than the time she kissed Grayson Teal during the high school play they'd both won starring roles in. Grayson had been attractive, too. It hadn't repulsed her to kiss him, but it hadn't been exciting, either.

The door of the mansion opened and a man in a dark suit called to them, "Mrs. Westerly will see you now."

Spencer looked down at her and mouthed, "Thank you."

Alisha smiled up at him. "Glass and lemon juice?"

He shuddered against her. "You'll understand when you meet her."

His arm dropped away, and they all made their way toward the entrance. As they did, Spencer lowered his voice and donned that of an old woman. "Spencer, sit up straight. How do you expect to be taken seriously if you slouch? You shouldn't play football, you know. It causes brain damage. If you're going to stay in a public school, you'll need every bit of your wits or you'll never make anything of yourself."

Alisha coughed back a laugh. "She can't be that bad."

Nicolette piped in. "Just wait. I hope you brought your cloak of confidence with you. If not, we'll carry whatever is left of you and your self-esteem back to the car after lunch."

Stephanie and Rachelle led the way into the home while Alisha, Spencer, and Nicolette trailed behind. Had they been there for any other reason, Alisha would have exclaimed in wonder at the grand foyer and the stairway that flanked it. An entire party could be hosted right here without any need of the rest of the house.

Beside them, the butler said, "Please follow me to the parlor."

The room they entered was every bit as awe-inspiring as the entrance had been, overlooking a grassy lawn that led to the ocean. Spectacular. Everywhere Alisha turned there were antiques, expensive cloth wallpaper, and woodwork so intricate it belonged on a museum tour. Alisha was glad she'd worn one of her best dresses. She felt as if she were about to meet royalty.

*Even if it's an evil queen.* She smiled a little nervously and reminded herself that the buildup was likely far worse than any grandmother could actually be.

Everyone stayed standing, although there were seats available. They seemed equally apprehensive. Even Stephanie's cheerful chatter was strained.

The woman who entered the room wasn't at all imposing in stature. Alisha guessed she stood only as high as Stephanie's chin, but she had the air of someone important. It bothered Alisha that the family she loved so much seemed to wilt in her presence. All laughing stopped and an oppressive silence hung over them for a long moment.

Stephanie was the first to speak. "It's so good to see you, Delinda."

"Yes," the old woman said without a shred of warmth. "Why are we standing about? Sit."

They all took their seats like obedient children, following her command so mechanically that Alisha and Spencer forgot to sit together. Delinda sat in an uncomfortable-looking formal chair and turned to the butler. "Michael, have the tea and sandwiches served in here. And quickly—my granddaughter looks as if she's wasting away. You do feed your children, don't you, Stephanie?"

The butler slipped out of the room.

Stephanie opened her mouth to say something, but closed it instead and merely smiled. Rachelle said, "I'm twenty-eight, Grandmother. I feed myself now."

Delinda looked her over. "You'll never find a husband if you don't fill out."

"I eat fine," Rachelle answered, her tone lowering as her temper rose.

Alisha intervened quickly, "Your home is beautiful, Mrs. Westerly. The view of the ocean is absolutely stunning."

Delinda's attention snapped to her. "Thank you. You must be Alisha Coventry." She looked her over from head to toe. "May I see your ring?"

Alisha stood, walked over, and held out her left hand. When the older woman's perfectly manicured hand gripped hers, Alisha was suddenly aware of the fact that her nails were unpainted and hadn't seen a professional in months. The half-carat diamond on her hand was far outshone by the mammoth stones in Delinda's rings. "I wanted something simple," Alisha said.

"Apparently," Delinda answered and dropped her hand. "Spencer, my mother's engagement ring or her mother's would be much more suitable." She waved a hand at Alisha as if dismissing her. "Of course, they would have to stay in the family if anything happened between the two of you. Do be smart enough to protect them for future generations."

Spencer straightened in his chair. "Thank you, but the ring I bought Alisha is good enough."

Delinda shook her head sadly. "Good enough? Spencer, when will you stop settling for the first thing that comes along?"

A rush of heat flooded Alisha as Delinda's gaze fell on her again with clear meaning. Alisha almost told her what she thought of her, but caught Stephanie's eyes and swallowed her anger. *Today isn't about me; it's for them. I thought I was patient, but if Stephanie actually translates shit like that into kind words, she's a saint.*

The entrance of a woman rolling in a serving tray provided a temporary reprieve.

Between bites of her sandwich, Nicolette said, "Grandmother, happy belated birthday."

Delinda's chin rose. "A person doesn't turn eighty every day. You could have celebrated it with me had your mother passed along my invitation to you."

"She did—" Nicolette began, but Delinda waved a hand as if she didn't believe her.

"No matter. You're here now. Are you still trying to make a living as a photographer? In my day it was a profession, but now everyone has a camera in their phones and all they do is snap photos of themselves. What do you even do with all those pictures?"

"I publish them in online magazines. One shot is even on display at the Boston Museum of Fine Arts."

"Everything is art nowadays, isn't it? Well, good for you. I know most of the board of directors at the museum. It's nice to see they're taking care of my family."

"It's there because it won an award—"

"So Alisha and I are getting married next weekend," Spencer interrupted. "Family will be invited of course, but we're having a small ceremony."

Alisha choked on a piece of bread. When Spencer had said something similar to Brett, it had sounded like a joke. This time he was serious.

Delinda's attention once again riveted to Alisha. "Is there a reason for the rush?"

Her meaning wasn't missed by Spencer, who flushed. "We simply don't want to wait."

After blinking a few times, Delinda rose to her feet. "Stephanie, would you mind walking with me to the library? I'd like to have a word with you."

Stephanie rose to go with her. Her children were instantly at her side.

"Alone," Delinda said with a tight smile.

"Of course." Stephanie shot them a look that said *stay*. "We'll be right back."

Spencer stepped in her way. "Mom—"

Stephanie gave his arm a pat. "I'm fine. Why don't you show Alisha the garden? In fact, why don't you all go out into the sun for a moment? It's a beautiful day." She forced a smile, then followed Delinda out of the room.

In the absence of their grandmother, a laugh of relief started with Rachelle and was echoed by the rest. "We shouldn't have let Mom come. Why doesn't she just tell her off?"

"Why don't we all?" Nicolette asked, then, turning to Alisha, said, "Are you okay?"

"Of course," Alisha said and meant it. The old woman's opinion of her didn't matter, but she felt for the rest of them. "How did you all end up so nice?"

Spencer looked toward the door. "Because my mother was wise enough to remove us from this toxic world."

Rachelle made a face. "And still you want to be rich."

"It's not about being wealthy. It's about having a successful company," Spencer protested. "Money doesn't have to corrupt you."

"It's power that corrupts," Nicolette interjected. "Isn't that what they say? 'Absolute power corrupts absolutely.'"

"You'd have to ask Brett," Spencer said, then seemed to regret his slip.

Alisha shook her head with sadness. Even though she'd practically grown up in their home, she'd been insulated from this part of their lives. The more she entered into it, the more she felt sorry for them.

Abuse came in many forms; it didn't need a bruise to leave damage. She still cringed when she heard a man raise his voice in anger. Her father's fists never came first. No, the vitriol that came from his mouth preceded his physical rage. Sarcasm. Degradation. *Then the bruises.* She couldn't let Stephanie face whatever Delinda was spewing any more than she could have stayed hidden when her own father had gone after her mother. "My hands are sticky. Do you mind if I find a place to wash them and meet you all in the garden? I can find my own way."

"I could use the fresh air," Spencer said.

"Me, too," Rachelle said. "Come on, Nikki. Alisha, there's a washroom off the main foyer to the left. Do you want me to go with you?"

"No. I'm good, really. I'll see you outside in a few."


Brett left his car in his grandmother's driveway and strode toward the house. The front door opened as he approached it, and the butler welcomed him. "We weren't expecting you, sir, but it's a pleasure to see you."

"Thank you, Michael. Is my mother here?"

"She's in the library with your grandmother. Would you like me to announce you?"

"No, I'll see myself in. Who else is here?"

"Your mother, Rachelle, Nicolette, and Spencer. Most are out in the garden."

"Did Spencer bring his fiancée?"

"He did, sir. Seems like he chose well. When she smiles, it's genuine, if you know what I mean."

"I do. That'll be all, Michael."

"Of course, sir." With that, he faded into the background as all staff there did. Grandmother ran a tight ship.

Brett heard his grandmother's voice from the library and headed that way. As soon as he'd heard that Spencer was officially presenting Alisha, he decided to intervene. His younger siblings didn't know how to deal with the matriarch of the family. She acted like a petulant child at times, testing the limits of what she could get away with, but she wasn't nearly as strong as they believed her to be. All they needed to do was stand up to her. He'd meant to arrive before them and speak to his grandmother first, to ease the way for them, but a business call had delayed his departure from the office. He saw his mother leave the library, looking upset. His father's words came back to him. *"She deserved better."* He cursed himself for being late.

He had just changed direction to go after his mother, hoping to hell he knew what to say that would alleviate whatever his grandmother had said, when he saw Alisha slip into the library. He was at the door swiftly, but hung back, more than a little curious to see if his brother's fiancée revealed a less savory side of herself.

"Mrs. Westerly," Alisha said in much the same tone she'd used with him days earlier. "May I speak to you for a moment?"

"You look flushed. Is the house too warm for you? I'll have Michael turn on the air."

"I'm not too warm. I came in here because—"

"Yes?"

"I don't like the way you speak to your family, and I'm hoping you don't know how hurtful the things you say are."

Brett let out a silent whistle of admiration. His grandmother's cheeks reddened. He would have stepped forward, but Alisha was doing exactly what he'd hoped his siblings would one day do. If she actually married into the family, things would go smoother for her if she stood up for herself. He stayed, though, prepared to bring it to a stop if the conversation turned ugly.

"Who are you to have an opinion about anything? You should sit back and be grateful my grandson is marrying you at all," his grandmother said.

Brett saw the steadying breath Alisha took. "See, that was cruel and unnecessary. But you're wasting your time if you think you can intimidate me. I'm here because I love the people out there. They are the nicest, most giving souls probably ever born. They're a lot nicer than I am, or you are, and they don't deserve the way you treat them. Those are *your* grandchildren. You're supposed to love them."

"And I do." His grandmother's tone was haughty.

"You don't seem to. Everything you say is a little dig. Can't you celebrate anything they do?"

"If you celebrate mediocrity, you plateau at mediocre. I want better for them. My family didn't get to where we are by cheering our children to second place."

Alisha shook her head and expelled an audible breath. "Life isn't a race you win or lose."

"That's exactly what people say who've never come in first."

Scenes from Brett's life flashed through his mind as he connected his grandmother's philosophy to his father's. And his own. Nothing but the best was of any value. It was a core belief he'd always held without realizing it, and now he saw its source. He thought about how he'd spoken to Spencer, how he often spoke to his siblings, and didn't like how much of what he said sounded scripted. *How did I never see it?* He stepped forward to end the conversation he didn't want to hear more of, but stopped when Alisha began to speak again.

"If you truly believe that, I feel sorry for you and for them, because you will never know how amazing your family is. They are second to none. Rachelle is shaping future generations one class at a time. Nicolette is capturing real moments that touch the people who see them through her lens. Spencer is brilliant, and he'll succeed at whatever he does. And Stephanie provided them the confidence to be whoever they wanted to be. They love her. I love her. I hope you were kind to her just now, because if you weren't, then you may very well lose your grandchildren over it."

"You don't need to tell me how wonderful my grandchildren are. I'm proud of each and every one of them."

"Don't tell me," Alisha said in a softer tone. "Tell them."

She turned and her eyes widened as she saw Brett standing in the doorway. He almost said he was proud of her, that she'd found a way to put into words what he was only just discovering himself. He opened his mouth to speak, but she rushed by him without meeting his eyes. He would have followed her, but it wasn't his place to applaud or console her. Instead, he'd handle the other end of the issue.

"Brett." His grandmother's happiness at seeing him lit her face. She shook her head as if to erase the last few moments. "Leave it to Spencer to want to marry a woman like that."

Brett closed the distance between them and took the hand she held out to him. His love for her didn't stop him, however, from saying, "I agreed with everything she said. I saw my mother leaving you. She looked upset. What did you say to her?"

His grandmother dropped his hand and fanned her face. "You know how sensitive she is."

"What did you say?"

Just as he knew she would, his grandmother softened beneath pressure. "I told her that my goal is to bring everyone back together, and to do that I'm willing to forget what she did to my son."

Brett pinched the bridge of his nose. "I'm sure that went well."

With a loud sigh, his grandmother said, "Don't blame me. This is Alessandro Andrade's fault. He suggested I speak to her."

"I'm sure that's not what he *suggested* you say."

His grandmother's eyes narrowed like a child being told something she had no argument against. "Do you know how many of my grandchildren came to my eightieth birthday celebration? Not one of them. Alessandro was here with all the Andrades. He said if I forgave Stephanie, things would change. He was wrong. She wants nothing to do with me." She sighed and took Brett's hand in hers again. "How can you and I get along so well, but everything I say to my other grandchildren is taken as an attack?"

Brett and his grandmother had always been blunt with each other. In a dry tone he said, "They're nicer than we are. They say supportive things to each other. Leave each other feeling good about themselves."

She laughed. "You make me sound horrible."

Giving his grandmother's hand a gentle squeeze, he said, "I'm beginning to think *we* are."

"Well, at least you include yourself. I asked my mother once why she picked apart everything I did. She told me the greatest gift a parent could give a child was to have high expectations for them. Children these days stop pooping their pants and they think they deserve a gold medal. That's not reality. I only push the ones I love."

*I agree and have done the same, but where has it brought our family?* "I understand that, Grandmother, but if something doesn't change, you may end up dying alone."

His grandmother gasped. "You're awful."

He smiled. "I get it from you."

A reluctant smile stretched her lips. "You do, I'm afraid."

"Is there hope for either one of us?" he joked, more serious than not.

Still holding his hand, his grandmother said, "Oliver always knew just what to say to make people feel better. I see him in you."

"Me?" Brett asked, not too sure he appreciated the comparison. *Especially now that I know how my grandfather died.*

"And your father. Dereck worshipped his father. He was so much like him when he was younger. Always laughing. Seeing the bright side of everything. Your mother's betrayal made Dereck so unhappy he lost himself, and he's never found his way back." Delinda had never believed her son had cheated on his wife. Dereck's protests that the dissolution of his marriage had been his fault had fueled Delinda's distrust of Stephanie.

As Brett listened, he understood his father's decision to keep his grandfather's dark secrets to himself. There would have been no benefit to destroying his grandmother's version of her husband. "We need to talk about the letter you sent everyone. You realize Spencer took it to heart."

"Good. Alessandro says his family was healed when his nephews and nieces found love. He thinks the same could happen with us."

Brett put an arm around a woman who needed him more than he'd ever realized. "That's what the marriage clause is about? How many glasses of wine in was Alessandro when he gave you this advice?"

She rolled her eyes. "It worked for them. I'm giving it a try." She waved a finger at him. "Who knows, even *you* might finally settle down. Then maybe you'll come around more."

He smiled at her gently. "I don't need your money." He guided her toward the door. "But I will try to get here more often. At eighty, you're already living on borrowed time."

His grandmother swatted at him and laughed. "I intend to live to one hundred."

"Good," he said. "Now, we're going to find everyone else, and you will be nice. Keep all of your helpful advice to yourself. Say things like, 'That's great' and—"

"Bravo," his grandmother said with forced enthusiasm.

"We'll work on your delivery," Brett said as they entered the foyer.

Michael met them. "Pardon the interruption, but it seems that there was an emergency somewhere that required everyone to leave."

"They're gone?" Delinda asked and slumped against Brett.

"Yes," Michael answered simply.

"Thank you, Michael," Brett said.

"Will you be staying for lunch?" Michael asked.

41

Normally, Brett would have declined, but the more he learned about his grandmother, the more he felt sorry for her. She was living by a stern philosophy her parents had passed down to her, and there she was, after a life of being doted on, alone and confused as to how it happened.

No different than his father.

*No different than me.*

"Would you like me to, Grandmother?"

A smile returned to her face. "I would. I would like it very much."

A short time later, Brett bit into a lobster salad sandwich and encouraged his grandmother to tell him another story of what life had been like before his grandfather had died. The way she glowed as she spoke of that time made him smile, but he was also sad for how it had all turned out.

He wished he'd met his grandfather.

*Would he be the weak man Father described or the loving paragon Grandmother remembers?*

*Could a man be both?*

# Chapter Four

Monday afternoon Alisha left school a few minutes after her last student was picked up. Before pulling out of the parking lot, she sent a text to Rachelle to say she wasn't feeling well and wouldn't be working out with her that evening. Physically, Alisha was fine, but emotionally she'd only made it through the day by pushing back how raw the weekend had left her.

Although on the surface her childhood had certainly looked different, the gut-wrenching guilt of watching someone she loved be treated badly was familiar enough to bring back memories Alisha could usually keep at bay. Telling Delinda Westerly what she thought of her behavior should have felt cathartic, but it remained tangled in a cluster of other feelings.

Marrying Spencer had been easy to agree to. At the time it had felt like a helpful deed without consequences. She hadn't expected for everything to go so fast. He wanted to move the wedding date to the following weekend. She wasn't ready.

Which felt ridiculous, because there was nothing to get ready for. In fact, the sooner they did it, the sooner they could end it.

Alisha drove toward her sanctuary. Had it gone to her mother, her father would have sold it. She was thankful her grandmother had wisely bypassed her own daughter and left Alisha the three-hundred-square-foot, one-bedroom cabin on a tiny slip of land by Lake Serenity. Over time the land around it had been built up with extravagant homes plus docks that jutted out well beyond the shore. The cabin was often confused for a utility shed for one of the neighboring properties, but to Alisha it was heaven. The thick brush surrounding it gave the illusion of privacy on an otherwise overpopulated shoreline.

And Alisha needed a place to hide, even if only for a few hours.

After leaving Delinda's home, she had gone back to Stephanie's place with the rest of the siblings. Emotions had been running high for everyone.

Stephanie had taken Spencer and Alisha aside to talk about slowing down their plans to marry. "It's a big decision, and not one anyone should rush into."

Spencer had argued that some things were better done quickly, decisively.

Never happy being left out, Rachelle and Nicolette had joined the awkward conversation, and soon the length of the engagement was being debated from all sides. The whole thing began to feel like a train speeding down tracks without brakes, and instead of helping Alisha gain control of it, the multiple opinions only added more fuel. The more arguments Spencer heard against marrying fast, the more determined he became that they should do it the following weekend.

"What does Alisha want?" Stephanie had asked, and all eyes turned to her.

Unable to voice the truth and unwilling to lie, Alisha had excused herself from the conversation and bolted to the porch. It was Rachelle who'd joined her there, but what she said had cut through her even though Rachelle hadn't intended it to. She'd said, "Crazy day, huh? Aren't you glad we're not really your family?"

With a whoosh, her words had knocked the breath clear out of Alisha. When she'd stood up to Delinda for the people she loved, in that moment they'd been her family. *But they're not.*

*They're friends. Good friends, but Stephanie is not my mother. As much as I love Rachelle and Nicolette, they are not my sisters.*

She'd looked down at the ring on her finger. *I don't really even have a fiancé.*

*If this goes badly, I could end up with no one.*

Her thoughts must have shone on her face because Rachelle quickly said, "Oh my God, Alisha, I didn't mean it that way. I was trying to make you feel better. I'm an idiot."

Alisha had forced a bright smile. "What? Don't be silly. I knew what you meant. I'm probably fighting something, because I'm tired and cranky all of a sudden."

Rachelle had placed the back of her hand across Alisha's forehead. "You don't feel feverish, but there are all sorts of colds going around my classroom. You should get to bed early tonight."

Alisha had stood, brushed off the back of her dress, and promised to do just that.

Sleep hadn't helped, though. Nor had her busy day at school. She was hoping a few hours at the lake house would clear her head.

A while later, she was sitting by the edge of her lawn, throwing pebbles into the water. Once summer started and school ended, peace would be impossible to find here, but today it was blissfully quiet.

*If I marry Spencer, will Stephanie forever see* me *as the woman who divorced her son? Will she come to hate me the way Delinda hates her?*

*I could tell Spencer that I'll only do this for him if we can be honest with her. And Nicolette.*

Alisha remembered Brett's expression when he caught her standing up to his grandmother. He looked . . . proud of her. *Someone should tell him, too; then he might stop seeing me as a potential gold digger.*

*Why would I care what he thinks? He doesn't come across as someone who'd be above stretching the truth to get what he wants.*

*And I'm doing this to help someone.*

*What do they say about good deeds? They never go unpunished?*

*How can something that felt right a week ago feel wrong now?*

Her phone beeped with a text from Rachelle. She wanted to know how Alisha felt and if she needed anything.

Alisha thanked her, but stressed that she was all set.

Chicken soup? Is your throat sore?

I'm fine. I love you for asking, but I'm going to sleep now.

Do you have your substitute lesson plans ready in case you can't make it in tomorrow? If not, I can go to your school first and make sure everything is there and ready.

*I should tell her I'm not sick so she'll stop worrying, but then I'd have to lie about why I don't want to see her today.*

I'm just tired, Rachelle. I'll be in school tomorrow. Thank you.

Call me in the morning.

I will. Love you.

Love you, too.

Alisha turned off her phone, put it down on the grass beside her, and threw another stone into the water. *Are you in a better place, Mom? Can you hear me where you are?*

*I'm sorry I focus on the worst of who you were, but that's because I don't want to miss you.*

*It hurts like hell when I do.*

Alisha lay back in the grass with an arm over her eyes. *I have a good life, Mom. I love my job. I have amazing friends who care about me.*

*And I'm getting married.*

*How is it possible to have all that and still feel alone?*

Brett had surprised his secretary by leaving the office at five o'clock. He drove to Braintree, where Spencer's office was located. After a long night of thinking, he'd decided it was time to make some changes in his personal life.

Like his grandmother, he was no longer willing to settle for the fractured state of his family.

In business, Brett went after what he wanted one hundred percent. Because he held nothing back, he won where others lost. Before Alisha, he would have said he lived by his own rules, but there was definitely a pattern playing out in his family, and it would stop with him. If he could run a multibillion-dollar corporation, he could damn well have a conversation with his brother that didn't end with one of them walking off.

A receptionist greeted him as he exited the elevator. The large glass walls behind her with the WorkChat decal had the feel of a start-up business, albeit a good one. He automatically assessed the professionalism of the conversations around him and nodded. "I'm here to see Spencer Westerly."

The woman held up a gadget about the size of a phone and scanned him. "Brett Westerly?"

"Yes."

She tapped something into the gadget. "He's not available to meet with you in person."

"Where is he?" Brett demanded. He didn't like wasting time.

The young woman gave him an odd look as if it were not the norm to hear a raised voice. "He's in the lab, but he said he's willing to meet with you if you're not afraid of heights."

*What the hell?* "Fine."

The woman stood and led him to what looked like a closet door. "Please step inside. Your session will automatically commence once the door closes. If you become disoriented or nervous, touch the wall with a flat hand for ten seconds and your session will end. Please don't try to run out of the room while still in session, since the floor is a rolling one and will only move you through the setting you've chosen. However, the floor freezes when the session terminates, so please remember to touch the wall when you would like to leave."

Giving in to his curiosity, Brett stepped inside and closed the door. He stood motionless inside what appeared to be a tan cylinder that was wide enough for him to extend his arms fully, but not much more. The room dimmed and what he'd thought was a painted surface became a 360-degree screen that flashed the words "WorkChat." He found himself standing in a grassy field that stretched in all directions without interruption. It was essentially a virtual reality experience he could move through by walking. He took a few steps and was impressed by how real the landscape around him looked. It adjusted with him. There was even an image on the floor that completed the landscape.

A female computer voice asked, "Spencer Westerly would like to join your session. Accept or deny?"

Brett said, "Accept."

In jeans and a T-shirt, Spencer appeared beside him and was cropped into the background as a second player in a video game would be. He started walking and his image blurred until he returned to Brett's side. "You have to keep pace with me or our sessions will separate. We're working on that glitch."

Brett fell into step beside his brother. "This is WorkChat? I'm impressed. I had no idea."

A look of surprise turned to a smile of pleasure. "It's the next step in productivity optimization. My goal is to integrate this technology into the workplace so seamlessly that companies won't know what they did before it was available." He lifted his hand and pressed a button on a small handheld device. They were suddenly walking down the hallway of an office building. "The workplace today is global, but flying people back and forth across the ocean is a waste of time. WorkChat allows real-time movement through space. It's also a healthier and safer option for many." They walked into a conference room. "Have a seat," Spencer said.

Brett walked over to one of the chairs. Since he physically couldn't touch it, he stepped next to it and heard a click behind him. Although it was nothing more than a flat board that appeared from the wall, when he sat on it all of his senses told him he was sitting on one of the chairs. Another plank lowered in front of him. On it there was a virtual notepad.

Brett stood, and the planks disappeared back into the wall. "Amazing."

"It will be. To be taken seriously, we need to get out of the prototype phase and smooth out the programming. We already have enough to market it as a game, but I want it to be so much more than that. Every meeting can be recorded. Every setting can be designed to the client's specs. The possibilities are endless. Ever look around the boardroom and wonder how to wake everyone up?" He hit a button, and Brett stumbled back as the conference room disappeared and they were standing on a cloud. The cloud dissolved, and even though Brett knew he was still standing on a solid floor, when a burst of air was added to the visual fall, it felt real. Real enough that when it ended, his heart was pumping.

Pride at what Spencer had accomplished drew a huge smile on Brett's face. Normally, he would have offered him advice, even if he didn't want it. Like his grandmother, Brett only pushed those he cared about. Yet he held his tongue this time. Spencer was doing just fine.

"What do you think?"

"I'm impressed."

"We still have a long way to go, but an infusion of capital would move us along while allowing me to maintain full control."

"Which is why you need your inheritance now."

"Exactly."

Letting out a breath, Brett plowed forward. "That's part of why I'm here. I know things didn't go as you'd hoped on Sunday, but I talked to Grandmother. We're both happy that you found a woman who truly loves you."

"I did?" Spencer asked with a frown, then corrected himself. "I mean, I did."

"What does Alisha think of all this?" Brett asked, waving a hand around the space, even though he didn't want to think about her with his brother.

Spencer shrugged. "She's never seen it. Because of the competitive nature of the business, there are only a handful of people who actually know what WorkChat is capable of. You lucked out and came on a day when we were testing our newest installation. The receptionist today is actually one of our engineers."

Interesting as that was, Brett couldn't get over the fact that his brother hadn't shared the nature of his work with his fiancée. He knew many men who kept their work and home life separate, but Alisha didn't seem like the kind of woman who would be content with that. She didn't sit quietly on the sidelines. He tried to stop himself from probing more, but said, "I hope Sunday didn't upset her."

"Who? Alisha? I don't think so."

"You don't know?" Brett tried to curb the impatience he heard in his own voice.

Spencer looked down at his watch. "Hey, I have a meeting in two minutes with one of my designers in Thailand. I have to go. Thanks for coming by, Brett. It's nice to finally show you what I do." He disappeared from the screen.

Brett placed his hand on the wall and left it there for the count of ten. When the session ended, the door opened. The receptionist was at his side almost immediately. "Mr. Westerly left instructions for you to be allowed another session if you'd like to experience a different location."

Adjusting his tie, Brett shook his head. "All set, thank you. I prefer reality."

*And the truth.*

*Spencer isn't in love with Alisha.*

*What the hell is he doing?*

On the way out of the building, Brett took out his phone. Someone had to know if Alisha was okay. Brett told himself it wasn't his business, but that didn't stop him from calling Rachelle.

# Chapter Five

Although Alisha hadn't come to a single conclusion about what she wanted to do, she did feel more relaxed. The lake house, or lake *shack* as she sometimes jokingly referred to it, always had that effect on her. She didn't have memories of the place. Her mother hadn't taken her there, perhaps because it had been her sanctuary, too, but her grandmother had said her mother had spent summers there when she was a child. Alisha liked to think that when she visited, she was connecting with a time when her mother had been happy. The sun was beginning to set across the water, and if she wasn't going to spend the night, Alisha knew she should leave soon, but she was too comfortable to move. Lying in the grass, propped up on her elbows, she had finally silenced the panic within her and was simply letting herself be in the moment.

"I thought you might be here," a deep male voice said behind her.

*What the hell?* Alisha screamed and jumped to her feet. *What is Brett doing here?* "You scared me."

His eyebrows rose and fell, then one side of his mouth curled in irony. "That wasn't my intention. Rachelle said you weren't feeling well, and when you didn't answer your phone . . ."

*Since when do you talk to Rachelle? And why would you be calling me?* Alisha swallowed that question and lowered the hand that had naturally risen defensively. "How did you find me? No one knows about this place." He held her gaze without answering and an idea came to her. "Do you have some kind of creepy file on me?"

The other side of his mouth twitched as if he were fighting a smile. "Creepy, no. Detailed, yes."

Too much adrenaline was rushing through Alisha for her to appreciate his humor. "That is wrong on so many levels. Did your file say that I come here to be alone?"

"It's not *that* detailed." He looked her over, either not getting her hint for him to leave or dismissing it. "You look like you're feeling better."

Alisha's face warmed as did the rest of her beneath his sustained attention. She clasped her hands in front of her and hoped her response to him wasn't obvious. "I am. Thank you." She swallowed hard as he gazed at her, and her heart began to beat fast. This time not from fear. "If you're here to offer to pay me off again, I'm still not interested." She watched for a reaction to her words, but his expression betrayed none of his thoughts. "I'm also not sorry about what I said to your grandmother, if you're expecting an apology."

"My grandmother needed to hear what you had to say, and I thought you handled her well. She respects you—that's the first step toward her liking you."

Alisha looked away, not wanting him to see how confused she was by his praise. "I'll take your word for that. She didn't look happy with me on Sunday."

"No one likes to hear the truth, but it's better than a lie."

"I guess," Alisha said, not sure where the conversation was going but positive it would be better if she ended it rather than found out. "Now that you've seen I'm fine, I'm sure you have somewhere you need to be."

He looked her over again. Although he was a man who played his cards close to his chest, Alisha would have sworn he was genuinely concerned about her. "Rachelle thought you might call in sick to work tomorrow."

"I'm not sick."

"She told me you'd already gone to bed for the evening because you weren't feeling well."

With a sigh, Alisha ran a hand across her brow. "I lied, okay? I needed a little time alone, and if I tried to tell her that, she would have thought I was upset."

"Are you?"

Alisha turned away from him and looked out over the water. "What could I have to be upset about? I'm getting married in less than a week."

He came to stand beside her. Alisha glanced at him out of the corner of her eye. With his jacket pushed back and his hands in his trouser pockets, he looked every bit like the confident, successful man he was. "If you have any doubts, you should postpone it."

Folding her arms across her chest, Alisha turned her attention back to the peaceful view of the lake. "I really don't want to discuss this with you."

"Marriage is—"

"Why are you here? What is it that you want me to say?" Spinning on him, Alisha dropped her hands to her hips.

His intense blue eyes sought and held hers. "The truth."

Alisha's chest heaved as she began to feel cornered. "What truth?"

He turned fully toward her. "I don't believe you're in love with my brother."

The peaceful lake setting faded into the background as Alisha's senses filled with Brett and how he made her feel. *I don't believe you're in love with my brother.* She knew she couldn't admit to that and should feel horrified that he could see through her so easily. Yet it was his presence she was most affected by, not his closeness to the truth. His nearness sent tingles of unexplainable pleasure through her. It was impossible to look up at his mouth and not wonder how it would feel on hers. Alisha's lips parted and her breath turned shallow. She couldn't move. Didn't want to move. Nothing she'd felt for any of the men she'd been with had prepared her for how easily Brett erased her coherent thoughts and replaced them with wicked images.

His mouth hovered above hers, the warmth of his breath teasing her. She felt herself swaying closer to him. "Well?"

*I need to push him away, tell him he's wrong.*

*God help me, I don't want to.*

"Brett—" She stopped only because she didn't know what to say. She couldn't tell him how she felt. She couldn't lift up on her toes and taste his lips, even if she was shaking from the need to. His eyes burned with a wild hunger. Anything they started wouldn't end with one kiss.

*Sorry, Spencer. I know I promised to marry you to help you, but I accidentally slept with your brother. My bad.*

Alisha took a step back, raised a flat hand up between them. "You need to go."

He held her eyes a moment longer, then nodded. "Are you staying here tonight?"

"No," Alisha said in a thick voice. "I'm going home."

"It's late. I'll follow you in my car," he said.

"You don't have to." There was an unyielding look in his expression that she recognized. "But you *will.*"

His sexy lips curled ever so slightly. "Just to your driveway. I'll sleep better if I know you made it home safely."

*Do you really care about me? Do I want you to?* Alisha nodded, then gathered her purse and phone. *Sleep? Not going to happen.*

*I plan to lie awake questioning my moral compass, then indulge in a fantasy or two about us engaging in carnal acts, and finally round off the night by listing all the reasons why giving in to how you make me feel would be the wrong choice.*

*Wrong for Spencer.*

*Wrong for my relationship with the people I love like family.*

*I should have gone with my first reaction and said no to marrying Spencer.*

*I can't add another layer to that mistake.*

After sliding into her car, Alisha started the engine and watched Brett get into his vehicle. She let herself imagine for a moment what could have been had they met under different circumstances. Would they have come together for one night or become lovers? Could someone like her have ever fit into his life and vice versa? She tried to imagine him chaperoning a field trip and smiled. Tough as he looked on the outside, she had a feeling her students would walk all over him. She sensed a gentleness in him. Strength, but kindness. It was a combination she wished her father had possessed.

Brett pulled far enough back onto the road so that she could pull out in front of him. Alisha did, then drove off, knowing he would follow.

She glanced back often during the drive, and he was there, watching out for her. For as long as Alisha could remember, she'd taken care of others: her mother, her friends—*Spencer*. She kept her pain hidden even from Rachelle, because her friend had also had her own share. Although Rachelle had been raised by a loving mother and a loving stepfather, she'd known her biological father only through court-ordered visits. As soon as she was of age, Rachelle had stopped seeing her father.

Alisha had never asked her why. Talking about Dereck Westerly would have opened the door to a conversation about her own father, and she'd never told anyone about her father's rage. She'd been too afraid she would be taken from her mother if anyone found out. She'd needed to stay and keep her mother safe the best she could.

She wasn't used to anyone watching out for her. Brett had come looking for her because he'd been worried. He was following her home to make sure she was okay. It was old-fashioned and unnecessary.

She didn't need a protector, not anymore.

And yet, a part of her wanted to call and thank him.

*He called me. I have his number now. Shouldn't I say something?*
He made her feel safe in a way she hadn't realized she craved.
And for that one ride home, she didn't feel alone.


*The best way to reconnect with Spencer is definitely not by spending more time with Alisha.* Brett ground his gears as he pulled out of her driveway. He'd followed her home to make sure she got there safely and stayed in his car to make sure he didn't do something he knew he'd regret—kiss her. Technically, he hadn't done anything but make sure Alisha was okay.

But it felt wrong.

Brett wasn't a man who second-guessed himself. He assessed situations and acted on them with swift and unforgiving force. He couldn't remember the last time he hadn't known what his next step should be.

No matter how attractive Alisha was, if she was his brother's fiancée, he wouldn't normally give her a second look.

*But is she?*

*And should she be?*

*And why can't I convince myself it's none of my business?*

*Because they aren't in love.* Brett took a corner too tightly, and the wheels of his sports car squealed in protest.

*Which has nothing to do with me.*

*Unless he's only marrying her to get his inheritance. But I don't know that for sure.*

His hands gripped the steering wheel.

*Why can't he see that he doesn't need to do this? He could get a loan from me. Or Dad. He has options when it comes to funding his company to the next level.*

*He's a man, not a child. If he wants to make a mistake like that, he should be allowed to.*

*Unless Alisha believes their engagement is real.*

*I can't stand back and watch him hurt her.*

He growled as he tried to find his footing on the subject. He considered his instincts first-rate when it came to people, but he was at a loss with Alisha.

*She says she loves Spencer, but the way she looked at me says otherwise. Is the whole guardian angel routine an act?*

*It can't be. She's been Rachelle's friend for too long. Rachelle would see through something like that.*

Could she be marrying Spencer simply to help him?

*There is no way anyone is that nice.*

Brett was under no illusion that he was perfect. Like his father, he'd put more time and value into growing the family business than into his private life. He didn't have what people would consider real friends. He had associates, connections. Loyalty went hand in hand with proven financial benefits.

He doubted many would describe him as a generous or kind man. He did what needed to be done and didn't waste time or emotion on how he felt about much.

Except when it came to his family. Nothing had ever come between him and what he considered his duty to them.

*Family.*

*Duty.*

For a long time he'd excluded his mother from his definition of family. She had not only cheated; she'd left and started over—without Eric and him. *How could my father still love her?* There was no denying that he did. It had been in his eyes every time he spoke of her.

Brett thought of his grandfather and how his father seemed to hate him. Did he? Or was anger easier?

He parked his car in the garage beneath his apartment building and sat in the quiet darkness. Love and loss. Anger and isolation. The pattern was woven through three generations of his family now. It had taken the appearance of Alisha to wake Brett up to how he'd unwillingly allowed the pattern to repeat for himself.

*Is that why I don't want to see her hurt?*

Gentle, but fierce.

Loyal.

Kind, even when reprimanding someone. She left one with the sense that she knew they could do better.

*And we could.*

If she was marrying Spencer for a reason other than love, there was one person who would know. He dialed a number he hadn't in a very long time.

His mother sounded worried when she answered, "Brett?"

"Mother."

"What's wrong? Are you okay?"

Brett closed his eyes for a moment at how his mother assumed he wouldn't call her unless something bad had happened. "I'm fine." He cleared his throat. "I arrived at Grandmother's just as you were leaving on Sunday."

"I know. I saw your car," she said, sounding a little sad about it.

"She means well."

"That's what I tell myself."

His mother's sadness touched him in a way he hadn't expected it to. *I thought I hated her, but maybe I only hated that she left.* "How are you?"

"Me?" she answered breathlessly. She seemed surprised to be asked such a simple question, as if she'd waited a long time to be asked. What had Alisha said about her? *"Stephanie provided them the confidence to be whoever they wanted to be. They love her. I hope you were kind to her, because if you weren't, then you may very well lose your family over it."*

When he compared his mother's personality to his father's, it was easy to see where the disconnect had happened. The miracle was how they had gotten together in the first place. *Is there any of her in me? A shred of her kindness?*

"I'm fine. I've known your grandmother for a long time. I shouldn't be surprised by what she says." *Forgiving*.

There was a time when Brett would have immediately taken his grandmother's side, but he was beginning to see that nothing was quite that simple. "We talked about it after you left. Her intentions are good. She really does want to patch things up. It may take her a few tries to figure out how, though."

His mother sighed. "She thinks I've turned her grandchildren against her. I haven't."

He might have doubted her in the past, but this time he said, "I know."

"I'm glad you called. I don't know if Spencer told you, but he was thrilled that you went to see him. He looks up to you."

"He hides it well," Brett volleyed back and then wished he hadn't. His humor was often lost on his mother.

"Does he?" she answered in a gentle tone. "You played football; he played football. You were at the top of your class; he followed in your footsteps. He's determined to do as well as you in business. I hope you're where you want to be, Brett, because being like you is all Spencer seems to care about."

The elevator opened. It was the top floor in the most elite Back Bay condominium building. A week ago he would have cared that it was the best, but he wanted more for Spencer. How Shakespearean would it be if Spencer made it to the top only to realize that the cost of getting and staying there was painfully steep?

As Brett walked through his full-floor penthouse condo, he felt no attachment. If a larger, better place sprang up across the street, he would move on without looking back. He felt the same about his car and everything else money had bought him.

He wondered if his father felt the same.

Brett sat down heavily on his white leather couch and loosened his tie. "Do you ever regret marrying Dad?"

His mother inhaled audibly. "I regret many things, but never that. Your father and I had some bad years, but we had good ones, too."

"He still loves you." Brett didn't know what he was hoping to hear, but he held his breath as he waited for her reaction.

"I know. That was never the problem," she said, then sniffed. "Are you sure you're okay, Brett? You don't sound like yourself."

In business, information was power. There were things Brett needed to understand before he could move forward. "Did you love him?"

"How could you ask that? Of course I did. A part of me always will."

"Yet you cheated on him and ultimately left him for that man. What kind of love is that?" Although his words were harsh, his tone wasn't.

"Oh, Brett." His mother was quiet for a moment, but then she said, "I'm not perfect, and marriage is hard. Your father and I started off blissfully, crazy in love. We had two really good years where I used to wonder if anyone had the right to be as happy as we were. Then his father died, and he changed. He pulled away and no matter how I tried, I couldn't reach him. I don't know what you're looking for, Brett, but I'm just a woman who married a man she loved, then felt desperately, utterly alone in her marriage. I should have left him years before I did, but I kept hoping it would get better. In the end, staying made it worse. Your father is a good man, but we couldn't make each other happy."

"Do you think Spencer loves Alisha?"

"Oh," his mother said. "He's known her for most of his life."

*That's not what I'm asking.* "So, yes?"

She sighed. "You're worried about him. I'm worried, too. If I tell you something, Brett, you have to promise that it will stay between the two of us."

*I'm not five, but fine.* "Okay."

"I've always encouraged all of you to make choices for yourselves, but Spencer needs guidance right now. Please don't take what I'm about to say to your grandmother."

"I believe that was covered by my earlier promise." As usual his mother didn't laugh, so he added, "I won't say anything to her."

She lowered her voice. "I think he's only marrying Alisha to get his inheritance."

"Does she know that?" he asked, relieved that his mother shared his opinion. And confused by his own reaction.

"I don't know, and that worries me. Alisha has always been a bit of a lost soul. She wants to belong so badly, and I'm afraid that's why she agreed. I hope Spencer is being honest with her. I've tried to talk to both of them, but they say they're in love. I don't want to see her hurt. Is there anything you could say to him that would encourage him to go slower? I feel like if they have more time, they'd both realize that this isn't what they want."

Brett paced the living room of his penthouse long after he hung up with his mother. He hadn't agreed to talk to Spencer about pushing his wedding date back, because he was sure he shouldn't be the one to question how Spencer felt about Alisha. Objectivity was impossible when one had a vested interest in the outcome.

And despite how Brett tried to deny it, Alisha was becoming an obsession. His nights were lost to imagining her beside him. His ability to concentrate on work was constantly threatened by thoughts of where she might be and a need to know she was okay. He not only spent an insane amount of time thinking about her, but she was also affecting him in ways he hadn't expected.

In all the years he'd known about his mother's infidelity, he'd never asked her about it. Her cheating had joined a long list of things he'd never questioned—along with why she hadn't fought for him to go with her.

Why had it been so easy to leave him behind? *Did Dad force her to? Did he need to groom me to take over Westerly Corp.?* He'd always assumed she hadn't wanted him enough to fight for him, but how much choice had either of them had? Twenty years of anger . . .

Talking to his mother had answered some of Brett's questions. *She still loved my father. Had never stopped. I knew why he had pulled away from her, how he had effectively sacrificed his marriage, his family, to save the business. A business . . . over family. Something he still held fast to.* But Brett still had more questions, and he wasn't sure where that left him.

*What kind of man am I?*

*I don't want to be like my father. Rich. Bitter.*

*Alone.*

*Unlike Spencer. If he marries Alisha.*

*Fucking Alisha.*

*How do I get her out of my head?*

# Chapter Six

"Hello? Spencer?" Alisha knocked on the door to Spencer's brownstone apartment a second time. "I know you're in there. Open the door." His lights were on. His car was on the street. Why wasn't he answering? *This is ridiculous.* She knocked harder. Since speaking to Spencer briefly on Tuesday, he'd gone MIA. The last thing he'd said was that they needed to get a marriage license, and that might delay their plans another week. He'd suggested they go together to get it on Thursday or Friday, but she hadn't heard from him since. No text. No phone call. Nothing. If he'd changed his mind about marrying her that was certainly not a reason to hide. She'd be relieved. *Which he would know if he wasn't avoiding me.* She raised her voice. "I am not leaving until you talk to me, so you might as well open the door."

His door finally opened, and Spencer stood there dripping wet with a sheepish smile on his face, wearing nothing more than a towel. Another woman might have found him irresistible like that, but Alisha felt nothing beyond irritation. "Sorry, Alisha. Would you believe I was on a business call?"

She rolled her eyes. "In the shower?"

His grin widened. "You got me. Hey, I don't mean to be rude, but can we talk later?"

She put her hands on her hips and mimicked his voice, "Hey, I don't mean to be rude, either, but no." She stepped by him and into the entrance of his apartment. "What happened? Why aren't you answering my calls?"

He reluctantly closed the door. "I needed some time to think. Last weekend was a lot to process."

"Spencer, are you coming back or should I turn the shower off?" a female voice called out from up the stairs.

Alisha shook her head. Spencer had always been popular with women, and she was under no illusion about the nature of their engagement. Still, finding him with a woman when he was telling the world he wanted to marry her was insulting. She gave him a long, measured look that she hoped conveyed her feelings.

He shrugged like a child caught in the act of something he knew he shouldn't do, but would also do again without hesitation. "Monica is a friend of mine from California. I forgot she was coming. We get together whenever she has a conference in Boston." He studied Alisha's expression again. "You're not upset, are you?"

"About her? No."

"I figured that once we get married, I should at least try to not be with other women, out of respect for you. But we could be married a while. That's a long time to go without—" He stopped, then cocked his head to one side. "Because we would never . . . You're not expecting to . . ."

"No."

"Thank God," Spencer said, then made a pained face. "I don't mean that the way it sounds. You are completely fuckable; it would just feel wrong."

Alisha sighed. *Fuckable? I'm fuckable? Not pretty, gorgeous . . . fuckable.* She knew what he meant. *Still, not an ego builder.*

"Spencer?" Monica called from halfway down the stairs. She froze when she saw Alisha, then smiled and purred, "Is this what you were trying to tell me earlier? Oh, I'm in. She's beautiful."

Alisha took a quick step back. "I'm not here for—"

Spencer laughed. "You should see your face, Alisha. Who knew you were such a prude?"

Alisha swatted at Spencer and took another step toward the door. "I'm flattered and completely accepting of other people's preferences, but I came by to ask Spencer a question."

The woman dropped her towel and ran a hand across her ample breasts. "Are you sure? I haven't been with a woman in a while, but I know we'd have fun."

After a quick fumble with the door, Alisha escaped through it. Spencer followed her, looking over his shoulder and then back at Alisha apologetically. "See why I couldn't say no? She doesn't care that I'm engaged. This is guilt-free. Like one last ice-cream cone before cutting out sugar."

Alisha was on the bottom of the steps, looking up at him. "At least I know why you weren't taking my calls."

A hand snaked around his shoulder and across his bare chest as he stood there, and his towel began to tent. "I meant to. Time flies when you're having fun. She leaves on Sunday night. I'll call you then."

"Fine," Alisha said as she turned away.

"Alisha," Spencer called out.

Alisha glanced over her shoulder in his direction but refused to actually look at him. "What?"

"Thanks for understanding."

"No problem," she answered automatically.

"Hey, I told you, you were fuckable. Monica is disappointed." His tone was the teasing one they often used with each other.

Facing forward again, Alisha shot her middle finger back at him. The past couple of weeks had been emotional, and she'd begun to worry that they'd overwhelmed Spencer.

Apparently, he was fine.

*I'm going to be, too. When Spencer surfaces from—that—we'll talk. I'll tell him the concerns I have about how little we've thought through this marriage-and-divorce thing. How I don't want to lie to his mother or to anyone else.*

*And we'll figure out where we go from there.*

The more she thought about it, the more relieved she was at the reason Spencer hadn't been calling her. He looked happy and confident, and that was what mattered most to Alisha.

She smiled. *And Monica thinks I'm hot.*

*So at least I know the yoga is working.*

After telling himself all week that he wouldn't, Brett parked his car in front of Spencer's brownstone and planned what he would say to his brother. It was Friday, and no one had heard from Spencer all week.

*He better not already be married.*

*Or?*

*Or I'll be forced to be happy for him.*

*I don't know if I can do that.*

Brett rang the doorbell, but there was no answer. He searched the street for Spencer's car. *Shit.* He was preparing to leave when Spencer's car pulled up. His gut twisted painfully when he saw Spencer lean over and kiss Alisha. He'd never respected a man who lusted after another man's woman, but there he was, suffering from a full-blown case of jealousy over a woman he barely knew.

Spencer exited and walked around to let Alisha out. It was only then that Brett realized the woman who wrapped herself about Spencer was a brunette. Anger replaced jealousy as Brett strode toward them.

"Spencer," Brett growled his brother's name.

"Brett." Spencer's eyes rounded. "Monica, this is my brother, Brett. Brett, meet Monica."

"What the hell are you doing?" Brett demanded.

Monica brought a hand to her chin. Her eyes danced with mischief. "Do you really want to know? Maybe watch?"

Spencer frowned at the woman. "Monica, that's my *brother*. And you shouldn't joke like that. He'll think we're more than friends."

Monica shrugged. "I'm confused. Other women can know about me, but you don't want your brother to?"

"Other women?" *This is too much.* "Excuse us, Monica. I need a moment with Spencer."

Spencer looked uncertain. "Monica, I'll get you the notes later. Wait in my car."

"Sure." Monica laughed. "Whatever." She slid into the car, but before the door closed, she said, "When you're married, would you mind if he and I—"

Spencer shut the door before she finished. He leaned against the side of the car and folded his arms across his chest. "You've never come here, Brett. What do you want?"

"You could start with an explanation."

The look he gave Brett was cold and steely. "The thing is, I don't owe you one. How I live my life is none of your business."

Brett counted to ten and pocketed his hands. Spencer was stonewalling him on a personal level, so Brett shifted automatically to handling it as he would any difficult negotiation: he plowed ahead. "Are you still getting married this weekend?"

After a brief pause, Spencer shook his head. "The paperwork is more time-consuming than we had anticipated. We're putting it off for a couple of weeks."

*Thank God.* He almost called Spencer out on what he was actually spending his time on, or rather who, but he didn't. He was willing to keep some thoughts to himself if it got him what he wanted in the end. And what he wanted was for Spencer to see that Alisha deserved to be treated better. "I may not have been receptive to the idea of Alisha when you first said you were marrying her, but if you're going to do this, you should do it right."

"Relationship advice from you? Am I supposed to take this seriously?"

"You're supposed to be the kind of man who gives a shit about his fiancée."

Spencer straightened. "You don't know anything about me or Alisha. I don't need your money or your advice. Now, if you'll excuse me, this conversation is over."

Brett stepped closer to him until they were in a nose-to-nose stand-off. The truth was obvious, but Brett wanted to hear it voiced. "You're better than this, Spencer. You know it, and so do I. What you're doing today shows a lack of respect for whatever you have with Alisha. You're not fucking invisible. People see what you do. Those same people will go back and say things to her. Ask yourself how that will be for her. You say you love her, but then you do something that is guaranteed to hurt her. If her feelings don't matter, why the hell are you marrying her?"

Spencer looked away first, and Brett knew he had been heard. That's all he could do. He wouldn't tell Spencer not to marry her. He sure as hell wasn't going to encourage him to do it, either. Hopefully, what he said woke his brother up to the fact that actions had consequences.

Brett started to walk away, but stopped and turned back. *How could he cheat on Alisha? Monica was pretty, but Alisha . . . she was the real deal. Beautiful inside and out.* If he started comparing the two, Brett was certain his feelings for Alisha would quickly become apparent. *And he made a valid point earlier.* "This shouldn't have been my first time here. I should have gone with you when you were house hunting."

A funny expression spread across Spencer's face. "Are you okay?"

In the past, Brett would have assured him that he was. Westerlys didn't talk about their feelings. His mother's words came back to him, though. If Spencer's goal really was to emulate him, he needed to know that it wasn't all gold coins and roses. How different might everyone's life have been had his father let his mother in instead of walling her out. Perceived impossibilities. They were simply obstacles he smashed through in business. *The distance between us appears insurmountable.*

*But is it?*

*One systemic policy modification can change the course of a company.*

He'd often told his directors that clear goals are the most powerful. Vision inspires effort. Focused vision inspires focused effort, which produces success.

*Our family has unhealthy patterns.*

*They stop now.*

*No walls. No lies.*

"You asked me why I came. I'm here because I care about you. I want things to work out for you and for your company. And if you need help, I'm always only a phone call away." He expelled a harsh breath. "But you need to know that Alisha is an amazing woman. She's intelligent, caring, and beautiful. If you don't treat her well, you'll lose her to someone who will. Dad learned that the hard way."

With that, Brett walked away. He'd said his piece. What happened next was up to Spencer.

# Chapter Seven

On Saturday morning, Alisha put the thermometer on the counter near the bathroom sink and looked at herself in the mirror. *This is what I get for lying about being sick.* Taking her temperature hadn't been necessary. She shivered with cold, her face flushed, and her eyes glazed from fever.

She downed a couple of Tylenol and dragged her feet back to bed. *I'll sleep it off and be fine by Monday morning.*

Her phone beeped with a text. She groaned and rolled over to read it. Spencer wanted to talk. She dropped the phone beside her without answering him. *He was fine not talking last week. He can wait another day.*

Still on top of her bedsheets, she closed her eyes and drifted to sleep. Her phone beeped again. Rachelle wanted to know if she wanted to go to breakfast. Alisha typed back that she was sick.

*Again?!? I'm worried about you. I'm coming over.*

Alisha swore. She felt miserable. If Rachelle came over, Alisha would have to get up and try to look less like she wanted to die. Not because Rachelle wouldn't allow her friend to wallow, but because Alisha wouldn't want to put the weight of how she felt onto her.

Alisha had learned at a young age to hide her pain, smile when she wanted to cry, and put her feelings aside for others. She didn't want to do that today. All she wanted to do was stay in her pajamas, leave her bed only to use the bathroom, and not think or worry about another person until Monday. She texted back. *Please don't. I just want to crash and sleep it off.*

If Rachelle was put off by her blunt response, Alisha was prepared to apologize for it. *Monday.* She closed her eyes and instantly fell back asleep.

She woke to a pounding headache and the sound of her doorbell ringing over and over. At first she pulled a pillow over her head, but the ringing didn't stop. Swearing, she stumbled out of bed to answer it. She felt cold and hated whoever had ended the reprieve she'd found in sleep. She looked out the peephole in the front door.

There, in a gray polo shirt and dark slacks was—*Brett?*

*Shit.*

*If I don't answer the door, will he go away?*

"Alisha, open the door."

"I can't," she said lamely. "I'm contagious. I don't want to give it to anyone."

"If you're actually ill this time, you need to open the door. How sick are you?"

Alisha raised a hand to her throbbing forehead. *Too sick for this.* "Thank you for checking on me, but I'm fine."

"I'm not leaving."

"Go away, Brett."

"Show me how sick you are, and I will."

Alisha straightened. "Oh, for God's sake." If seeing her in her full germ-infested glory would get him to leave, then fine. *Let him look.* She swung the door open and put an arm up. "I'm fine. See?"

He looked her over from head to toe and frowned. "You look awful."

She would have glared at him if she'd had the energy. "That's sweet, but there's no need to heap on the compliments."

He stepped inside and closed the door behind him. "I'm serious. You're definitely sick."

She waved a hand at him. "Thank you, Doctor Obvious."

He raised a hand to her forehead. "You're burning up."

"I'm aware of that, too." She pushed his hand away. "Which is why I'm home sleeping it off."

"Alone?"

Irritated that he wouldn't leave, she snapped, "Yes, my therapeutic orgy ended an hour ago, and they all went home."

His smile didn't help her mood. "I'll have to try that the next time I'm sick." His smile faded. "I thought Spencer might be here. Does he know you're sick?"

Alisha shook her head and turned away. Pretending was beyond her at the moment. "I can't do this right now. Could you let yourself out and lock the door behind you, please?" She trudged back to her bed and collapsed, facedown, on top of it.

A few minutes later, Brett's voice pulled her back awake. "Roll over."

Alisha did and opened her eyes. The glass of water he held out to her was the solution to the dry mouth she hadn't realized she was suffering from. She pushed herself up to a seated position and sipped it. "Thanks."

He held two pills toward her. "Take these. Do you want me to call Spencer?"

She dutifully swallowed them. "No. It's just a fever. I'll be fine by tomorrow." She met his eyes and saw the same stubborn look he'd had the night he followed her home a week ago. Had it been that long ago? "I don't mind being alone."

"He should be here."

Alisha put the glass of water on the bedside table and flopped back. She was shivering but too tired to do anything about it. Her feverish brain defaulted to honesty. "Don't call him. I don't want to argue. I don't want to lie. I just want to sleep." She sighed in bliss when she felt him place a light comforter over her.

"What are you lying about?" he asked in such a gentle tone that she answered him without hesitation.

"Everything."

"Does that include why you're marrying him?" The corner of the bed dipped beneath his weight.

*Double shit.* Alisha's eyes flew to his. "When my mother passed, I swore I'd never lie again. For anyone. It eats away at me. Do you know what I mean?"

He frowned. "I think so."

Her eyes closed again and the rest drifted out of her like a confession. "But some lies are good, right? I mean, if they help people. That's all I wanted to do—help Spencer. I didn't know it would become this . . . all of this. I should have thought it through. How will Stephanie feel when we divorce? Can we tell the truth after he gets his inheritance? Will they hate me for lying? Spencer is counting on me, but I don't know if I can go through with this." A tear escaped the corner of her eye. "He has been so good to me. Your whole family has. I would do anything for them. I want Spencer to have his money. He deserves the same kind of chance you had." She turned on her side and cried softly into the pillow.

"Shh," Brett said from beside her as he placed a hand on her back. "I'll make sure Spencer has what he needs. Go to sleep."

He continued to speak to her, but his voice sounded far away. She knew she should force her eyes to open again, but she didn't want to think about how wrong it was to have him there. She didn't want to worry about Spencer or Brett at that moment. Normally, she wouldn't be able to sleep with someone hovering over her. She never allowed herself to feel vulnerable like that.

That day, though, it was comforting. She fell asleep on her side to the soothing touch of Brett gently rubbing her back.

She woke in a sweat a few hours later. Instantly Brett was beside her, laying a hand on her forehead. "Looks like the fever broke. Good."

Her eyes fluttered as she strove to remember why he was there with her. Bits and pieces of their conversation before she fell asleep came back to her. She took his hand in hers. "Brett, what I said earlier . . ."

"Yes?" he asked, his expression inscrutable.

"Please don't say anything to anyone. Spencer is counting on me."

He gave her hand a gentle squeeze, but didn't promise anything. "How do you feel?"

"Better."

"You still look like shit."

She smiled weakly and dropped his hand. "You're an ass."

"I called my doctor. He's coming by on his way to dinner."

"That's not necessary."

"It's done."

She rubbed a hand across her forehead. "Did anyone ever tell you that you're bossy?"

"When you have a dick they call it commanding."

Alisha chuckled. Brett was funny. Who knew? And nurturing. She was still trying to get over the fact that he'd spent the day at her house while she likely snored her fever away.

*Unless I'm still sleeping.* She brought a hand self-consciously up to her hair and groaned at her tangled mane of curls. *If this were a fever-induced dream, I'd look better, and he'd be naked.* Her face warmed at the thought, and she looked away.

*I guess I'm feeling better.*

"What are you thinking?" he asked and sat on the edge of her bed again.

She shook her head and regretted the move when her forehead began to pound again. "Nothing." *That I can say.* "Thank you for staying."

He smiled. "Don't tell anyone. I have a reputation to uphold."

It almost felt as if he was flirting with her, but Alisha told herself she was imagining it. *In his own words, I look like shit. He's not here because he's attracted to me.* "It'll be our secret." Only after the words came out of her mouth did they sound wrong. "I didn't mean to make it sound . . ."

"Alisha, about what you said earlier—"

The sound of her doorbell ringing cut off whatever he was going to say. He looked down at his phone and said, "That's Dr. Earl."

Alisha sat up and was going to stand when Brett stopped her by putting a hand on her shoulder.

"I'll get it," he said. "No need to get up."

"I didn't realize doctors still made house calls."

"Then you don't know the right doctors," he said with a smile that told her he was throwing her own words back at her.

"I guess not," she said. Brett left the room to let the doctor in, and Alisha adjusted the comforter around her. *Or the right men.* This wasn't her first rodeo. She'd known her share of men, slept with a handful of them, even fancied herself in love once or twice. None of them had ever taken care of her when she was sick. As she looked back at her relationships, she realized she was as much at fault as they were. She didn't let them close because she didn't want to need them.

It was different with Brett.

*But he's Spencer's brother*, she reminded herself.

A man who is now and will always be off-limits. *So enjoy the idea of him, but it can't go past that.* She scooted to sit on the edge of her bed.

A thin white-haired man with an easy smile and a small leather bag followed Brett into Alisha's bedroom. "Let's take a look at your sick friend."

Alisha stood to greet him, but felt weak as she did. She raised a hand to her wild hair, embarrassed to be meeting anyone looking the way she did. "Thank you for coming to see me. It's probably just a virus that'll be gone by tomorrow. I'm Alisha Coventry."

"Dr. Earl." He put his bag down on the corner of her bed. He looked around the room, then back at her. "I didn't realize you went to school for medicine. Where's your diploma?"

Alisha's mouth rounded in offended surprise until she saw a spark of humor in his eyes. "I'm a kindergarten teacher. This isn't my first cold."

"Ah," he said as he nodded in agreement. "You work in a petri dish of germs, so you're a pro at this. Why don't I have a look anyway?"

Brett stayed by the door while Dr. Earl took Alisha's temperature, looked down her throat, and took her blood pressure. She had a feeling Brett would leave the room if she hinted that she didn't want him there, but he stayed in case she needed him.

She answered question after question from the doctor and was relieved when he started gathering his instruments. "Probably a virus. Sounds like you're over the worst of it and hopefully it'll be gone by tomorrow," the doctor said, then wagged a finger at her. "But don't go getting cocky. If you're still sick on Monday, give me a call."

"I will," Alisha said and took the card he offered her.

He gave her one last assessing look that ended on her left hand. "So when is the wedding? I hope I'm invited."

Alisha quickly covered her engagement ring with her other hand. "Oh, we're not—" *We're not . . .* What struck Alisha silent was the sadness that accompanied her denial. *We're not engaged.*

*We're not anything.*

*And we can't ever be.*

"I'll walk you out," Brett said smoothly and led the doctor out of the room.

Alisha covered her face with both hands. *What am I doing?*

Beside her bed her phone beeped with an incoming message. *Spencer.*

**Rachelle said you're sick so I won't come by. Unless you need something.**

She wrote back: I'm good. Sleeping it off.

Hey, I'm sorry about Monica.
Don't be. It didn't bother me.
You said that, but I'm still sorry. You're doing me a favor by marrying me, and I'm acting like a complete ass. I was thinking with my dick and not my head. I should have thought about how it might make you feel. I won't do anything to embarrass you while we're married.

*About that.* Alisha took a deep breath and typed: I'm not sure we should get married. Before she had time to hit "Send," though, another message from him came through.

I want you to know how much I appreciate you doing this for me. You are the most generous and caring person I know. All joking aside, I owe you big for this.

Alisha deleted her last message instead of sending it. The talk they needed to have would wait until it could happen in person.

Talk to you later, Spence
Later, Al

Brett held the door of Alisha's home open, but Dr. Earl didn't move to exit through it. He stood there, looking as if he wanted to say something. When he finally spoke, it was in a tone that sounded more fatherly than professional. "I've known your family a long time, Brett. Most of my career, in fact."

"That's why I knew I could call you about this."

"Who is she engaged to?"

Brett flexed his shoulders. "A man she doesn't love."

77

The doctor put a hand on Brett's arm. "Are you sure?"

"Yes."

He studied Brett's face for a moment. "Then you'd better do something about that. I hate to advise on so little information, but I can tell by the way you look at her that you'll be one miserable son of a bitch if you let her get away."

Brett closed the door after the doctor left and leaned against it. As usual, Dr. Earl was spot-on with his diagnosis. After pushing off the door, Brett paced Alisha's small living room. The truth about Spencer and Alisha's engagement was a game changer.

*All Spencer wants is his inheritance.*

*Alisha wants to help the family who was kind to her during her troubled childhood.*

*No fucking way does this end with the two of them getting married.*

As he headed back to Alisha, he heard the door of her bedroom close, followed by the sound of the shower turning on. It was impossible not to imagine how she would look, naked and luscious beneath the spray. That's all it took for his body to become fully excited. He groaned, walked back to the living room, and read e-mails on his phone in an attempt to distract himself.

Eventually it worked. He calmed, lost track of the time, and only noticed that the sun had set when he looked up and the room was dark. Alisha's room was silent again. Brett stood and stretched.

Most likely she'd fallen asleep after her shower, but he couldn't be sure. How could he leave without knowing if she was safe in her bed or had collapsed in her shower? He opened her bedroom door and called her name.

No answer.

He stepped inside the dark room. As his eyes adjusted, he saw the outline of her on her bed, cuddled beneath her comforter. He stepped closer and marveled at her natural beauty. With no makeup and hair still damp from the shower, she effortlessly took his breath away.

He told himself to leave, but instead he sat on the edge of her bed and laid a hand across her forehead. It was finally cool to the touch.

Her eyes fluttered open. "Brett?"

"Yes."

"Thank you for staying."

The simplicity of her gratitude moved him. He wanted to tell her there wasn't a limit to what he would do for her, but neither of them was ready for such declarations. He touched her hair. "It's still wet," he said in gentle reprimand.

Her eyes met his.

If only she wasn't sick.

If only he wasn't Spencer's brother.

Despite the circumstances, their attraction for each other was present, a slow steady beat in the background. "I meant to dry it, but I was tired. I thought I could lay down for a minute."

He stood, turned on her bedroom lamp, walked to the bathroom, and returned with her hair dryer. After plugging it into the outlet she had by her bed, he said, "Sit up and turn around."

"You are not blow-drying my hair."

Another man might have accepted that answer, but in the time it had taken to retrieve her hair dryer, he'd indulged in a full fantasy of how much he'd enjoy running his hands through her hair. "Sit up."

A smile tugged at her lips. "Your tone of voice alone makes me want to say no."

His heart thudded in his chest. "Funny, the way you look at me makes me want to hear you say yes."

Suddenly, she was all eyes. She sat up and pulled her knees protectively to her chest. "You should go."

He placed the hair dryer on the bedside table. "Don't marry Spencer. I understand why you want to. You think it's the only way to help him. It doesn't have to be that way."

She chewed her bottom lip. "I shouldn't have said anything. I don't know why I did."

He sat on the bed beside her. "I do." He picked up her hand, brought it to his mouth, and gently kissed the inside of her wrist. Her pulse beat wildly against his lips. "It's this."

She let out a shaky breath. "I've already decided I can't go through with the wedding, but I can't do this, either." She removed her hand from his. "Spencer would never forgive me. He'd think I chose you over him. He's been in competition with you his whole life. I couldn't do that to him."

"What about what you want?" he growled softly.

She went back to hugging her legs. "You asked me once if I loved Spencer and I said yes. I wasn't lying. I do love him . . . like a brother. His happiness is important to me, just as it should be to you. We can't do this. I won't do this. I'm sorry."

His pride kicked in and he stood. "I hope he is as loyal to you as you are to him. We'll find out as soon as you tell him no." He hated the uncertainty his words brought to her eyes. He wanted to crawl into the bed and ask her to forgive him, but that wasn't yet an option. Before walking out of her bedroom, he paused. *What kind of an ass hurts a woman like her? She has more decency in her pinkie than I've ever had.* "Do you need anything before I go?"

She shook her head and looked away.

Brett told himself to leave but couldn't. He thought about the first time he met her and how she had stayed true to his initial impression of her. Money couldn't buy her. Desire came second to her principles. He hadn't thought people like her existed.

She was the kind of woman Brett would want to marry, if he believed in marriage. *And what do I do? I insult her. I try to pay her off. Then, to top it all off, all I can think about is sleeping with her, regardless of how my brother feels or how sick she is.*

She was a decent person, and he didn't know how to walk away from how she made him feel. It was more than a physical attraction. He felt good when he was with her—hopeful. At a time in his life when he wasn't sure what he believed in anymore, he believed in her.

She met his eyes again. "Thank you, Brett. For staying with me when I was sick. No one has ever done that."

Brett's generosity had never extended beyond his family, but he would have spent a week at her bedside if she needed him to. He nodded once in acknowledgment of her comment and left. As a man, as well as a child, he was used to getting what he wanted. He'd known how to win in almost every situation he'd ever been put in.

Except this one.

Every problem had a solution.

With determination, every obstacle fell away.

There was a way to have Alisha without hurting Spencer.

And he would find it.

# Chapter Eight

Alisha woke late after a fitful night of sleep that had nothing to do with the virus that had plagued her the day before. She trudged to the bathroom and made a face at how her hair had dried into a wild mess. She looked pale, but felt a hundred times better. *I don't even want to think about how I must have looked yesterday.*

Pink filled her cheeks as she remembered the kiss Brett had given her wrist. Despite feeling weak from her fever, her body had tingled from that brief touch. She'd wanted nothing more than to pull his face to hers and finally taste those strong lips of his.

*Why couldn't he be the asshole Spencer said he was? This would all be easy.*

Brett didn't hide that he was used to things going his way, but he didn't push her. In fact, he was unexpectedly tender at times.

No one in her entire life had ever cared for her the way he did. Not her mother. Definitely not her father. Alisha went back through the boyfriends she'd had since high school. Not one had made her feel the way Brett did. Of course, he was the polar opposite of what she'd always thought she wanted in a man. She'd never wanted a powerful man in her life.

She hadn't realized until then that she'd always chosen men she thought she could control. She'd even dated a man in college who had cried every time they watched sad movies together. At the time, Alisha had told herself his emotionalism meant he would be more sensitive to her needs, but that wasn't the case. He'd seen every disagreement they had, every bump in their shared road, in terms of how it made *him* feel.

*Brett listens to me, goes out of his way to make sure I'm okay.*

*And the way he looks at me—like I'm already his.*

*Oh yes.*

*He's there for me even when I tell him he doesn't have to be.*

*Stubborn about what he wants, and he wants me.*

*Why?*

*Because I stood up to him? Refused to be bought?*

*It can't be because I told his grandmother off.*

*Or because I look good when I'm sick. How many times did he say I looked awful?*

*I hardly know him, but I feel like I do.*

*What's this connection we have? It's more than lust.*

*Although, that is certainly there.*

She flushed.

*I wish I could say yes to you, Brett, but I still have to find a way to say no to Spencer.*


The next few days Alisha tried to push Brett out of her thoughts. Nothing could dislodge him. Not the last-days-of-school chaos. Not the advanced yoga class Rachelle convinced her she was ready for. Her attempt at meditation failed, and she spent the hour feeling guilty even though she hadn't yet done anything.

She hadn't spoken to Brett or Spencer.

Three days away from both of them should have given her clarity, but all she'd done was pine over one while she felt guilty about the other.

On the first afternoon of her summer vacation she was running errands when she thought, *This is ridiculous.*

*I was perfectly fine before I met Brett. I'll be fine if I never see him again.*

*I can't marry Spencer, and I can't keep avoiding him because I don't want to disappoint him.*

*His grandmother says she loves him.*

*If that's true, she wouldn't want him to marry a woman he doesn't love. That's it.*

*I'll go see Delinda Westerly. I'll explain all of this . . . well, some of this, to her and she'll see why simply giving him his inheritance is the only solution.*

She sprinted back to her car and sped along, following the directions her GPS gave her. She didn't second-guess her decision until she was standing on the stone steps of Delinda Westerly's mansion by the sea.

*Spencer needs that money. If I simply break it off with him, he may get nothing. This is the only way.*

The butler answered the door. "Miss Coventry. Is Mrs. Westerly expecting you this afternoon?"

Alisha smiled politely. "No, but I'm sure she'll want to see me. I have something very important to tell her."

"One moment please," he said, and then he was back in an instant. "She'll see you in the solarium."

"Thank you," Alisha said as she followed him in.

Delinda was sitting when Alisha entered the room. She waved at a chair near her. "Don't dawdle near the door. Come in."

Alisha approached and told herself she wasn't intimidated. Delinda certainly had a presence. "I hope you don't mind that I dropped by without calling."

"Whether I mind or not doesn't change that you're here, does it, dear?" Delinda asked with a thin smile.

Alisha remembered what Brett had said about Delinda respecting her for speaking up. "You could pretend you're happy to see me."

Shrewd eyes flew to Alisha's. "Whoever said I wasn't?"

Alisha leaned in. "If you don't say something nice, I may hug you."

Delinda's eyes rounded, then humor filled her eyes, and it transformed her face. "You are a spirited young woman, to say the least."

Up until then, Alisha hadn't thought of herself as spirited. Yes, she gave herself tough pep talks, but she did so out of fear that she'd succumb again to her childhood feelings of powerlessness. *No one will ever make me feel that way again.* Taking a seat across from her, Alisha smiled. "I'll take that compliment. I have a feeling you were described the same way when you were my age."

A sincere smile stretched across Delinda's face. "I was. I wouldn't have been able to marry my husband if I'd been afraid of what anyone thought of me."

"Really?" Alisha asked in surprise. Could understanding Delinda's own choices help Alisha convince her to change her mind about the wedding clause?

"Oliver worked in one of my father's factories. He was a floor manager. My father was angry when he heard I was dating Oliver. He wanted me to choose someone from our social circle. He threatened to disown me if I went on another date with him. You can imagine the fit he had when I married him."

"But he didn't disown you."

"No, he didn't. In the end he saw how much I loved Oliver, and that was all that mattered."

*Deep breath.* "I'm glad to hear that because there's something I need to tell you."

Delinda folded her hands on her lap. It was a move that might be confused with docility, but Delinda was far from embodying that. "Well, say what you came here to say, child."

"You *have* to give Spencer his inheritance no matter what happens between me and him. That money will make his dream company a reality. Spencer wants desperately to prove himself to be as good as his older brothers. He doesn't just want it; he needs it. I can't leave here today unless I convince you of that."

"Forgive me, but I was under the assumption you two were about to be married. Did something happen?"

Alisha stood, paced, then sat again. "Promise me that no matter what happens, whether he marries or not, that you'll give him his inheritance."

"Are you saying you're not marrying him?" Sharp eyes watched Alisha intently.

*Spencer needs this. I need this.* "Please. I can't tell you why, but you have to see that he deserves it either way."

Delinda's lips pressed in a determined line before she said, "Young woman, you don't need to tell me what Spencer does or doesn't deserve. I've always treated him as one of my grandchildren even though . . ."

"Even though?" Spencer said from the door of the solarium.

Delinda pushed herself out of her chair and stood. "Spencer, I didn't know you were here."

There was no trace of the quick-to-humor Spencer. He stood frozen in the doorway with a tone that was just as cold. "Even though what, Grandmother?"

"Surely your mother told you. She married the man, for God's sake."

"What are you saying?" he barked.

Alisha rushed to Spencer's side, but he was oblivious to her presence.

Delinda went pale. "I'm sorry. I assumed you knew. I—" She sat down heavily in her chair.

Spencer's face tightened with anger. "Dad was the one who cheated."

"I'm sorry if that's what you've all been led to believe." Delinda shook her head and raised a shaking hand to her mouth. "I would have never said a word had I known your mother hadn't."

"You're lying," Spencer boomed.

Delinda came to her feet unsteadily. "It never changed how much I loved you. It never mattered to Dereck, either. He would have raised you as his own if your mother had let him."

Spencer turned and strode out of the room. Alisha followed him, grabbing at his arm. "Are you okay?"

Spencer stopped and snarled, "I came here to confess to her that our engagement was a sham. I hoped to persuade her to drop the condition. Turns out, I'm not even her grandchild." He pulled his arm away from Alisha.

"I'm so sorry, Spencer."

He marched out of the house as he said, "Don't be. You did me a favor. I never have to see her again."

Alisha stood on the steps and watched him peel out of the driveway without looking back. She slid the engagement ring off her finger and pocketed it. Something told her the break-it-off conversation she'd been rehearsing in her head would no longer be necessary.

She numbly walked to her car and started it, but didn't know where to go. On her drive home, she called Rachelle. "I made a huge mistake, Rachelle, and I don't know how to fix it."

Brett had been at work when his grandmother called. She'd sounded upset and asked him to come right away. Leaving work required some tricky rescheduling, but he did it and was at her house in less than an hour.

As soon as he saw her, he was glad he'd come. She was visibly distraught to the point where he called Dr. Earl. She refused to lie down, but he was able to settle her onto a couch in her living room. He'd never seen her worked up the way she was. Brett called his father and told him to come as well. "What's wrong? Tell me."

She kept shaking her head as if she were in shock. He sat beside her and put a comforting arm around her. As soon as he did, she began to cry against his chest. "Whatever it is, we'll fix it."

"You can't. I never would have said something if I had known she hadn't told him. It never mattered to me. I love him. I should have told him sooner."

"Who? Grandmother, who are you talking about?"

She raised her face and wiped the tears from her fragile cheeks. "Spencer. I never meant to hurt him. I wanted all of you to be more a part of my life, but all I did was make it worse." She started to cry again.

"I don't understand. What did you tell Spencer?"

"That Dereck isn't his father. Mark is. I thought he knew. I thought you all knew. Stephanie married him. He raised Spencer. Why would I think he *didn't* know?"

He stopped asking questions and simply held her as he processed a truth a part of him had always suspected. Spencer was blond, like Mark. Spencer was quick to laugh and just as quick to forgive. Usually. Brett had no idea how Spencer would handle something like this, though.

Part of Brett wanted to rewind the last few weeks and go back to thinking only about business. Taking care of his family then had been hands-off and clean. This was messy, emotional, and everything Brett wasn't comfortable with.

His grandmother never cried, but she was sobbing in his arms.

He'd thought he knew his father, but now he questioned if he knew anyone at all. His opinion of his mother was so convoluted now that he didn't know what he thought about her. Why had she stayed with his father after her affair? Was Nicolette Mark's? What else had his parents lied about or failed to disclose? In his mind it was the same thing.

He doubted his own ability to protect his family. How could he not have known about Spencer? And if he had, what would he have done differently?

Would he have let Spencer go on believing they had the same father or would Brett have found a less painful way for him to find out? Was there one?

By the time his father arrived, his grandmother had already met with the doctor. She refused sedatives and told the doctor where to go when he suggested she lie down. After their heated exchange wherein she threatened everything from his life to his medical license, he diagnosed her healthy enough to handle it without his assistance.

His father asked for a moment alone and spoke to Delinda quietly on the other side of the room. He nodded a few times, then stood.

Brett was at his side in a few strides. "This is a problem."

His father sighed. "Yes, it is."

Brett swayed back onto his heels. "It wasn't fair for Spencer to hear it this way."

One of his father's eyebrows rose, then fell. "That wasn't my decision to make."

"Wasn't it? If you knew, then you could have said something. Or did you think none of us had the right to know? We did."

Dereck looked sadly from his mother to Brett. "I hoped she didn't know. I thought only your mother and I did."

"You were wrong, and Spencer paid the price for that cowardice."

Brett's voice brought his father's eyes to his with anger. "You think I said nothing because I was afraid? I didn't care that Spencer came from an affair your mother had. He is my son."

"How many times have you seen him in the past ten years? A handful, I'd guess. Don't try to sell a version of this where you are the victim. He deserved to know that he was living with his real father."

His father's shoulders slumped. "When he left with your mother and she married Mark, I did close a door on him. It was too much. That doesn't mean I don't consider him my son or that I would have had him find out this way." He rubbed a hand over his chin as his eyes blurred with emotion. "I have never denied him a single thing. He has always been in my will as well as your grandmother's. We'll fix this. You and I have always been good with damage control."

Brett shook his head as the full extent of how little his father understood became clear to him. "Dad, the last thing Spencer is thinking about right now is your fucking will. There is no damage control plan for this. He just found out his life has been a lie."

"I never lied to him."

"You never told him the truth. That's the same thing."

"Your mother made that choice, and I honored it."

"What about Nicolette?"

"Mine," his father said in a low tone. "At least I believe so."

Brett was temporarily finished with lies that seemed to have no end or justification. "Stay with Grandmother. She needs you."

"I realize that."

*Do you?* Brett wasn't so sure. "For as long as I can remember, you've been telling me that family is all that matters. What we want comes second. You also said you learn a lot about a man when you step into his shoes. I can't imagine what you went through when your father died and you learned the truth about him. I know it forced you to do things you wouldn't have. Maybe you had to close off a piece of yourself to do it. I don't know. But I'm standing in your shoes now, and your legacy is also a tragedy. You need to make sure your mother understands that this was not her fault. You left her in the dark, and her assumptions were valid. We do many things well, you and I, but this is where we fail. You taught me to never give up. Fight for what I want. Fight for the family. Where's your fight now? Because I don't see it."

"Your mother . . ."

"Needed you. Just like Grandmother needs you now. Just like Spencer needed you. You raised me to not accept excuses. I don't accept yours. We can't fix this, Dad, but we can sure as hell be honest with each other from this point on. You and Mom made choices that you'll soon have to defend, but not to me." He turned to leave.

"Where are you going?" his father asked.

"To find my brother."

# Chapter Nine

After leaving Delinda's house, Alisha drove to her lake cabin. She needed the peace of that place to sort through the storm of emotions swirling within her. Her heart was breaking for Spencer. Mark couldn't have known. He wouldn't have been able to keep something like that a secret from his own son.

Could he?

Why wouldn't Stephanie want Spencer to know Mark was his biological father? It wasn't about money. She'd turned her back on that.

Alisha couldn't imagine how confused Spencer must be.

*And it's my fault. I never should have gone there.*

On the drive over she rehashed the conversation she'd had with Rachelle. She'd told her what had happened in a rush, afraid if she didn't say it all, she'd find a reason to say nothing. They didn't keep secrets, and Rachelle deserved to know what she'd done, especially if it helped her prepare herself, Nicolette, and Stephanie for what was surely coming.

She hadn't told Rachelle about Brett because she didn't know what to say when it came to him. Technically, nothing had happened between them. She didn't need Rachelle to forgive her, but her friend had to know what happened and deserved to hear it from her.

When Alisha had finished talking, Rachelle was quiet for several long minutes. "You must have misunderstood what was said."

"I didn't. Your grandmother kept saying that she thought Spencer knew. That your mother had married Mark."

"You're wrong. Did you actually hear her say Mark was his father?"

"No, but—"

"Then there's a chance that this is one big misunderstanding. We all loved Mark. If it were true, why wouldn't my mother tell us?"

"I don't know, but Spencer took it hard."

"Where is he now?"

"He's not answering his phone." After another long pause, Alisha said, "I shouldn't have gone to your grandmother's."

"Now, that I agree with."

"I'm so sorry, Rachelle. Do you want me to help you look for him?"

"No, I'll find him."

"Should I say something to Stephanie?"

"We don't even know if what you heard was true. The best thing you can do right now is nothing. We need to figure this out."

*In other words, without me.*

And just like that, a frightening truth hit Alisha. *I'm alone.*

*I should have said no when Rachelle joked that I should marry Spencer.*

*Once I said yes, I should have stayed away from Brett because how he makes me feel clearly confuses me.*

*Only I know the truth: I didn't want to marry Spencer because I didn't want to lose the chance that I could be with Brett.*

*There, I said it.*

*I'm a selfish, awful person who probably deserves to lose all of them.*

*And I just may have.*


Alisha sat on the grass near the water and waited for peace to come, but it didn't. Instead, she flashed back to her childhood.

*"Don't tell your teachers, Al."*

*"But Mommy, Daddy h-hurt you again."*

*"Don't get involved; it'll only make things worse. Baby, this needs to be our secret. Can you do that for Mommy? Be brave for me."*

*I stayed quiet, Mom. For you. It didn't make anything better.*

*I thought keeping my silence was wrong. I vowed to never quietly stand by again.*

*How can that be equally wrong?*

No answer came, but Alisha hadn't expected one. She knew that, whether it was deserved or not, she was alone.


Brett went to Spencer's office. His secretary said he wasn't in, but Brett knew he was. Work was where Brett would have gone if he'd been handed something as big as Spencer had. When you need to find your footing, you go to stable ground.

"Tell him I'm not leaving until he sees me."

"I would if he were here," his secretary, or engineer—really it didn't matter—said firmly.

When Brett walked past her desk, she rushed to stand in his way. "He told me that he was not to be disturbed for any reason."

Brett looked her straight in the eye and said, "I'm his brother. I'm going in."

She looked uncertain, then stepped aside. "I should at least tell him—"

"No need. I'll do it myself," Brett said as he opened the door.

"I told you—" Spencer looked up from his computer with irritation. He stopped as he saw Brett. "Whatever you have to say, save it. I'm not in the mood to hear it."

"Then we don't have to talk."

Spencer told his secretary to close the door, and she left. "Grandmother must have told you. Oh, wait. I can't call her that anymore. Delinda."

"You can call her whatever you want. She considers you her grandchild."

"Tell her she doesn't have to. Not having her in my life will be a relief."

*He doesn't mean that.* "Your anger is justifiable. No one should hear something like that the way you did."

Spencer laid his hands flat on his desk. "Why are you here, Brett? Seriously? What the fuck do you want from me?"

"I don't want anything. I'm here because you're my brother."

"Half brother."

"Same thing."

"Are you kidding me? I thought I knew who I was. I just found out my father isn't really my father. The man who raised me was, but apparently Mom didn't think I needed to know that. No wonder Dad kept you and Eric with him but let me go. I always wondered why I was shipped off with the girls. I'm no longer confused about any of it. I get why he can't be bothered to call me and why he doesn't give a shit about my company. I'm not even his."

"There are things you don't know about Dad. Things maybe you should."

"Dad? Spare me. I don't want to know more about Dereck Westerly. All he ever gave me was his name."

Brett pinched the top of his nose and told himself Spencer would need some time to process this shock. "I'm here if you need me. I called Eric and told him to come home for a few days. He said he could be here by the weekend. You don't have to deal with this alone."

Spencer stood. "There's nothing to deal with. I appreciate you coming here, but I'm done. My real father is dead. My mother is a liar. No need to get married. Got it. I'm moving on."

Although he hated to admit it, the last part was a relief to hear. Brett rose to his feet. "You're calling off the wedding? Does Alisha know?"

"I'm sure she does." He glared at Brett. "She was only marrying me to fulfill Gran—Delinda's conditions for inheritance, but I'd already decided I couldn't go through with that, anyway." He laughed with self-deprecation. "I went there because I thought about what you said about it not being fair to Alisha to put her through this. I thought if I was honest with Delinda and told her the truth, she might waive the marriage condition. I'm such a fool. No one gives a shit about honesty."

"Your inheritance is still yours. You can still have that conversation."

"I don't want her money."

Brett cleared his throat. "I've never seen Grandmother cry, but she did today. She does love you."

Spencer studied his brother's face. "Did she send you? What do you get out of this?"

"Nothing. I'm here because I care."

With a wave of his hand, Spencer said, "Don't bother. I'm done with everyone."

"Even Alisha? She was upset, also." Brett needed to know where his brother stood with her.

"Alisha is the last thing on my mind. If she's upset, she'll get over it."

"Are you sure? She takes things harder than you think."

Spencer gave Brett a long look. "What is your fascination with her?"

*And this is where I step up to the plate.* "Honesty is something our family hasn't had enough of. You need to know that I have feelings for Alisha. I don't want to add to what you're dealing with, but I'm going from here to her unless you tell me that you have feelings for her, too."

Spencer's hands fisted at his sides. "You want my fiancée?"

"Fake fiancée. Unless you tell me differently."

Spencer ran a hand through his hair. "This is so fucked up. You know what, you can have her. I don't care about her, you, or any of this shit. Do me a favor, though, and stay the hell away from me."

Brett felt his brother's pain and didn't let his words deter him from saying what he'd come to say. "You're angry. Be angry. I would be. None of this changes the fact that you're my brother, and I love you. I will always be there when you need me. Always."

Spencer's face tightened, and he slammed a fist down on his desk. "Go. Just go."

Brett started out the door.

Spencer called to him. "Brett."

Brett turned.

Spencer took a step toward him, then stopped. "Alisha is the nicest person I know. Don't hurt her."

*At least you recognize that.* Brett nodded at his brother as he left. His life had become complicated, and he'd always kept things simple. When it came to his personal life, he'd never been willing to invest much of himself.

*My grandfather chose to end his life rather than admit he'd failed.*

*Dad chose the company over his family, even if he may never see it that way.*

*Why didn't Mom tell Spencer that Mark was his father? Because she would have had to admit to cheating on Dad? She's more of a Westerly than she knows. Westerlys never lose; they admit to no weakness, no matter the cost.*

Just as he was exiting the building, Brett saw Rachelle walking toward the entrance. He stepped in front of her on the sidewalk. They'd recently started talking on the phone. He was disappointed she hadn't called him when this storm hit their family, but what could he expect? He hadn't been a presence in their lives. With Eric out of the country most of the time and Brett's investment in work, Rachelle probably felt like she was the eldest child. "Rachelle."

She looked up, and for a split second the wall that had always been between them held strong, but then her features softened and she smiled at him sadly. "It's true."

He didn't need to ask what she was referring to. "I know."

"How is he?"

"Understandably angry."

"I had no idea. Did you?"

"No, but Grandmother thought we knew. She wouldn't have said anything if she'd known he didn't."

Rachelle rolled her eyes. "I'm not so sure about that, but it doesn't matter now. The damage is done."

"She loves him. Dad does, too."

"They suck at showing it."

"Mom was just as wrong."

Rachelle tensed and looked about to defend her, then hugged her purse to her stomach. "I don't understand any of it. When I tried to talk to her, she started crying. She said she'd tried to make the best choice for everyone. But how could she lie to all of us for so long? How was that for the best?"

"I don't know. I called Eric and told him what's going on."

"You did?" She looked sad yet hopeful. "I almost did, but I didn't want to interrupt his shoot. Is he coming back?"

"He said he would. Some things are more important than work."

She looked up at him in shock. "Wait. Who are you? You do not sound like my brother Brett."

He shrugged. "People change."

She looked him over and nodded knowingly. "You met someone, didn't you?"

He neither acknowledged nor denied her claim. There would be time to tell her after he figured out what he and Alisha would be to each other.

"You did; I can see it in your eyes."

Instead of admitting anything, he nodded toward the office building behind him. "Do you want me to go back in with you?"

She took the hint and changed the subject. "Not if you've already talked it out. I'm glad you did, though. He needs to know that this doesn't change anything."

"That's not how he sees it, and he may not for a while."

Rachelle squared her shoulders. "I hope I say the right thing. It doesn't feel real. What did you say?"

A month ago Brett would have never left work to talk to his siblings. He certainly wouldn't have had this conversation or known what to say to Spencer. His first responsibility to the family had always been to take care of the company. Everything else came second. Did they need more from him? *They don't know how I've always watched over them. Did keeping my influence behind the scenes hurt them as much as it helped?* "I told him I love him, and I'll always be there when he needs me."

Her eyes bright with tears, Rachelle hugged him. "Whoever you're seeing, don't you dare break up with her. I like this new you."

He hugged her back. "Me, too. Call me later."

"I will."

Brett cleared his throat. "Have you talked to Alisha?"

"Briefly. She's the one who told me what happened."

"How was she?"

Rachelle shrugged. "Apologetic."

"She did nothing wrong."

Nodding, Rachelle hugged her purse again. "I know. I did. I suggested she marry Spencer. If I hadn't done that, she would have never even met Grandmother and none of this would have happened."

Brett understood guilt. He'd mentally flogged himself many times for staying with his father instead of going with his siblings. Not one good thing had sprung from his regret. He was beginning to see that, as in business, intention didn't matter as much as action. "Was she upset?"

Cocking her head to one side, Rachelle studied her brother's face before answering. "Why the sudden interest in my friend?"

Unblinking, Brett held her gaze. He didn't have to tell her.

"Alisha? But she's . . ." Her mouth rounded. "Not anymore. Of course she's not marrying Spencer anymore." She frowned. "You didn't tell Spencer, did you?"

"It's the only thing Spencer was fine with."

"You don't even know her."

"That's what I intend to change."

Rachelle's mouth opened and closed a few times. "I don't know what to say."

A corner of Brett's mouth lifted in a half smile. "How about good luck?"

Shaking her head, Rachelle turned and walked into the office building. She glanced back at him with an unhappy expression on her face, before disappearing into the foyer.

He wouldn't have chosen to meet Alisha the way he had or when he had, but that didn't change how he felt about her. He was going to her, and nothing would stop him from making her his.

# Chapter Ten

Dangling her feet into the water off the edge of the dock, Alisha watched the sun set on the lake. The peace of the location was broken by laughter from a group of people gathered around a fire pit two houses down. Voices rang out from the other direction as someone playfully threw someone else in the water. It was impossible to begrudge families for having fun simply because she wasn't. In a way, their happiness comforted her. *Someday, someday I'll feel like that again.*

*Just not today.*

Rachelle hadn't called her back. Not even a text. Alisha was tempted to call her and apologize again, but Rachelle had asked for time.

Spencer hadn't called, but Alisha hadn't expected him to. He was dealing with his own issues.

*Does he blame me, too?*

*Does it matter?*

*Nothing will ever be the same.*

She lay back on the dock and watched the stars as they began to appear in the sky. *I should go somewhere. Somewhere far away.*

*Is that running away?*

*What's the alternative? Stay here and feel sorry for myself?*

*There's an upside to having no one in my life. I don't have to ask anyone for permission to do whatever the hell I want to do.*

She sat up, took her phone out of her pocket, and began to search for last-minute vacation destinations. She wanted to go somewhere easy. No planning. No thinking. *Just take me away.*

A cruise?

She searched for ships that left from somewhere on the East Coast within driving distance. A seven-night cruise to Grand Turk and the Bahamas? She clicked through an itinerary and its accompanying photos. The reviews were positive. "Walk off the boat onto the beach. Escape to paradise."

*That sounds pretty damn good right about now.*

She clicked through the website.

"Number of passengers?" Alisha blinked back tears and entered, "1."

"Inside. Balcony. Suite." She read about each and chose the middle option. A few more thousand dollars just to have a butler? *Balcony is fine.*

The constant state of uncertainty and fear in her childhood made Alisha avoid anything resembling irresponsibility. She'd worked hard to put herself through school. She'd saved diligently and bought her own home a few years ago. Although she was far from rich, she had a decent rainy-day savings account. She also had a current passport.

*I'm doing this.*

She chose the earliest available cruise, filled out her personal and credit card information, and then hesitated.

*What do I have to lose?*

*I don't have anything left here.*

She confirmed the purchase and tucked her phone back into her pocket.

*Paradise, here I come.*

◆　◆　◆

Brett pulled into the small driveway of Alisha's lake house and parked behind her car. He'd guessed she would be there, and seeing her validated what his gut was telling him. They might not have had much time together, but he *knew* her. Their connection was real.

He saw her outline on the dock, illuminated by lights from the neighboring house, and walked down to where she was. Before stepping onto the dock, he slipped off his Louis Vuitton loafers and socks and rolled his pants up. She was deep in thought and didn't realize he was there until he sat down on her left side.

She bounced a foot into the air and screamed before realizing it was him, then she punched him in the arm—hard. "Stop sneaking up on me."

He laughed and rubbed his arm. "Ouch."

She settled back down beside him. "Seriously, don't do that again. I aged about five years."

He frowned. "You shouldn't be out here alone. I could have been anyone."

She turned to look back over the water. "I can take care of myself."

The way she said it made him realize how often she probably had, and it saddened him. "You shouldn't have to."

She folded her arms in front of herself. "When has life ever been about what should be?"

He wanted to put an arm around her, to comfort her, but he knew she wasn't ready. "Most of my family would agree with you today."

She sighed and her voice softened. "Sorry. I know it wasn't an easy day for any of you."

"Or you."

"Or me," she agreed.

"There was no way you could have known."

She laughed sadly and covered her face with one hand. "You don't have to sugarcoat it for me. I should have stayed out of it."

That wasn't how he saw it, but what mattered was that she did. "Maybe, but you went to see my grandmother because you care about my family." He took her left hand in his and ran his thumb over her now-bare ring finger. "I've never known anyone like you."

Her hand went cold and stiff beneath his touch. "Brett, just because I'm not marrying your brother doesn't mean . . ." Her voice trailed off, then she said, "The only way I could possibly screw this situation up more is if I sleep with you."

He couldn't help the grin that spread across his face. "I'm flattered that your mind went there, but we could start with dinner." She went to pull her hand away, but he held on to it, brought it to his lips, and kissed her knuckles. "Before you throw me in the lake, this is a new suit."

She laughed and their fingers laced. "I'm serious."

"So am I."

Her smile faded. "I can't, Brett."

"But you want to."

She gave him a look so full of yearning he almost kissed her, but then she said, "All I want right now is to get as far away from here as I can."

"Where would you go?" Wherever it was, he'd take her there.

"Oh, I'm going. I already bought my ticket. I leave on Sunday for a week."

His hand tightened on hers. "Where?"

"On a cruise."

"Alone?"

She pressed her lips and slid her hand away from his. "Yes, alone. I want to sit on a beach, sip frozen drinks, get a tan, and forget about everything else."

"I have a two-hundred-fifty-foot yacht."

"Good for you."

She wasn't making it easy for him, and that was a novel experience. Too many women offered themselves to him before he had a chance to learn their names. Alisha was going to make him work to be with her, and he liked it. "There's no need to suffer through being shuttled like cattle when you could go there on a private craft with a crew dedicated to anticipating your every need."

"Quick, say something plebeian, your entitlement is showing."

He thought about what he'd said and grunted. Like his father and grandmother, he'd been raised with money. He generally didn't think much about it, but lately he was aware of how it had shaped him. Seeing himself through Alisha's eyes was often uncomfortable, but in an honest way that left him feeling invigorated. "The cattle reference was too much?"

With her finger and thumb she measured an inch. "Just a little."

He was tempted to smile, but held it back. She was serious and adorable all at once. "Where does this perfectly wonderful cruise go?"

"Now you're being sarcastic."

He felt like a young man trying desperately to impress his first crush. "But in a humble, everyman kind of way."

Her answering smile was reluctant, but it was there. "Fine." She took out her phone and opened a photo of one of the cruise's excursions. "Grand Turk. Look at that beach. Doesn't it look amazing?"

All he saw was a herd of drunk college students, a hundred screaming children, and their sweaty parents all crammed onto a very crowded beach, but he wasn't about to say it. "Hmm . . ."

She pointed to a lounge chair beneath an umbrella. "That's where I'm going to be. Right there. Hopefully with a nice buzz."

It would take a few drinks to make the setting appealing to Brett, but if she wanted to be on that beach, he wanted to be beside her. "And you already bought your ticket?"

She put her phone away. "I did. I never do anything wild or crazy, but I'm doing this. I leave this Sunday. I can't wait."

Sunday to Sunday.

*I'd have to clear my schedule at work.*

*And find out what cabin she's in. I'm sure the people in the next room would love to spend a week on my yacht instead.*

*Okay, then.*

"Are you staying here or heading home?" he asked.

A kind of hopeful expression filled her eyes. "Going home."

"I'll follow you to make sure you get there safely." He stood and offered her his hand. She took it and came to her feet close enough that with a dip of his head he could have claimed her lips with his. Their eyes met and held. He wanted her, but strangely he didn't want to rush it. He wanted to savor every moment with her before he tasted every inch of her. Being with her felt that good.

"Thank you." Those two softly spoken, heartfelt words warmed him in a way that he welcomed even as they scared him a little, too.

Whatever they had, however this thing between them worked out, he knew he would never be the same. *And that is not a bad thing.*

# Chapter Eleven

Alisha was up early reading countless blogs and passenger reviews to help her decide what to take with her. She didn't want to pack so much that she couldn't handle the luggage herself, but she couldn't turn off the side of her that needed to be prepared. Armed with a long list, Alisha showered and rushed out the door.

She was halfway down the steps when she registered having passed something on her porch. She turned and her jaw dropped open. A three-piece set of luggage patterned with delicate flowers stood proudly, each wrapped in white ribbon and sporting a huge bow. She read the card she found propped against them.

*I took a chance you didn't already have luggage.*
*Consider these your first flowers from me.*
*—Brett*

Blinking back tears, Alisha smiled. She texted a polite: Thank you. She knew if she called, she'd probably cry. In the years of watching her father and mother interact, she had rarely seen selfless kindness. *If ever.* But here was Brett, consistently showing that he cared in ways that were truly touching.

If you don't like them, I have the receipt, he texted back.

They're perfect.
I'm glad. What are your plans today?
Busy. Packing. Shopping. More packing.
Dinner?

She wanted to say yes, but she didn't want to open the door to more. There couldn't be more. I can't. *At least that's honest.*

Tomorrow?

*Is this a test? Because remembering why to say no to him is hard when all I want to do is say yes.* Sorry, no.
Don't be sorry. I don't mind waiting. It'll make being with you that much sweeter.
*Holy crap. That's hot.* Alisha tucked her phone into her jeans pocket, leaned against the railing of her porch, and fanned her face.

She stashed the luggage just inside her front door and headed back out with the list of what she needed, one item now crossed off. Thank God she had the list. She found it difficult to think of much beyond Brett as she drove. *Sleeping with Brett would only make things worse.*

Rachelle had mentioned him over the years, but not usually in a favorable way. She'd always described him as judgmental, arrogant, and impossible to talk to without arguing. Rachelle had led Alisha to think he was the type who cared only about money and himself.

She couldn't reconcile Rachelle's version of Brett with her own experience of him. The Brett she knew went out of his way to take care of people. He was thoughtful. Funny. Sexy as hell.

But off-limits.

There was no way she'd risk making things worse between Rachelle and her. Rachelle hadn't called her back to confirm that it had been a misunderstanding, so it must be true. Spencer wasn't Dereck's son. *And I brought that fact to light.*

She pulled into the parking lot of the local pharmacy, grabbed her purse, and headed in while giving herself a mental shake.

*Rachelle said she needed time. I'll give her time.*

*Focus on the cruise.*

Alisha walked up and down the aisles, filling her basket with travel-sized items. She accidentally walked down the contraceptive aisle, paused in front of the condom section, and blushed as she remembered how she'd told Brett she couldn't sleep with him. *I don't even know what he sees in me. So far I've yelled at him, told his grandmother off, cried all over him while I was sick, and practically destroyed his family. I'm a hot mess.*

The memory of how his lips had felt as they grazed across her knuckles vividly came back to her. She warmed from head to toe as she imagined how good his mouth would feel on hers, or anywhere else it roamed.

Although she'd been dating a man until a short time ago, she hadn't slept with him. He'd been nice enough, and attractive, but his kisses hadn't left her craving more. That was never a good sign.

She wasn't a virgin. Like many of her friends, she'd lost her virginity to a high school boyfriend who hadn't wanted much more than sex. She slept with a college boyfriend she'd imagined herself in love with until she caught him screwing one of her friends in the bathroom at a party she'd said she couldn't attend because she had to study. Studying always took priority over men after that. There had been two more men since college, but neither had made her feel all tingly and alive the way Brett did.

Unlike the men she'd dated, Brett wouldn't be tentative in bed. No, he was definitely a man who would know what he wanted and how to please a woman. She had nothing to base that on but a gut feeling. *And the way he looks at me. Like he wants to devour me.*

*I want to be taken like that.*

Alisha licked her bottom lip as she pictured him picking her up and carrying her to his bed. She wasn't the type who gave control to someone else, but imagining being with a powerful man like Brett was exciting. She didn't think it would be scary because she couldn't imagine him ever hurting her.

She ran her hand over the front of a box of extra-large condoms. Was Brett as big in reality as he was in the naughty dreams he'd inspired the night before? Images of the two of them naked and rolling around passionately on her bed circled in her mind. The fantasy was so good she could almost taste him.

From the corner of her eye she caught a movement and saw a man in his early twenties watching her. She realized she'd been caressing the front of the condom box and hastily dropped her hand. Feeling like she should say something, she smiled sheepishly at him. "It's a good brand."

He nodded and blushed.

She turned away, but as she left the aisle, she saw him toss two boxes of that brand into his cart. She waited until she was around the corner before she laughed into her hand. *There is always a bright side. At least I know I could do condom commercials.*

She hurried to the cashier and paid for her items.

*Now I need new underwear, a bathing suit, and a few dresses. Hopefully, I can buy those without making a spectacle of myself.*

Back in her car, she started the engine and said, "Brett Westerly, get out of my head. I'm trying to do the right thing."

*Not that I'm totally sure what that is anymore. I know one thing: I shouldn't leave without talking to Rachelle.* She dialed the number.

"Hello?" Rachelle said as she answered.

"It's me."

"I know."

"How are you? How is everyone else?"

"You were right."

"I'm sorry."

"My mother is still upset. Nicolette is in shock. Spencer isn't talking to anyone. All in all, it's pretty bad."

"Do you need—"

"Are you seeing Brett?"

Wham. The question hit Alisha like a punch. "No. We talk sometimes. That's it."

"Is that the truth?"

*Since fantasies don't count, and I've told him I wouldn't go out with him, yes.* "Why would I lie to you? When have I ever lied to you?"

Rachelle sighed. "Never. It's just that he said some things that made it sound like . . . Alisha, my family is falling apart over here. I feel like one more tap and we'll shatter. Please, stay away from Brett. Spencer is already hurting enough."

Her request was a painful slap that sent Alisha momentarily off-balance. *Apart from agreeing to go along with a scam to help Spencer receive his inheritance early, why am I the pariah here? I was helping him. How did I end up as the outsider?* Alisha started to feel angry. And it showed as she said, "So stay away from you, your mother, your sister, the brother you're close to, and the brother you never talk to. In general, just stay away."

"Alisha, that's not what I'm saying—"

"No, I get it." She gripped the steering wheel. "You know what? It's fine. I'm going away for a week. If you want to talk when I get back, call me." Alisha hung up the phone and threw it on the seat next to her.

*Two more days until the cruise.*

*Just two more days.*

*Feels like forever.*

Organizing his office and global teams so all would run smoothly while he stepped away for a week kept him busy enough that his day passed quickly. When he finally looked up from his computer, after answering the last of his e-mails, the sun had already set.

He stood, stretched, and walked to the window of his office. The Boston skyline at night was impressive, but he was lost in thought.

He'd never needed to pursue a woman, so it was difficult to judge how he was doing. Alisha had liked his gift enough to thank him for it. He'd expected her to agree to have dinner with him. His plan was to take her on a couple of dates, the last of which ended with her spending the night at his place, and then surprise her with the fact that he was going away with her. Her refusal made his booking the suite adjoining hers a little less romantic and a little more stalkerish.

*She's interested. I can't be wrong about that. What did she say? Sleeping with me was the only way she could make things worse?*

*Because she feels guilty about something that wasn't her fault.* His family was imploding, but it wasn't by her hand. *There has to be a way to make her see that.*

*To make* everyone *see that.*

So far, he wasn't impressed with how his family was handling the fallout from the other day. His father was in stoic denial that anything significant had happened. His grandmother saw the event only in terms of how it affected her. Eric's return was delayed by an unavoidable filming issue. His mother and younger siblings had circled their wagons as if they'd somehow been threatened. And Spencer was doing his best to follow in their father's footsteps, by hiding at work.

*Really, how could sleeping with me make anything worse? It's already a shitfest.*

"I told you he'd be here," Victor Andrade's voice boomed through the doorway even before he entered it.

Brett turned from the window and groaned. Victor and his brother, Alessandro, were his father's age and friends of the family, but they'd chosen the wrong time to visit. "Gentlemen."

Alessandro crossed the office and hugged Brett. "Is that any way to greet family?"

Brett had never been, and would never be, someone who hugged other men, but these two old coots had broken him down over the last thirty-two years. There was no family tree that linked the Westerlys to the Andrades, but that fact was lost on them. Their mother had been a good friend of his grandmother's and that was enough by their definition. Victor was next, with a loud backslapping embrace that always left Brett wondering if muggers used the same technique to disorient their victims.

When Victor stepped back, he was beaming with pride. "I still picture you hiding behind the couch in diapers, but you look good in your father's office."

Brett shook his head at the image.

"You're embarrassing him, Victor," Alessandro said, as if Brett needed his support. "He's a man now."

"What can I do for you two?" Brett asked. The Andrades were like a summer storm. There was no avoiding them; all one could do was buckle down and hope they didn't last long.

Victor made himself at home in one of the chairs in front of Brett's desk as Alessandro followed suit in the other. "We're here to see how you're doing," Victor said.

"Just checking in," Alessandro added.

"My grandmother called you," Brett said dryly.

Alessandro shrugged. "She worries."

Brett sat on the front edge of his desk and folded his arms across his chest. "She'd have less to worry about if you kept more of your advice to yourself."

The brothers exchanged a pained look. Alessandro waved an expressive hand in the air. "Love is always the answer."

Victor slapped a hand on his thigh. "Unless it involves your brother's fiancée. What is this nonsense we're hearing about you squabbling over the same woman?"

Brett looked skyward for assistance but received none. When he looked down, they were still there. "I'm not discussing this with you."

"He doesn't look guilty," Victor said.

Alessandro rubbed his chin as he studied Brett. "So Delinda was right, and it wasn't a real engagement?"

Brett said nothing.

Victor went back to waving his hands as he spoke. "You have to admire Spencer for finding a fiancée that fast, even if it wasn't for real."

"Delinda says she's a spitfire. My Elise is never afraid to say what she wants. I love that in a woman." Alessandro's expression turned dreamy.

Brett closed his eyes and counted to ten. There were few people he tapped into his patience reserve for, but Victor and Alessandro had always been good to his family, good to him. Loyalty like that gave them a special place in his heart. Still, he didn't want to imagine either of them with their wives. He shuddered. "I hate to cut this visit short, but it's been a long day and I'm beat."

Neither man moved to leave.

"So tell us about this Alisha Coventry," Alessandro said.

*Never going to happen.* Brett pushed off the desk. If he walked out of the office, they might follow him.

They didn't.

From the other room he heard Victor make a tsk-tsk sound. "He thinks we're too old to remember what he's going through."

"Or that he knows women better than we do."

"Who understands women better than men who have been happily married for over thirty years?" Victor chided. "Our résumés speak for themselves. What's your track record, Brett?"

Brett walked back into his office. The Andrade storm was not yet abating. "Although I appreciate your concern, I don't need your help."

Alessandro smiled. "We've heard that before."

Nodding, Victor said, "We sure have. How do you feel about this woman?"

Brett kept his silence, which did nothing to break their stride. Alessandro leaned forward in his seat and spread one hand in the air, then the other as he spoke. "Are you at the pop-the-question or the make-up-after-the-breakup stage?"

"Neither," Brett answered abruptly.

Victor said, "He doesn't look excited or nervous enough to be about to propose."

Alessandro shook his head in confusion. "He's not sad, so he's not fighting with her."

Victor's eyes rounded, and he slapped his knee. "She turned him down. That's it, isn't it?"

Brett sat in the empty chair across from them. *Their slow torture techniques should be registered with the government.*

Alessandro's eyebrows shot to his hairline. "She did? This is worse than I thought."

There was an irony to his claim that Brett couldn't let pass. "Worse than when you thought I was stealing Spencer's fiancée?"

"We never really believed that," Victor said. "We've known you your whole life. You're a good boy. That's why we're here. We want to see you happy."

"Who is ever really fucking happy?" Brett countered.

Victor frowned. "I am." He looked to his brother. "Alessandro, are you?"

"I have my health, a beautiful wife, grandchildren, and good people who are family through love if not through blood. What do I have to be unhappy about?"

This wasn't the first time Victor and Alessandro had shared their view of the world with him, but it was the first time Brett didn't dismiss it as utter bullshit. They weren't feeding a teenage boy an unrealistic version of life in an attempt to cheer him up. They genuinely were that fucking happy.

"Nothing, apparently." If they were comparing personal lives, theirs were, in fact, better than his. What did he have to lose? "You're right. She turned me down."

Alessandro clapped his hands together. "So? What did you do?"

"I sent her luggage."

Victor made a face. Alessandro waved him off and encouraged Brett to continue. "Maybe it's not so bad. Was it full of jewelry? Flowers? Expensive dresses? Did you include an invitation she couldn't resist?"

"No," Brett said and began to wonder if he'd missed the mark with his gift. "It had flowers on it, so I told her to consider them the first flowers I gave her."

Seesawing his hand back and forth, Victor said, "That's not horrible. But luggage?"

"She's leaving on a cruise on Sunday."

"That you bought for her?" Victor continued his interview as Alessandro sat back and listened intently.

"No."

"That you're going on together?"

"No. Yes. It's complicated."

Alessandro cut in, "I have a feeling you need to start from the beginning for us to be able to help you."

"I don't need—"

"You do, Brett. You gave her luggage," Victor said blandly.

*Touché, old man.*

*Touché.*

Brett got up and poured them all a glass of scotch. Then he sat back down and began to tell them about the time Alisha walked into his office.

# Chapter Twelve

The next day Alisha was on her way home from leaving the engagement ring, tucked into a handwritten apology, with Spencer's secretary. She didn't know if he'd actually not been there or if he simply hadn't wanted to see her, but either way it was over. She couldn't go back in time and stop him from hearing the truth about his parentage, but she did let him know how much she regretted the way he'd learned about it. She wished she could have spared him that.

*I can't change what happened.*

*I can't make anyone forgive me.*

*But I can look at myself in the mirror now. I did everything I could to make amends.*

When she pulled into her driveway, there was a limo parked off to one side. The driver straightened and replaced his hat when he saw her. *Is Brett here?*

Her heart beat double time, and she could barely breathe as she parked her car. The driver opened the door of her car for her and handed her a card.

Alisha opened it.

*Let me pamper you today.*
*— Brett*

She looked from the driver to the limo. "Is he here?"

"No, ma'am, but I'm at your disposal for the day."

Alisha had never ridden in a limo. Feeling awkward, she shrugged. "I don't have anywhere I need to go."

He reached into his pocket, pulled out a piece of paper, and unfolded it. "I believe this might help."

It had the name of a spa and two high-end stores. "I'm sorry. I don't understand."

"Mr. Westerly has arranged a surprise for you at each of the places listed. You may choose to go to any or all of the locations. Now or when it is more convenient for you. As I said, I'm at your disposal today."

"What kind of surprises?" she asked.

The driver gave her a bland smile. "I really can't say."

Alisha chewed her bottom lip and weighed her curiosity against her common sense. Accepting gifts from Brett would give him the wrong idea. She should have refused the luggage.

*But they were so perfect. Exactly what I would have chosen.*

*I have to say no to this. I don't want him to think I'll change my mind about us.*

"I'm sorry. I can't accept this." She handed him back the list.

He took it and tucked it into his suit pocket. She leaned on her car and waited for him to climb into the limo and drive off.

*I have no choice. I have to say no.*

The driver returned to where he'd been standing when she pulled in, near the front of the limo beside the passenger door. He removed his hat and tucked it beneath his arm.

"Aren't you leaving?" she asked.

"My instructions are to stay all day in case you change your mind."

*Okay, I'm good, but I'm only human.* She took out her phone and sent a text to Brett.

I can't do this, Brett.

Yes, you can. Let someone do something nice for you for
a change.

She remembered how Rachelle had asked her to stay away from her
brother and told herself to be strong.

I don't want you to think . . .
Let me worry about what I think. Start your vacation early.
Get in the limo. See if I guessed correctly about what would
make you smile.

*One day. One indulgence. The driver will wait here all day unless I
agree. This is harmless. Fun. Don't I deserve a little happiness?*
*I'd ask Rachelle if this is out of line, but she's not talking to me.*
*Which is a horrible reason to do something I know she wouldn't want
me to do.*
*But how could saying yes to this hurt anyone?*
*He just wants to make me smile.*

Okay, but I need to be clear about something. All we can
be is friends.
I hear there is no better place to start.

He didn't write more, and Alisha had no idea what to say in
response, so she pocketed her phone and grabbed her purse. "I've
changed my mind," she told the driver.

He opened the back door of the limo, professional enough that it
was as if they'd never had their earlier conversation. He gave her the list,
closed the door, and went around to the driver's side. Once inside, he
lowered the window between the front and the back. "Would you like
to go in the order it's listed or do you have another preference?"

Alisha's mouth went dry as she answered, "This order is fine." She took a deep calming breath and settled against the plush leather seat.

The first stop was a local spa she'd driven by many times but had never allowed herself the luxury of stepping inside. Brett had arranged for her to choose any service. She was willing to settle for a simple manicure, but when the owner of the spa came out to greet her, she talked her into adding a pedicure and then a massage. Although Alisha declined a makeover, they did wash, trim, and blow-dry her hair. A few hours later, one very relaxed Alisha plopped into the back of the limo.

She wrote to Brett: The spa was amazing. Thank you. I didn't realize how tense I was. What a great way to start my vacation.

You're smiling.
Yes.
So am I.

She looked at the next stop on the list. It was a clothing store. You don't need to buy me clothes. I bought plenty for the trip.
Do you always have to say no before you say yes?
No. She read her response, laughed, and added: Yes.

Funny. Text me once you see my gift. I want to know what you think of it.
I'll go see it, but I can't accept anything more.

She was still telling herself that when she walked into the boutique clothing store. A saleswoman rushed over to her as if she'd been waiting for her. She led her to a changing room. Alisha was torn between feeling ridiculous and thinking Brett could have walked straight out of a romance novel. Who did things like this? No one she'd ever dated.

The dress the woman brought her was elegant and sexy at the same time. It revealed very little skin, but clung to her curves. Normally, Alisha would have felt more comfortable in a looser dress, but this one complemented her full figure. If she had spent a month hunting for a formal dress for the last night of the cruise, she couldn't have found a more perfect one. She spun around before the mirror. It made her feel beautiful.

As did Brett.

Still wearing the dress, she typed: I love it. Did you pick it out?

I did.
How did you know my size?

I put a lot of thought into it. A lot. His dry humor came through even in a text. Still, what man knew dress sizes?

You showed a picture of me to the sales clerk.
That, too.
The dress is perfect for the formal night. I'm going to buy it myself.
Sorry, it's already sold.

She laughed loud enough that the clerk inquired if she needed anything. She assured her she didn't before continuing to text. Then I'll pay you back.

I'm sure we can work something out.
That's not what I meant.
Leave a man with some hope.

Alisha laughed again. What am I going to do with you?
I have a few ideas.

She placed the phone down so she could unzip the dress and caught a glimpse of her expression in the changing-room mirror. Her eyes were dancing with humor, her cheeks were pink, and the smile on her face said it all: *I can't do this partway; it's too easy to forget that this can't go further.*

Once she was in her own clothing again, she held up the dress in front of her and let herself imagine what it would be like to wear it for him. To dance, to flirt, to spend an evening on his arm, feeling beautiful, like she belonged there.

She called him instead of texting. "Brett?"

"Yes."

She sat down on the chair in the changing room and pulled her legs up in front of her. "All joking aside, thank you for today."

"All joking aside, you're welcome."

"I can't go to the third place. I hope you don't think I'm ungrateful. I just need to go home. I shouldn't have accepted any of this. I know I'm sending you mixed signals, but . . ."

"Alisha."

"Yes?"

"Take the dress on the cruise." He hung up without saying more.

Alisha stood, gathered the dress and her purse, and stepped outside the dressing room. She handed the dress to the clerk, who returned moments later with it in a box. "Is there anything else you need?"

"Yes," Alisha said as she remembered she hadn't seen a price tag. "How much was the dress?"

"Twelve thousand dollars." The woman handed her the box.

"Thousand." Alisha choked and crushed the sides of the box in her hands. *"Thousand?"*

"Yes. Is that a problem?"

*Only if that's half of what you have in the bank.* She almost handed the box back to the woman. To a man like Brett Westerly, $12,000 was probably equivalent to twelve of her dollars. *I'll still pay him back, but in installments until I'm fifty.* "No, everything is wonderful. Thank you."

Only everything wasn't wonderful.

After instructing the limo driver to take her home, Alisha opened the box and ran her hand over the dress. Just like Brett, it had been too tempting to say no to.

*Thank God I'm leaving tomorrow.*

*Or I'd be taking more than this dress home with me.*

*And then where would I be?*


On his way home from work, Brett stopped by the third shop, the one Alisha had declined. He'd written the name of a department store on the list, but the limo driver had been instructed to take her to the jewelry store next to it. A phone call would have been enough to have the present delivered to his office or apartment, but he was feeling restless, and the errand would keep him from driving to Alisha's home to see her.

He had a plan now. He'd been reluctant to take any advice from Alessandro or Victor, but they had compelling arguments for each suggestion they put forth. At first Brett had held back details of his reasons for seeing Alisha. He wasn't proud of how he'd offered her money, but her refusal was significant, so he ended up sharing that story as well.

When he'd finished talking, Alessandro had looked at Victor and said, "She sounds like a good girl. I don't think we should get involved unless he's serious about her."

Victor had given Brett a stern look. "Do you see yourself marrying this woman?"

"I don't see myself marrying anyone," Brett had answered honestly.

Victor cut a hand through the air. "Then we want nothing to do with this."

Relieved, Brett had said, "I'll muddle through it myself, I guess."

Alessandro had stood, paced, then come to stand over Brett. "Describe Alisha in five words. Don't think about it. Just tell me the first five words that come to you when you hear her name."

*Easy.* Brett had said, "Brave. Resilient. Funny. Beautiful. Loyal."

Victor had nodded in approval. "You respect her. That's the foundation all good marriages are built on."

"I'm not getting married."

Not giving much credit to Brett's declaration, Alessandro said, "When you marry, Brett, only do so with a woman you also consider your friend. A lover leaves you if your finances change or your health takes a turn. They are there for the pleasure only."

Brett groaned, already regretting that he'd shared as much with them as he had. "Thank you for the sage advice, but as I said—"

Victor clapped his hands together once. "Okay, we will help you, but be generous with your wedding invitations when it comes to our family. We prefer to include the children. It's important that they are a part of these things, you understand?"

"Absolutely." Brett had promised because, as far as he was concerned, it wasn't going to happen. He wanted to be with Alisha, get to know her better, date her, possibly have a long-term relationship with her—but none of that changed his lack of faith in the institution of marriage.

Alessandro had sat down again and said, "Brett, winning a woman is not complicated. I don't care if you are trying to woo the CEO of a company or someone who likes to change diapers and stay home—they want the same things from their men. They want to be appreciated, and they want a real partner, not a puppy. Have fun. Dare them. Challenge them. Savor each layer, each new thing you learn about her."

"It's not the gift that matters," Victor added. "It's the way it leaves her feeling. Make a woman feel beautiful, and she will dance for you. Make her feel loved, and she'd die for you. No woman leaves a man who makes her feel this way."

As Brett entered the jewelry store, he was still mulling over Victor's theory on women and love. Love wasn't something he'd put much thought into since he'd always lumped it with castle-in-the-sky stocks: overvalued and very likely to fail. Look at his parents' marriage and the complexity of its demise.

His father, lost to his own pain, had closed his mother out. What had she found in Mark that his father hadn't given her? Had Mark made her feel beautiful? Special? He thought back to the conversation he'd overheard between his parents all those years ago and tried to hear it again as a man. His father had begged her to stay. How hadn't that made her feel loved?

She'd said she couldn't take it anymore. Take what? His father had given her a life of luxury most people dream about. He struggled to see how she could justify being anything but grateful. She'd made leaving sound like it had been a long time in coming.

*My grandfather died the year I was born.*

*Was my mother unhappy for twelve years?*

He pocketed the jewelry box after paying for Alisha's gift. He wanted to make her happy, but he didn't need her to love him. Things were a hell of a lot simpler if that word was kept out of the equation. What had love done for his parents? Nothing. It hadn't stopped his mother from cheating. It hadn't kept his parents together.

No, love was a word people threw around to justify doing whatever was in their best interest. Why had his mother kept Spencer's real father a secret? Brett was willing to bet his mother would say she loved him too much to hurt him with the truth.

Love was fickle and malleable.

*Sorry, Victor, I can make Alisha happy without relying on unrealistic, archaic traditions of promising the impossible. That's where my father failed. He should have been more honest.*

*I won't lie to Alisha. She'll have to take me as I am.*

*I won't promise her forever, but I can make her feel damn good for as long as we last.*

He paused as he stepped out of the store into the evening heat. Part of him resisted leaving while his family was in turmoil, but he couldn't work this mess out for them. He couldn't wrap his own head around most of it, and there was no amount of money that could fix it.

*My family will be fine. This is old news that won't matter once the sting of the reveal passes. By Thanksgiving we'll all be back to awkwardly finding reasons we can't gather.*

*None of that matters now. I'm on vacation.*

A lusty smile curled his lips.

*Alisha Coventry, prepare yourself for a week of pleasure.*

# Chapter Thirteen

The morning of the cruise, Alisha double-checked that she'd packed everything, rolled her luggage onto the porch, and firmly locked the door. She'd read blogs about cruising alone, but most of them were geared toward single people who were looking to hook up with someone.

A quick image of Brett popped into her head. She couldn't imagine meeting anyone who would make her feel as good as he did with a simple text. *Which is why it's probably best that we can't be together. I could lose myself in someone like that. Isn't that what my mother did? She put how my father made her feel above protecting herself—or me. She called it love, but it wasn't.*

Her mother had never looked happier than when her father first returned to her. She soared with him, happy beyond caring about anyone or anything else, but that euphoria was always followed by an ugly crash.

He'd been her addiction.

*But she gave him that power.*

*That importance.*

*No man will ever reduce me to that.*

As she walked toward her car, a limo pulled in, and her heart started beating wildly. The same driver who'd taken her on the shopping excursion the day before exited and walked toward her. He stopped next to her and removed his hat.

"What's your name?" she asked, suddenly conscious that he'd driven her around and she hadn't thought to ask.

"Todd," he answered.

"I'm sorry, Todd, but I can't go anywhere today. I'm leaving right now for a cruise."

Todd held her gaze with a professional lack of emotion. "I was instructed to drive you to the port."

Alisha blinked a few times rapidly as she took that in. "Brett—Mr. Westerly sent you to take me?"

"Yes," he answered patiently.

She looked from her car to the limo. "I am perfectly capable of driving myself."

He merely nodded.

She chewed the corner of her thumb as she chose her next words. *This is my fault. I shouldn't have gone to the spa or accepted the dress.* She remembered his joke about how she could pay him back. Was he merely being kind to her, or was he pursuing her? She didn't consider herself the type to inspire the latter from a man like him, so she assured herself it was the former. Still, it had to stop. "So please thank Mr. Westerly, but tell him I didn't require your services."

Todd handed her a folded note.

She opened it and laughed out loud as she read:

*Still saying no before you say yes? Get in the damn limo.*

She met Todd's unblinking gaze and shrugged. "He's unexpectedly funny." When Todd didn't respond, Alisha continued, "Does he do this kind of thing often? Send limos to pick people up and take them places?"

"I wouldn't know."

"Wouldn't know or wouldn't say?"

A corner of Todd's mouth twitched in amusement. "Whichever keeps me employed."

Alisha put a hand on one hip. "Gotcha. You're a vault. But if this were something you've done before and you, say, dropped your hat to signify that it was—who would know?"

Todd placed his hat firmly on his head. "Would you like me to place your luggage in the trunk?"

"I'm sorry, but as I said—"

"Of your vehicle or the limo."

Alisha handed the note back to Todd. "Neither." He nodded again and went to stand beside the passenger door of the limo.

After hunting through her purse for her phone, Alisha texted Brett: Thank you, but I want to drive myself.

His answer came a few seconds later. Poor Todd. I hired him to drive you around. What will he tell his wife and eight hungry children?

Alisha looked over Todd with a critical eye. He's twenty-five at best.

Maybe he started early.

No wedding ring.

He couldn't afford one.

"You're not married, are you, Todd?" Alisha asked across the driveway.

The uncomfortable expression that entered Todd's eyes was the first emotion she'd seen there. "I'm sorry?"

Suddenly aware of how her question could come across, Alisha was slightly embarrassed but found herself laughing. You're making me crazy. I just asked him if he's married.

And?

He thinks I was coming on to him.

128

He's fired.

You're not serious. When Brett didn't respond, Alisha texted, You would never do that.

Depends on what he said to you.
He said nothing. That was my guess at what he thought.
Good. Then he still has a job.

Alisha lowered her hands and took a deep breath. As usual, talking to Brett only confused her more. Although some of what he'd said was a joke, the last part hadn't been. He would have fired Todd for offending her.

She struggled with how conflicted that made her feel. He should have sounded like a pompous, entitled ass, but he didn't. There was an edge of possessiveness to how he spoke to her. She wanted to tell him she wasn't his to protect even as a part of her wanted to be protected.

Seriously, Todd has been nothing but completely professional.
Prove it and accept the ride to the port.
One has nothing to do with the other.
I want to do this for you.
You have a problem with the word no.
So do you.

She laughed at his quick wit. Just when she thought he'd gone too far, he threw out a funny comment that softened his arrogance—made him likable.

He was a man no woman would ever control.

That should have made him less attractive, but Alisha closed her eyes briefly as flashes of what it would be like to be taken by him assaulted her imagination. Would he give as much pleasure as he took? Could any man live up to the fantasies he inspired? She'd always told herself she preferred gentle men who took their time, but her body quivered as she imagined being ravished against a wall. She saw herself clinging to him, still partially dressed, kissing him desperately as he thrust so deeply into her that she cried out into his mouth.

She bit her bottom lip, forced her eyes to open, and gave herself an inner smack. Todd looked even more uncomfortable, which made her decision easier. I'd stay and debate this with you, but I have a cruise to catch.

Tell me something.

His request was unexpected. Curious, she texted back: What?

Are you tempted?

Her fingers hovered over her cell phone as she took in his question. He wasn't asking about the limo, and she knew it. If she said no maybe he'd move on to another woman.

No.

*Doesn't he at least deserve an honest answer?*

Yes.

As she waited for his answer, she called herself all kinds of an idiot. *Why am I encouraging him? Because I want him to want me even if I know I can't have him?*

*I really do need to get out of here.*

Good.

He didn't say more, and she didn't, either. She threw her phone back in her purse, placed her luggage in the trunk of her car, and waved to Todd as she backed down her driveway. *Sorry, Todd, you'll have to find another way to feed your eight imaginary children.*

As she merged into traffic, she thought about his response to her admission.

*Good? What is that supposed to mean?*

◆　◆　◆

Brett shook hands with the captain of the cruise ship and feigned interest in the tour of the bridge he'd agreed to out of politeness. Brett wasn't one to do anything he didn't want to, but he had contacted an old friend, who was the CEO of the cruise line, and was relying on the captain to ensure his requests were implemented seamlessly. The least he could do was listen to the man gush about their level of technical sophistication matching or surpassing those of naval warships. Electronic charts. Wind speed. Traffic. Navigators with overhead monitors. Thrusters.

Brett's thoughts were thrown back to Alisha when he heard the captain say *thrusters*. There was only one thing on his mind, and it had very little to do with accurately maneuvering the ship. He had his own ideas about maneuvering and maintaining his position . . .

Brett shook his head and followed the captain to his chair in the dead center of the bridge. Locating the helmsman in front, where he could see better while steering the ship, was interesting. The computerized maneuvering system allowed for precision within decimeters, which was impressive considering the size of the craft, but no amount of joysticks or knobs could take the edge off the anticipation bubbling within Brett.

Alisha had been tempted.

Her admission had removed all doubt from Brett that he'd made the right decision. He'd never been a big fan of vacations, but the idea of having seven nights of uninterrupted time with Alisha was enough to sell him on the merits of cruising.

Would she fall into his bed that night or make him wait a day more? The uncertainty was novel and thrilling. With her, he didn't feel like a man carrying the weight of his family's fortune on his shoulders. Alisha made the present more vibrant. He wanted to embrace that feeling, lose himself in the pleasure of her presence and her body, even if only for a week.

There wasn't a part of Alisha that he didn't crave to explore more. He'd make an hour-long feast of her luscious lips. Remembering the light scent of her, the feel of her soft skin beneath his lips, he wanted to taste, claim, and pleasure every inch of her. Alisha, lying naked across his bed, offering herself to him, brought him to an uncomfortable level of excitement—all while he pretended to listen to the tour of the bridge.

When the captain's monologue about the ship's remarkable updated equipment finally ended, Brett forced himself back to the present. He asked for a maneuverability comparison between his yacht's propulsion system and the cruise ship's. The captain's face lit up as he described the similarities and differences in painstaking detail.

"Everything is as I requested?" Brett asked when the captain finally asked if he had another question.

"I made sure of it myself. It's an honor to have you aboard."

"Thank you." His friend must have said something to the captain. It was nice to know he hadn't forgotten the boost Brett had given his career early on. "I'll retire to my suite, then. Thank you for the tour."

"My pleasure. I'll have First Mate Anderson show you the way. Unless, of course, you'd like to help navigate the ship out of port."

Some offers were too good to pass up, and he didn't want to run into Alisha before dinner. He'd planned their meeting to unfold in what he'd hoped was an impressively romantic way. Bumping into her in the hallway would ruin the effect.

Besides, steering a thousand-foot ship was something he'd never done. It was frivolous entertainment he normally wouldn't waste time on. It fit, though, with how he felt just then. He wanted to step away from his chronically serious, often cutthroat, business. For once, he wanted to see how the other half lived and simply have fun.

*Does everything have to make sense? I want this.*

*For now, that's enough.*

# Chapter Fourteen

After waiting in a long line to board the ship, Alisha did a quick, self-guided tour, then decided to get something to eat. Balancing a plate of food on one hand, she adjusted her purse on her shoulder and searched the busy lido deck restaurant for an empty table. She'd already checked the tables near the pool area. They were full as well. A man bumped into her, mumbling an excuse as he went. A group of teenage girls jostled her from the other side as they passed, one of them shooting her a glare as if Alisha had thrown herself intentionally in their way. Everything she'd read about cruises said that the first day was busy, but she was feeling overwhelmed and anxious for her room to be ready.

A blond-haired toddler ran straight into her and wrapped himself around her leg. A woman, with the same wild blond curls, rushed toward them. Clutching two plates in one hand and a large backpack in the other, she said, "Ethan, let go of that woman this instant."

Ethan clung to Alisha tighter. "Ice *meme*. Ice *meme*."

"No ice cream until after you eat your lunch. Come on."

He shook his head. "Ice *meme*."

Seeming as frazzled as Alisha felt, the woman looked up and said, "I'm so sorry. Could you follow us to our table? We're right there. I'll just put this down and grab him."

Considering the octopus hold Ethan had on her thigh, Alisha didn't see she had much of a choice. "Sure."

As Alisha moved to follow her, Ethan almost fell off. She looked around for a place to put her plate so she would have a free hand to help him, but he righted himself and smiled. "Go. Go. Go. Pony. Go."

She took another step, and he laughed and hung on, so she kept going. Alisha made it to the table where the woman was standing in time to hear her say to a man who was seated, "Yes, I need you. Look at Ethan. Do you think he should be doing that? Could you help me with him before you start eating?"

With an easy smile, the man unfolded himself from behind the table and bent down to talk to Ethan. "Let go of the nice lady, Ethan."

"Ice *meme*." His bottom lip jutted out.

The man reached over and started to pry Ethan off Alisha while saying, "I probably shouldn't have mentioned dessert so soon. Let go, Ethan. And don't you dare bite her."

Alisha froze and handed her plate off to a passing staff member. She helped the father loosen the child's hold. Ethan looked tired and about to cry. He sounded spoiled, but he probably felt as overwhelmed by the crowd as she did. Alisha sympathized with the little man and remembered something she had tucked into her purse the last week of school. "Would you like a sticker?"

His mouth rounded.

She dug in her purse. "I have puppies, kitties, and maybe even a Spider-Man."

Ethan clapped.

"All you have to do is sit down with your mommy, and I'll let you pick one. Would you like that?"

He nodded and climbed onto the bench beside his mother. Alisha laid out the stickers, and Ethan calmly chose one with a puppy on it.

"Wow," the child's mother said. "Are you someone's nanny?"

Alisha straightened and smiled. "Kindergarten teacher."

"Same thing," the father said.

"Not really," Alisha answered, but refused to elaborate on a topic that was one of her pet peeves. She had a job most people thought they could do, but only those who had ever done it, and done it well, understood the challenge. Comparing it to babysitting was insulting, but very few people understood that.

"You looked lost a moment ago. Who are you sitting with? Maybe we could help you find them," a beautifully made-up brunette asked from the other end of the table.

"Thank you, but I'm alone," Alisha said.

"Alone?" the blonde asked. Then cheerfully she said, "Well, not anymore. My name is Nadine. You've met my husband, Josh, and my son, Ethan, of course. Join us. We have two large tables. What's your name?"

"Alisha, but I don't want to intrude," Alisha hedged.

The brunette stood and came around beside her. "Are you kidding? We love meeting new people. Nadine and her husband renew their vows on a cruise every year."

*Oh boy, a bride who can't let go of her wedding day. I thought they only existed on TV.*

"My name is Brandi." She motioned toward the man in a bright Hawaiian shirt. "That's my husband. Freddy, come meet Alisha."

Alisha shook his hand, then the hands of eight more people, whose names evaporated as quickly as they were spoken. Parents, grandparents, cousins, friends. Before she had a chance to say no again, she was seated in the middle of them while someone went off to the buffet to get her a hamburger and lemonade she hadn't asked for.

"I know we sound crazy, but it makes us happy, and that's what matters, isn't it?" Nadine asked, then looked Alisha over expectantly. "Are you celebrating anything?"

"No," Alisha answered with a forced smile.

"Who are you here with?" Brandi asked as she scooted closer.

Nadine referenced the table of people near them. "We sometimes come alone, but this time we brought the whole gang since it's our ten-year anniversary."

"Just me."

"Just you?" Nadine's eyes rounded. "You mean for the whole cruise?" Brandi looked equally shocked.

"The whole thing."

There was a painfully sympathetic pause in the conversation.

"Well, that's nice," Brandi said in a supportive tone. "It frees you up for possibilities." She turned to her husband. "Your cousin Henry didn't bring his girlfriend. Did they break up?"

Alisha accepted the burger and drink that were handed to her and said, "I'm not looking to meet anyone."

Nadine fed a slice of apple to Ethan while nodding. "That recent, huh? Was it serious?"

*Oh, what the hell? It's not like I'll ever see these people again after this trip. Who cares what they know or think of me?* "I was engaged."

"That's awful," Nadine said. "But you're doing the right thing. You shouldn't stay home and wallow when something like that happens. It just makes it hurt more. Did he cheat on you? I was engaged before Josh. The loser slept with my roommate. Remember that, Brandi? I was heartbroken. But he did me a favor. I met Josh a month later. So don't waste another thought on that douche. You're better off without him."

Ethan said, "Douche. Douche. Douche."

Nadine picked him up and handed him off to her husband. "He's ready for ice cream."

"Ice *meme*!" Ethan exclaimed.

Josh laughed and took him. "I'll take him for a walk to get some, then check if the room is ready. If it is, I'll change him and take him down to the water park for a bit."

Nadine stood and kissed her husband briefly. "Are you sure?"

He wiggled his eyebrows suggestively. "If I tire him out now, he'll sleep for your mother later. We can leave him with her for a few hours."

Nadine laughed and swatted her husband's behind. "So we can go dancing?"

"Whatever you want to call it," he joked, then winked and walked away with his son in his arms.

"Men," Nadine said as she returned to her seat, but she was smiling. She looked across at Alisha. "I'm sorry to hear about your engagement."

"It's okay." It wasn't the broken engagement that had her suddenly feeling melancholy. Watching Nadine flirt with her husband inspired unwelcome visions of Brett.

Brett definitely had an imposing presence. She could imagine him intimidating a room of businessmen if he wanted to, but she'd also seen another side to him. He could be gentle and thoughtful. He was also often surprisingly funny.

*He'd probably make a great husband one day.*

Once again what she knew about him didn't match her experience of him. She remembered Rachelle once commenting on a photo of Brett that had shown up online. He'd attended one of Eric's movie premieres with a well-known actress on his arm. Rachelle had said she didn't bother to try and keep up with who he was dating, because none of them lasted long anyway.

*Which is the real Brett?*

*And since when do I care if a man is marriage material? I don't need one to make my life complete.*

Still, it was difficult to meet a family like Josh, Nadine, and Ethan and not wish that kind of love was possible in her life.

*Why am I torturing myself like this? Brett isn't looking for a relationship with me. At most, he wants sex. He's probably not used to women who say no to him. I was a challenge to him, that's all. One that will likely be replaced by the time I return home.*

*Enough of feeling sorry for myself. I have a cruise to enjoy.*

She checked her Fitbit and said, "Look at the time. I need to see guest services about something. I should probably head over there now." She worked her way out from the table and stood.

Brandi got up and hugged her briefly. "You are not alone on this cruise, honey. You have friends now. While you're at guest services, ask if they can move you to sit with us." She wrote her name on a paper napkin and handed it to Alisha. "Or just come over if you see us. We're forty people altogether. There's always some who don't make it to dinner. We'd love to have you."

"That's so kind, thank you." Alisha tucked the napkin into her purse. At that moment she had no desire to join them, but it was a long cruise. *Who knows? Right now all I want is to be alone, but maybe I'll be begging for company in a few days.* "It was very nice to meet you—all of you." She gave the group a general smile and a wave, and walked away.

An announcement stated that the rooms were ready, so she made her way to hers. She attended a muster where she and the other passengers were instructed on what to do in case of an emergency. Afterward, she ended her subsequent stroll around the ship when she thought she saw Brett getting into an elevator.

*I have to stop thinking about him or I'll never enjoy myself.*

She returned to her room, showered, changed, and headed down for the early dinner in her assigned dining room. When she gave her ID key to the receptionist, the woman said, "It looks like your assignment has been changed. I'll have someone show you to your new table." She waved a staff member over to her and spoke to her on the side.

*New table? As in with Brandi and Nadine's group? No. It can't be. I never gave them my last name.* She scanned the room and cringed when she saw that very group, now more than doubled in size, seated in the direction the receptionist pointed toward.

"Is there a way to refuse without appearing rude?" Alisha asked the staff member who was holding the menus.

"Refuse?"

"Yes. Is there a problem with my original table? Could I still sit there?"

Across the room, Brandi stood and waved. "Alisha."

Alisha waved back, but directed her comment to the staff member. "I'd love to join them another night, but not tonight."

"That party?" In scanning the room, the receptionist saw the woman waving to Alisha, and said, "That's not where I was told to take you."

*Thank God.* Alisha felt awful thinking it. She normally loved getting to know new people, but this was her week to escape. To hide. She could have stayed home if she wanted to pretend to be happy. She wanted to simply be by herself for a few days and not have to worry how anyone else felt, what they thought, or if they considered her responsible for anything.

No guilt. No expectations.

Just me.

"Okay, then, lead the way," Alisha said. She made an apologetic face toward Brandi and motioned that she had to follow the staff member.

The woman led her to the far corner of the dining room and up a wide, curved glass staircase. Alisha paused at the top to appreciate the floor-to-ceiling windows that provided a panoramic view of the ocean. All the tables were empty, and only one was set. "Are you sure this is the right table?"

"Miss Coventry?"

"That's me."

"Then, yes, this is the right table." She led her to the table and a waiter rushed over to hold the chair out for Alisha.

After taking her seat and putting the napkin on her lap, Alisha scanned the empty room again. "Is it because I'm traveling alone?" *This could be an overflow section.*

The woman smiled politely without answering, then walked away. The waiter coughed as if covering a laugh, then asked if Alisha would like something from the bar.

A drink sounded like the perfect way to make it through her solitary meal on the top floor of the dining room. "Yes, but I don't know what. Surprise me," she said.

The waiter nodded and stepped away.

"I'm glad you like surprises," a deep male voice said, and Alisha gasped as Brett took the seat across from her.

Brett.

Not imaginary Brett from the hallway. *Unless I've completely come unhinged.*

"How . . . why . . . what are you doing here?" Alisha asked in a strangled voice.

He placed his napkin on his lap and smiled. "Could I convince you that I was in the neighborhood?"

Alisha gripped her hands on her lap. Seeing him again shook her. She'd tried to tell herself that she'd imagined the effect he had on her, but there was no denying the flush that spread up her body or how she could barely breathe. "This isn't a joke to me, Brett."

His expression turned serious. "Nor me. I'm here because you're here. It's that simple." He reached into his pocket and pulled out the gift he'd picked up from the jewelry store. "I couldn't let you leave without giving you your third gift. I had it made especially for you." He placed it on the table between them. "Open it."

*I can't open it. I can't go down this road. I promised Rachelle I wouldn't. I told myself I was stronger than this.*

*My mother chose a man over everything that should have mattered more to her. She let him ruin her life, my life. Why? Because she felt like this?*

*I won't do it. I won't risk losing a lifelong friendship over a man.*

*Even this one.*

"No," she said weakly, then cleared her throat and pushed the box back toward him. "Thank you, but no."

The return of the waiter with a bottle of champagne provided a short reprieve during which Brett attempted to process her response to his appearance. He wasn't an egomaniac. It was conceivable to him that a woman might not find him attractive, but that wasn't the case with Alisha. He was experienced enough to recognize desire in a woman's eyes, and it had been there. When he'd first appeared, the look she'd given him had made him want to haul her to him and carry her off to the nearest bed.

In fact, she was still looking at him with hungry, take-me-now eyes. There was something else, though. An anger he couldn't understand. *Is she angry with me? My family?*

She stood. "I should go."

"No." He was at her side in a heartbeat, taking her hand in his. That touch, innocent as it was, sent flames of pleasure through him. "Have dinner with me."

Her hand trembled in his. "I can't."

His mouth twisted in a wry smile. "That's better, I suppose, than 'I don't want to.'"

"What I want doesn't matter."

"It does to me."

She blinked several times, pressed her lips together briefly, then said, "You're not making this easy."

"Good." He pulled her closer and wrapped an arm around her waist. She melted against him. Ever so slowly he traced the curve of her collarbone, the exposed length of her neck, then cupped the back of her head. *This. This is what I've been waiting for.* "Because not being with you is slowly killing me."

When he claimed her mouth, it was everything he'd imagined it would be. Fire leapt inside him, burning away all sense of where he was or who might be watching. There was only her mouth, eagerly opening to his, and the sweet taste of her. *Fuck food.* She was what he hungered for. Her hands landed on his chest beneath his jacket. The feel of her beneath the thin material of her dress. He wanted it all. Right there if he could pay the world to disappear around them.

She writhed against him, and his cock throbbed with need. Her hands moved upward to encircle the back of his neck as she arched against him. He adjusted his stance to take her more fully into his arms and knocked over a glass on the table.

She broke off the kiss and pulled out of his arms, covering her mouth with her hand. He moved to touch her, but she stepped away. Their ragged breathing drowned out the hum of conversation from the restaurant below. "We can't do this," she said, looking close to tears.

"Why?" he demanded.

She brought her hands beneath her eyes as if to wipe away any smeared mascara, then let out a long, shaky breath. "I promised to stay away from you."

"Who? Spencer? He knows about us."

Alisha shook her head and picked up a napkin to dab at the corners of her eyes. "There is no us. There can't be an us."

*Can't* wasn't a word he'd encountered many times in his life. "Who did you promise?" *A man?* The idea that she might have a man in her life that he didn't know about was a sucker punch to his gut.

"Rachelle."

Relief flooded him. "She'll get over it." He went to pull her back into his arms, but Alisha took another step back.

"She won't. She blames me for Spencer finding out about his father. It *was* my fault. He wouldn't know if I hadn't gone to see your grandmother. Now he's hurting. Your mother is hurting. Rachelle is trying to hold them all together. Rachelle has been my best friend for most of my life. Stephanie has been more of a mother to me than my own. I can't risk hurting any of them more than I already have. I love them. I'm sorry. Nothing I feel with you is more important than making sure they're okay."

And just like that, Brett felt like a complete and utter asshole. She was putting the happiness of his family before her own. She was easily a million times better a person than he'd ever been.

*How do you fuck that?*
*You don't.*

More than anything, he wanted her to understand that there was no reason for her to feel guilty. Not about going to his grandmother. Not about him. "Rachelle will realize that Spencer would have found out either way. It would have come out when he received his inheritance."

She gripped the back of one of the chairs to steady herself. "I guess it would have. I just hate how it happened."

"There was no way you could have known. Rachelle will see that when things calm down. My mother will, too."

Alisha nodded, then smiled sadly and looked around the empty room. "You arranged all this? Just to have dinner with me?"

He smiled ruefully and then tried to make her smile by saying, "I was hoping for more than dinner."

She threw her napkin at him. "That's—"

"Honest," he supplied.

She blushed an adorable shade of pink that made him want to kiss her all over again. "Are you staying on the ship?"

"That was the plan." Although, he was beginning to see that when it came to Alisha, nothing went as planned.

There was a pause while they both gathered their thoughts.

"And now?" she asked with a mixture of longing and sadness in her eyes.

"I could attempt the swim, but I should probably wait until we reach the first port and fly back from there."

She stayed silent for a long moment, seemingly torn between sadness and apology. "I feel horrible. If I did something that made you feel—"

"Not everything that happens is your fault, Alisha. Don't take it all on. Sometimes shit just happens, and all we can do is make the best of what we're dealt." It was a philosophy born in the realization that he couldn't protect his family, especially when the betrayals occurred within it.

She cocked her head to one side and frowned. "Really? I had you pegged for more of a control freak. Not *freak*. But you know what I mean."

He chuckled, although there was little about their conversation he found amusing. "I do. And I was, but lately I've come across several situations no amount of money can fix. That used to be my solution. If I threw enough cash at a problem, it went away. This has been quite the humbling summer for me."

Alisha looked down at the table and then met his eyes again. "You probably don't want to have dinner with me anymore, but since we're both here . . ."

Brett pulled out the chair for her. It took every bit of control in him not to kiss the curve of her neck revealed as her hair fell forward. He pushed her chair in with more force than he'd meant to, and she let out a small surprised sound. "Sorry, still getting my sea legs, I suppose."

She watched him cautiously as he took his seat across from her. "Just because we're sharing a meal doesn't mean that I've changed my mind. We can't . . . I don't want you to think . . ."

What he'd once seen as indecision was now tangible evidence of her loyalty to his family. As much as he wanted her, he also wanted her to stand strong with her principles. It was a confusing place to find himself. Never in his life had he ever imagined uttering the next words that came out of his mouth. "We have two days at sea before we reach the first port. Let's be friends. We can spend time together with no expectations of more. Would you like that?"

"Yes."

He groaned. It figured that she'd chosen then to finally say yes without first saying no.

# Chapter Fifteen

After gulping down a fruity glass of liquid courage, Alisha asked Brett if he liked what he did for a living. She expected to see a return of the cocky man she'd met when she'd accompanied Spencer to face the "dragon."

Instead, he sat back and took a moment to consider his answer. "I've never thought much about that. I knew I'd be the one to take over the company for as long as I can remember. It was never a question of if, but how well I'd do when I did."

She studied his face for a hint of how that made him feel, then guessed based on how she would have felt. "That's a lot of pressure."

"The price of being born wealthy," he said, with a hint of humor in his eyes.

There were layers to his answer that Alisha might have missed had she not spent most of her workday assessing the emotional state of those in her care. Five-year-olds were unfiltered versions of who they'd be later. She liked to think that understanding them gave her a deeper insight into adults who tried to conceal all the same basic drives—hope, fear, anger, pride, along with a desire to be loved and belong. She could read most people, but Brett was a confusing mix of nature and nurture. His confidence bordered on arrogance, but there was another side to him that made her wonder who he would have been had he not been raised with money. "If you weren't you and you could do anything, what would you do?"

His eyes twinkled, and she knew exactly what he'd thought and held back. It was that gentle humor that made their strong attraction less scary. He wanted her and knew she wanted him, but was playfully respecting her decision. In place of the innuendo, he said, "If I weren't me . . . I hope I'd be like Spencer. He is building his company from the ground up and doing an amazing job at it. His WorkChat truly has the potential of changing how business is done. He'll leave his mark on history, and I admire that."

Alisha's heart constricted at the sincerity of his appreciation for what his brother was doing. "Have you ever said that to him?"

His features tensed. "I should have. He's never wanted my input. Recent events have amplified that sentiment. Too little, too late . . . Isn't that what they say?"

Moved by his concern for Spencer, Alisha reached across the table and gave his hand a supportive squeeze. "He'll come around. He always felt like he'd been left behind, and discovering he had a different father must make him feel like that was why."

Brett laced his fingers through hers. "We all felt left behind. Although I didn't know that Mark was Spencer's father, I knew my mother had been the one who had cheated. It was why I chose to stay with my father, but I'll admit that the ease with which she left Eric and me there had a bit of a sting to it."

Her heart ached for him, and she sought the right words to lessen his pain. "You were older. She might have thought you didn't need her as much."

He smiled sadly. "For a long time, I would have agreed with her."

It was impossible not to fall a tiny bit in love with him right then. A strong man, raised to work for his family, struggled to connect with them. She'd always viewed the separation of the Westerlys from

Rachelle's side and thought it was sad for her, but it now felt unnecessarily tragic all around. He loved them. They loved him. How could that not be enough? "Is that what you discovered this summer? One of the things money can't fix?"

Appetizers arrived, and the moment was lost. They took in the glass tower of jumbo shrimp placed between them.

"Does one even need a meal after this?" he asked, looking relieved.

She decided to drop her earlier question and simply enjoy what was turning out to be a delightful evening. "I'm willing to find out." She dunked a shrimp into the sauce, then bit a large chunk of it off with exaggerated enthusiasm.

He laughed and reached for one. "You are a joy. I'm used to women who are so obsessed with how they look that they don't eat."

She froze.

He froze.

She waited.

He swallowed hard, then smiled with pride as if he'd just solved an impossible equation. "Luckily, you naturally have what they work for."

She tried not to smile back, but gave in to the charm of his attempt. "Good save. But it's not easy for me, either. You're looking at the product of three to five workouts a week."

His gaze roamed over her appreciatively. "Looking is the easy part. Not touching is where the challenge is."

"You got that right." A blush warmed Alisha's cheeks at her brash remark. She'd never considered herself a particularly flirtatious person, but he made her exquisitely aware of her sexuality. Even as she said no, he drew her to him.

"Was that a compliment?" Laughter mixed with desire in his eyes.

She dipped another shrimp into the sauce. "Do you need to hear one?"

His smile widened. "Maybe. What does it for you? My strong jaw?" He turned his head so she could appreciate his profile, then turned back and flexed beneath his expensive suit. "My build? Abs like mine require a committed effort. They're quite impressive if you change your mind and decide to feel them for yourself."

She popped the shrimp in her mouth and chewed it before answering cheekily. "I'll take your word for it. Did you need extra luggage to bring that oversize ego with you?"

"I bet it's my ass. I've been told I have a good one."

Alisha laughed. "You sound so serious."

He frowned. "I am."

She laughed harder. "I can't tell if you're kidding." When he didn't smile, she was sorry that she'd made fun of him. Most people, even good-looking people, were insecure about how they looked. She felt awful. "Oh my God, I'm sorry. I didn't mean to make you feel bad. You know you're gorgeous."

His smile returned, and he winked. "I knew I could get you to say I'm gorgeous."

It was impossible not to smile back at him. "You're so bad."

He wiggled his eyebrows up and down. "You have no idea."

She shook her head and laughed again. "I didn't picture you being this much fun."

His smile faded. "People don't tend to describe me that way."

She instinctively gave him the same encouraging smile she used on the first day of school with new students. "Then you should let them get to know this side of you. Your whole family is naturally very funny. Spencer is quick with a joke. Rachelle's humor is dry like yours. Nicolette has a cutting wit your mother is always trying to rein in." She paused as she realized what she was doing. "I'm sorry. I'm explaining your own family to you. It's not like you don't know them."

He reached over and took her hand. "Alisha, you are by far one of the nicest people I've ever known, and yet I've lost count of how many times you've apologized since we've met. Stop. If I have a problem with something, I'll say it. Trust me, speaking my mind has never been an issue." He caressed the inside of her wrist with his thumb. "But this is about you. What are you sorry for that makes you feel everything else is your fault as well?"

No one had ever looked beyond her "good friend, good person" reputation and asked her that. Certainly never a man. And she had never trusted people enough to let them bear witness to her private shame. There was something about Brett, though, that made her want to be honest with him. He'd taken care of her when she was sick, come to see her when she was sad. What they had, whatever it was, deserved that much. "My father was a sporadic and abusive presence in my life. My mother took what he dished out, and so did I. I never stood up to him. My mother died without ever doing that, either." She looked down at their linked hands. "Sometimes I wonder if it would have all been different if I had turned him in. It might have been enough to break my mother free of him. I'll never know."

If he could have, Brett would have gone back in time to stop her father from overdosing on heroin. The investigator he'd hired to track down her father had returned with the news that he'd died six months ago. Brett had considered that good news when he'd heard it, but now he wished he could give her the chance to face him. She may not realize it, but she was stronger than most people.

What he really wished, though, was that he could have saved her from him entirely. She should never have known a moment of pain or fear. It tore at him that she had. He wanted to swear then that no one would ever hurt her again. *But I don't have to look past my own family to see how little I actually know when it comes to protecting anyone.*

*I do understand regret, though.*

*And how to flog myself with the list of what I could have done differently.*

His hand tightened on hers. He hadn't expected to have as much in common with Alisha as he did. He saw her pain through the lens of his own and, for that reason, knew what she needed to hear. "You did what you had to do to survive. Forgive the child you were. She was an innocent in a situation she did nothing to create."

A tear spilled down her cheek. He wiped it away gently. "I try to tell myself that, but it's the believing that's the hard part."

He didn't allow her to hide behind the dry joke. "Believe it. I've never met anyone more loyal or brave than you. Everything you went through made you into the beautiful woman I can't stop following around like some smitten teenager." He cupped her cheek with his hand. He'd never been big on compliments or gushing about how he felt, but he sensed that Alisha's self-esteem needed bolstering. If being more open than he would normally be could help her see herself in a better light, then he would tell her everything he liked about her as often as she wanted to hear it.

"I *am* pretty fucking wonderful," she joked as she regained her composure.

She'd made a joke to ease the tension of the moment. "You got that right."

Their meals arrived, and as Alisha spoke with the waiter, Brett soaked in the deeper beauty of the woman sitting across from him. She could have let her childhood harden her, but she was stronger than that. The more he got to know her, the more he knew he'd never again meet a woman like her. The man who one day won her heart would never have to worry where her loyalties lay. She deserved someone who believed in forever, too.

*Not someone like me.*

A better man would have walked away from her then, but Brett wanted the next two days with her. Even if all they were was friends.

Victor's voice rang in his head, *"When you marry, Brett, only do so with a woman you also consider your friend."*

"I don't believe in marriage," Brett thought, not realizing he'd announced it aloud until he heard Alisha's response.

"I don't either," she said after a pause. "It didn't work out for my parents or yours. Most don't last. That's why I agreed to marry Spencer. It's nothing more than a piece of paper nowadays. It's easier to get out of a marriage than it is a mortgage."

"Exactly," Brett said, but he didn't like how easily she agreed with him. He frowned. "You surprise me, though. I picture you pining for a house in the suburbs with kids and a dog."

Her eyes narrowed. "First, I do have a house in the suburbs, and I want children. There is nothing wrong with that or the dog the kids will enjoy growing up with. I just don't need a man to make any of that possible."

His eyebrows shot up.

She added, "Besides the obvious contribution, but that can be done in a lab. It might even be better that way. I hate the idea of a man coming in and out of my child's life."

"Have you considered choosing one who'd stay?"

"This from a man who doesn't believe in marriage, either?"

She had a point, but he liked the idea of her finding the right man and having the complete family package.

No. On second thought, he hated that idea because it meant imagining her with another guy.

He pushed his half-finished steak aside and stood. "Let's get out of here. I need some air."

She gathered her purse and stood. "Sure." She studied his face, looking uncertain. "Don't feel like you have to ask me to go with you."

"Oh, you're coming with me."

She blinked in surprise, and her mouth opened as if to say she wasn't, but then it closed without saying a word.

*You don't have to say it; I know I sound like an ass.*

He cleared his throat and told himself to get a grip. *I'm thirty-two. I've dated more women than I can remember the names of. I'll survive not sleeping with you.*

She looked up at him with those big blue eyes, and he groaned. *Maybe.*

He offered her his arm, and only because the truth of what he was thinking would have confirmed what a dick he was, he said, "You haven't told me about your job. Kindergarten. I don't know how you do it. I doubt I could get one five-year-old to do anything. I read an article about how academic the lower grades are now. That must be a challenge."

"It is," she said with enough wonder in her voice that he would have felt worse if her hand on his arm didn't feel so damn good.

# Chapter Sixteen

A few minutes later, Alisha and Brett were standing in front of his room's door, which just so happened to be right next to hers. She put a hand on one hip and arched an eyebrow at him.

He grinned and shrugged a shoulder. "I was optimistic."

There it was, that unrepentant, boyish charm Alisha couldn't resist. "Apparently. Is that all it takes with most women? A connecting door?"

Still smiling, he crossed his arms in front of himself and leaned against the wall. "Usually much less. I've never had to work this hard to be with anyone."

Alisha inhaled sharply. "Well, you can stop working at it because we've already agreed nothing is going to happen."

He straightened and opened the door to his suite. "Which is why it's perfectly safe for you to come in and see the view from the balcony. It's spectacular."

"I'm sure it is." Even though she trusted him, going inside would test her resolve as well.

"Afraid?"

"No."

"Worried you won't be able to keep your hands off me?"

She made a sarcastic sound in her throat. "Hardly."

He stepped through the door and held it wide open. "Then come see the view."

"I'm right next door. I have the same view."

"Really?"

The way he asked piqued her curiosity. She peered inside. "Holy shit. This is what a suite looks like?" She stepped past him and craned her neck to see the second floor. The room was easily eight times the size of hers with floor-to-ceiling windows on two sides and a large balcony with a hot tub.

"I was pleasantly surprised myself."

After gazing out the window, Alisha spotted a baby grand piano in a corner of the large living room area and moved toward it. A butler appeared, temporarily occupying Brett's attention. Alisha ran her hand over the top of the piano, then pressed a few keys. It was nicely tuned.

Brett's voice at her side made her jump. "Do you play?" he asked.

"We all do. Your mother played when she was young. It was important to her that we all learned as well. She paid for my lessons because my mother couldn't afford them. She always made sure to include me." A sad thought occurred to her that prompted a question before she had time to reconsider asking, "Do you play?"

"No," he said abruptly.

"I'm—"

"Don't say it. My mother's choices are hers to apologize for."

Alisha tried to think of something to say that would make it better, but fell silent when she failed.

He sighed. "She might have asked me to take them. I don't remember. If she did, I'm sure I declined the offer. I didn't want any part of the new family she'd made for herself."

There was a longing in his voice that she understood all too well. Even though she loved Stephanie and her children, when things had fallen apart, they'd pulled together—without her. It hurt, and she saw that same pain reflected in Brett's eyes. More than anything, she wanted to give him a bridge to them. "Would you like to hear your mother's favorite song?"

Their eyes met and held for a long moment. "Yes."

That's all it took for her heart to beat wildly and her body to quiver with desire she refused to give in to. The air sizzled. She was aware of every inch of him so near, every breath he took. He was as focused on her. It was dangerously intoxicating.

Alisha gave herself an inner shake and took a step back. She quickly sat at the piano and began to play the melody she'd heard Brett's mother return to again and again over the years. The ragtime tune was exactly the distraction she was looking for. "It's called 'Blame It on the Blues.' Stephanie said it was her father's favorite. When her mother met him, he was playing in bars for extra money. That stopped when they got married, but he still wanted to smoke a cigar and have a whiskey while he played. Her mother hated that, but she hated the idea of him going off to a bar to play even more, so she'd open the windows and let him. I never met him, but there's a photo of him at your mother's house, and I can imagine him so clearly whenever I play the song."

"I've seen photos of him." Brett sat down on the bench beside Alisha. "He did love a cigar and a whiskey."

The warm expression in Brett's eyes had Alisha momentarily fumbling to remember the notes. *I can't think about how much I want those lips on mine or on any other part of me they'd like to wander to.*

*I shouldn't even be here.*

*I should have said no and gone straight to my room.*

*But we're not doing anything wrong.*

*I'm simply savoring the little time I'll have with him. I can do that without taking this anywhere I'll regret.*

*I won't forget about everyone back home.*

Alisha transitioned to a more modern beat. "Spencer always preferred contemporary artists." She flowed from one song into another as she spoke. "Rachelle loves holiday music. Nicolette is a huge Mozart fan because she loves numbers and puzzles."

"What about you?" he asked huskily.

His simple question was thick with intimate meaning, but she refused to acknowledge it. She was tempted to turn her head toward him, but if she did, she knew he'd kiss her.

And her resolve would crumble.

"I like jazz. I close my eyes and the peace of it sweeps over me."

Swept away was close to how Brett felt when Alisha played as she described and gave herself over to the music. There was nothing overtly sexual about what she was doing, but he was torturing himself with the image of her talented fingers dancing their way off the keyboard and onto him.

He reminded himself of his promise: they would spend the next two days together without the pressure of more. Which meant he couldn't give in to the urge to lean over and kiss her bare shoulder. He definitely couldn't run his hand from her bare knee up her thigh, slide it beneath the light material of her dress to cup her sex. Taking her by the shoulders, turning her to face him on the bench so he could ease her down onto her back, was also strictly off-limits. As was ripping away her underclothing and spreading her wide for his hungry mouth.

*If I'm not going to do anything, why the fuck did I invite her in?*
*Because no other woman has ever reduced me to this.*

"You need to go," he growled.

The music instantly stopped. Her eyes flew open, and her cheeks turned an embarrassed bright shade of red. "Oh. I didn't mean to give you a full concert. I'm—" This time she stopped herself. "I haven't played in a while, and it felt so good."

Brett's cock hardened at her choice of words. He stood. "I'll show you out."

He didn't let the disappointed expression on her face deter him from opening the suite door and hustling her out of it. She looked confused by the snap in his voice, but he wasn't about to explain that he was angry with himself for wanting to pull her back inside and fuck her against the door.

He was always in control—of himself and usually those around him. Alisha had somehow turned that all around. Turned him around. He could barely recognize himself when he was around her.

If the look in her eyes earlier was anything to go by, he was reasonably certain her no would turn to a moan of yes if he kissed her. She was as hot for him as he was for her, which only made it harder to keep his hands off her.

*So why not do it?*

*Do her.*

*One time.*

*Or two. Maybe three.*

*And then we'd both be able to think straight again.*

*But then what?*

*Her promise to Rachelle is important to her, and her loyalty is part of her beauty.*

*Do I really want to take that from her?*

"Good night." His finality might work in business situations, but instead of leaving, Alisha stepped closer.

She cocked her head to one side and asked, "Are you angry with me? Did I say something wrong?" *How could she think that?*

He took a deep, fortifying breath. *She's only asking because I'm acting like an utter ass.* "No. Tonight was great." *Just great.* "See you tomorrow."

"Sure."

After watching her walk to her room and let herself in, he closed the door with more force than he'd meant to. He spent a while looking at the connecting door on the inside wall. What would he do if she knocked?

*I'd let her in.*

*That was a stupid question.*

She didn't knock, so he made his way up the stairs to his bedroom, shed his clothes, and took a very cold shower.

# Chapter Seventeen

The first thing Alisha saw when she entered her room was the small gift box on the middle of her bed. She sat down and picked it up. It was the jewelry box she'd refused at dinner. Its presence confused her as much as the night had. He'd spent the first part of the evening convincing her that they should spend time together, then practically tossed her out of his suite.

Was it because she'd offended him by talking about his family as if they were strangers to him? In a way they were.

No. His response had been tender and sincere. *"You did what you had to do to survive. Forgive the child you were. She was an innocent in a situation she did nothing to create."* So was he, to some extent. Just a different but equally tragic one.

So, why the gift? Had he left it before he realized she wouldn't sleep with him? Was it supposed to be a high-priced thanks-for-the-romp gift? Something impersonal he ordered in bulk and gave to all his hookups?

*I'll never know if I don't open it.*

She hesitated. *I can't keep it, but I can't send it back without knowing what it is.*

She lifted the cover off. "Aww." It was a simple blue lanyard for her room key that was engraved with her initials. Not expensive but incredibly thoughtful—and perfect. She hadn't realized that it was necessary to have her room key with her at all times because it served as an ID and was used to purchase items on the ship. Most people bought simple plastic card holders. After hearing Brett describe a cruise as a way of being moved around like cattle, she doubted he'd been on one before. How would he know that she'd need a lanyard?

She hunted down her phone, signed up for the onboard Internet package, and sent him a text. I love it. Thank you.

He didn't answer right away, so she put her phone down and went to change into her pajamas. After brushing her teeth and attempting to read a book, she gave up and flopped back onto her bed. How would sleep be possible when all that separated her from Brett was one door?

*And my promise to Rachelle.*

Her phone finally pinged with an incoming message. I hoped you would.

It's perfect. How did you know I'd need one?
I read a blog about cruises after you told me you were going on one.

Alisha was so touched by the idea of him researching what she would need that she didn't know how to respond.

Up for a run in the morning? he asked.

She picked up the lanyard. There was nothing impersonal about his gift. He might not be a man who intended to stick around, but that didn't make being with him feel any less wonderful. Yes.

Eight o'clock.
I'll be ready.

Alisha lay in bed for a long time thinking about Rachelle and the request she'd made. Was it fair? *No.* Could she understand how Rachelle might feel that her dating Brett could make a bad situation even worse? *Yes.* Unfortunately, she could.

She eventually fell into a restless sleep. The next morning she woke, freshened up, gathered her hair up in a ponytail, donned a T-shirt and shorts, and was tying the shoelaces on her running shoes when a knock came at the door. Before opening it, she told herself she had done nothing wrong. She'd been honest with Rachelle. Honest with Brett. She hadn't invited him on the cruise, but he was there. What was she supposed to do? Ignore him?

She opened the door. If possible, Brett looked even better than he had the night before. His running shorts accentuated his muscular thighs and his T-shirt complemented the broad shoulders and flat stomach he'd jokingly boasted about the night before. There wasn't an inch of him that wasn't deliciously fit.

His eyes looked a little tired. She fantasized that sleeping with only a door separating them had been just as difficult for him as it had been for her.

He looked her over appreciatively, then smiled. "Ready?"

*To spend another day with you, pretending we're just friends?*

Their eyes met, and her heart began to thud in her chest. *Yes. I know I'm crazy to do this to myself, but I want to be with him—even if it's only like this.* She put her lanyard with her key around her neck and closed the door behind her. "Let's go."

"Did you sleep well?" he asked with an innocent expression on his face.

She could have lied, but she didn't. "Like crap."

They looked at each other and both laughed. He bent and placed a hand on one of his knees in preparation for racing. "I bet I can beat you to the elevator."

"I bet you can't," Alisha said, holding her room key so it wouldn't fly free as she took off in a run.

"What do I get if I win?" he asked, falling into stride beside her.

She quickened her pace. "No need to ask because you won't."

A couple opened their door and made sounds of disapproval as Alisha and Brett thundered by them. Their opinion didn't matter, though. Alisha felt young and free as she rounded the corner with Brett at her heels.

She was preparing to announce victory when he snaked an arm around her waist and swung her around. She came to a full, sudden stop against the length of him. Any protest she might have uttered against his last-minute cheat was forgotten as her body settled against his. She didn't wonder if he was as affected by her: evidence of his excitement surged against her stomach.

In a near whisper she said, "I won."

"Then what do you want?"

She bit her bottom lip. Would one kiss break her promise? What was a kiss in modern society? Little more than shaking hands, right? *As long as I don't sleep with him.* "One. One kiss. But only that."

With a groan he swooped down and claimed her mouth with his. It was the kind of kiss a woman might wait her whole life for—hungry and primal. She opened herself to it, gave herself over to the pleasure of it. Had they been anywhere else but in the elevator foyer, they would have been tearing each other's clothing off, but they confined their passion to the kiss.

"Eww, they're kissing," a young girl said.

"Don't look. Just keep walking. We'll take the other elevators," the woman, likely her mother, said firmly.

Alisha and Brett jumped back from each other. They both fought to catch their breath.

"You're killing me," he said in a strangled voice.

As she came back to her senses, Alisha was confused and embarrassed by her request. "Oh my God. I'm an idiot." *How do I expect him to believe I'm not going to sleep with him when I melt every time he touches me?*

He cupped her face with his hand and ran his thumb gently over her lips, silencing her. "I'm the idiot. I can't keep my hands off you."

"I wish—" Alisha stopped. *What do I wish? That being with him didn't feel as good as it does? I didn't know anyone could make me feel the way he does. Because of him I know I can trust a man, really trust him. He can be strong without being cruel. He's giving me back a piece of myself I hadn't realized I'd lost. How do I wish that away?* "I wish you weren't Rachelle's brother."

He let out a harsh breath. "Another unfortunate reality I can do nothing about."


Brett knew he wasn't being fair to Alisha. He listed the reasons in his head, again and again, why her request that they remain just friends was for the best.

But when she'd asked him for one kiss, every shred of sense left him. That was the wonder of being with her. Before he met her, he would have described himself in terms of who he was at work: relentless, focused, controlled. Not even the boy he'd been before he'd taken over his father's company had ever laughed too loud or raced down a hallway not caring what others might think. There'd been no room for foolishness in the life that had been mapped out for him.

Piano? Waste of time.

Vacation? Only if it had networking potential.

Relationships were private. Public displays of affection such as what he'd just indulged in with Alisha would have been considered below him. Westerlys had a reputation to uphold. They kept their feelings and their scandals to themselves, and they always came out on top. Always.

*But at what cost?*

*When it comes to what really matters—we lose every time.*

He sighed and pulled Alisha into his arms, this time simply holding her. He tucked her head beneath his chin. She was tense within his embrace for a moment, then relaxed and wrapped her arms around his waist, resting her cheek on his chest. "We'll figure it out, Alisha. It won't always be like this."

She nodded but didn't raise her head. He inhaled the light scent of her shampoo and nuzzled the side of her head before he could stop himself. That little indulgence was enough to affect their breathing, and he stepped away because if he didn't, he knew he couldn't resist tasting her sweet lips again. "I don't know about you, but I need that run."

She pressed the button on the elevator, then glanced at the stairs. "We're only five decks down from the track."

Without another word they both charged up the stairs and paused only to catch their breath when they reached the right floor. He opened the heavy glass doors, and they walked out together into the bright sunlight. As if they'd done it a hundred times before, they fell into a comfortable matched pace.

The workout felt good, even better with her company. He wasn't one who talked much as he ran. For him, half of the benefit was emptying his mind and letting the fall of his steps lull him into a sort of meditation. He always ran alone because the few people he'd tried to run with chattered nonstop, which had denied him what was usually the only peaceful part of his day. Alisha either understood that or also preferred the silence.

He normally ran five miles a few times a week, but the track on the ship was small. He lost count after about thirty times around and decided it was close enough. When he slowed to a walk, Alisha did as well. "Shower, then breakfast?"

Wide-eyed, she blushed. "Oh. Sure. That sounds great." She tucked a loose tendril of hair back into her ponytail. "It's really windy, but it's beautiful up here, isn't it?"

*It sure is.* He was enjoying every aspect of the cruise more than he'd ever imagined he would, but she was to blame for that. "What do you feel like doing today?"

"I had planned to check out the shops and then lose twenty dollars at the casino," she said.

"Only twenty? If you don't risk big, you can't win big."

"I'm okay with that. I've worked too hard for what I have to throw it away like that."

"At least tell me you play blackjack."

"Penny slots only. I dare you to try them and not have fun."

He'd try anything she suggested if she asked him in that cocky tone of hers. "You're on." He caught his reflection in the glass window of a restaurant they passed, and the expression on his face took him by surprise. His smile was wide and bright. The corners of his eyes were wrinkled with laugh lines. He looked—*happy?*

*My family is in a state of crisis. I'm lusting after a woman who has no intention of sleeping with me. Why am I smiling?*

He pulled open the glass door that led back to the stairs and had his answer as soon as he looked at Alisha. *Because she is.*

*It's that simple.*

*And that fucked up.*

A couple of hours later, Brett walked into the ship's jewelry store with Alisha. She'd said they could skip it, but he wanted to know her taste. "Do you prefer diamonds or rubies?" he asked.

She shrugged and tucked her hands into the front pockets of her jeans like a child who had been told not to touch anything. "I've never cared much about jewelry. I'd rather spend my money on a new lawn mower or a hot water heater."

He turned and frowned at her. He didn't see the world the way she did, but he liked the way she thought. Unless her practical side stemmed from desperation. "Do you need either of those?"

"Not yet, but when I do, I'll have the money to buy them because I didn't spend it here." Pride shone in her smile.

He tried to imagine the wives of his work associates saying something like that and doubted any of them ever had. They wore their diamonds like war trophies. Alisha wasn't like that. She wasn't in constant competition with the women around her. She was simply herself. And unlike the women he usually dated, the more time he spent with her, the more he found to like about her. Still, he wanted her to leave with something—a tangible reminder of this trip. "If you had the money, what would you buy?"

She gave him a funny look. "I don't need anything."

"It's not about need." He put his hand on her lower back and guided her toward a display. A salesperson came over and said all the precious stones were half-price for that one day only.

Alisha shot Brett an unimpressed look and said in a tone for only him to hear, "Which means they are all normally priced at twice the value."

He silently agreed, but it wasn't the cost that mattered. He wanted her to wear something he'd given her. Something more personal than the lanyard.

"Are you shopping for something in particular?" the salesperson asked.

Brett pursed his lips and kept his gut response to himself. *Yes, do you have a necklace or a bracelet that says, "Don't even look at me, because I'm taken by a man who has to sort out some family issues before we can fuck? He's not here with me because he flew home, but I'm definitely taken."*

"No, just looking," Alisha answered politely.

The salesperson not so subtly checked her left hand, then said, "We have our own jeweler aboard who designs incredible engagement rings for much less than you'll find in the United States. And they come with a guarantee. If you need it repaired or resized, it'll be covered. Cruises are a wonderful time to pop the question. We even have a wedding coordinator on board if you feel that spontaneous."

Alisha tensed beneath his hand and said in a rush, "We're not . . . he and I are . . . we're just friends."

Brett fought a sudden urge to punch the knowing smile off the salesperson's face. Instead, he said, "We'll call you over if we have any questions." The salesperson took the hint and set his sights on another couple. Once they were alone, Brett decided not to address the awkwardness of what the salesperson had said. He returned the focus to his original goal. "I know your taste."

She visibly relaxed, and her smile returned. "Really?"

He leaned in and pointed at a pair of two-carat diamond earrings. "You'd never wear those."

"You're right."

He hovered his hand over a large emerald pendant trimmed in diamonds. "Too flashy."

She nodded and leaned closer to inspect it. "It's beautiful, but you're right; that's not my style."

He walked to another case. "Now, these remind me of you. Blue diamonds. Rare. Colorful. You'd never wear the square stones because you're too practical and they'd catch on everything. You'd want beauty you could wear while you teach. Something simple. Understated, but built to endure. Like that one." He pointed to a bracelet with round blue diamonds spaced out between links of white gold. He nodded at a salesperson who came right over. "She'd like to try that one on."

"Of course."

"It's not necessary." Alisha protested as the woman opened the case and took out the bracelet. "I don't even wear—" She stopped, held her wrist out to the salesperson, and allowed her to put the bracelet on. "Wow, that's beautiful. I guess you do know my taste." She looked up. "How much is it?"

"Four thousand today. Eight tomorrow," the salesperson said.

"We'll take it," Brett said.

Alisha's eyes flew to his. "No. It's too expensive."

He shrugged. "Hardly."

She removed it, placed it on the case, and walked away. Never in his life had he chased a woman, but she was a confusing laundry list of firsts for him. He caught up to her in the hallway outside the store. "Alisha."

She stopped and clasped her hands in front of her. "Don't ruin the day by doing this. I said I don't want it, and I meant it."

*Then why do you look about to cry?* "Look at me, Alisha."

She raised her eyes to his.

"Talk to me." He didn't understand how offering to buy her something could have upset her.

"Don't push me. I already feel terrible that we're together." She rubbed a hand up one of her arms. "Could we go back to having a fun day? Maybe go to the casino or for a swim?"

He planted his feet and waited. "The bracelet was merely meant to be a souvenir of this trip."

She looked uncomfortable with his persistence, but the answer mattered to him. Finally she said, "Brett, I know it's not much money to you, but please, please don't buy me any more gifts." She looked away as if to compose herself, then added, "It only makes it worse," in a whisper.

"Worse? Because of Rachelle? It wouldn't affect her."

She went white. "It would affect me. This is about how I feel. None of this was supposed to happen. It's bad enough that I'm having so much fun with you when I told Rachelle I'd stay away from you. When I accept things from you, it says I'm not strong enough to do the right thing. I don't want another reason to feel that way."

*Loyal to a fault. She gives the feelings of others more importance than her own. A person like that deserves to have good things happen to them. If I want to spoil her, I damn well will.*

The hallway of the ship wasn't the place to talk out her feelings on the matter, so Brett asked, "Penny slots, then?"

"Yes," she said in a relieved tone. "Want to see who can make twenty dollars last longer?"

He nodded and was rewarded with a smile. He wondered if she realized how much her happiness was beginning to matter to him.

It was something he'd fought at first, but now saw as part of his newfound journey. There were many things he'd had to concede were beyond his ability to control. He couldn't change the past. He couldn't prevent the people he loved from disappointing one another. But he could put a smile on Alisha's face.

Somehow, that made everything else bearable.

# Chapter Eighteen

A short time later, Alisha laughed out loud at the frustrated expression on Brett's face when she won forty dollars on the penny slot machine. She'd led him to two identical machines that were side by side and unoccupied. After convincing him to only bet twenty dollars, she'd challenged him to match her spin for spin until one of them lost. He'd enjoyed it until his balance had gone below five dollars and hers was nearing sixty.

"Did you see that woman trip? I hope she's okay," he said as he pointed toward the other side of the casino.

Alisha scanned the room for a woman either on the floor or righting herself after a fall but didn't see either. "Where?"

"Next to the man in the orange shirt."

"I don't see a man in an orange shirt."

"They must have left."

She turned back and looked from his suspiciously happy expression to the credit balance on his machine. He now had sixty-three dollars and change. "You cheated!" She gave his shoulder a shove.

He continued to look pleased with himself. "I merely took advantage of a loophole in your rules. You stated that we both *start* with the same amount, but you never stated we couldn't add as we please."

"It was implied."

"Which may work in kindergarten, but would never hold up in the business world."

Alisha's chin rose. "You did *not* just go there."

His chin rose as well.

She folded her arms across her chest. "I don't care if you're five or fifty, cheating is cheating. If you want to play with me, go back down to your original balance or the game is over."

"You're taking this far too seriously." There he was, dismissing how she felt again. Her temper rose.

"And I expect an apology for the kindergarten dig."

Some of his smugness left. "I can see how that might have sounded—"

"Might have?" Oh no, he was not getting off that easily.

"Let's cash out and go for a walk."

"Seriously? You're so afraid of losing that if you can't cheat, you'll quit?" She told herself to drop it, but she couldn't. Rachelle had said that Spencer had always been in competition with Brett. Did it go both ways? She didn't like to think she might be a pawn in a game she had inadvertently wandered into.

A storm raged in his eyes that belied how he was attempting to rationalize his reaction. "It's just a game."

"Is it? Or are you a sore loser? How do you handle losing in real life?"

"I don't. I make sure I win."

"No matter what?" Nothing he was saying was making her feel better.

"You're naive if you think anyone in power follows the rules. We make them."

"Wow." The coldness in his tone was new to her experience with him. *Here is the dragon Spencer said destroys all in his way. How can this be the same man who seems so considerate the rest of the time?* "This is a side of you that's hard to like."

His eyes darkened, and he looked away. "I added money as a joke. I thought it would make you laugh. It didn't. Let's go." He punched the button to return his winnings to his card.

She didn't move. *He's not in charge of my emotions. I am. I may not like what he's saying, but how I respond is my choice. If he is looking for someone to cower and apologize whenever he is less than pleased, he picked the wrong woman to spend time with.* "I didn't take you for someone who runs away."

He froze. "I don't."

"Then don't dismiss what I said or how you made me feel. Don't talk down to me. I've seen you do it with Spencer, and it's why he doesn't go to you with his problems. You are not better than me, but you talk like you think you are. Which man are you? The kind, gentle man who took care of me when I was sick—or the condescending asshole I thought you were the first time we met?"

He turned toward her slowly, and one of his eyebrows arched. "I am not condescending."

She gave him a moment to internally review what had come out of his mouth a moment before. Then she said, "You owe me an apology."

His jaw tightened, then relaxed. "I respect your job. I shouldn't have used it to make my point." She held his eyes during a standoff that lasted a few long minutes. Finally, he sighed. "I'm sorry. I can see you're right about how I talk to Spencer, but I didn't see it until you challenged me that first day. When I heard my own words come out of my father's mouth, I didn't like the way they sounded."

She reached across and put her hand on his thigh. "I can understand that."

His hand covered hers, and the connection turned intimate. "I don't want to be the man you thought I was that first day."

"Then don't be." She said the words with conviction. Maybe she was nothing more to him than a win over his brother, but he seemed to genuinely want to be a better person. Like her, maybe he was on a journey of self-awareness and improvement.

*Or maybe that's what I want to believe.*

He chuckled. "You are not the least bit intimidated by me, are you?"

"Should I be?" Her breathing became shallow, and her body began to warm. She struggled to focus on the topic of their conversation, yet there was his nearness and the way he was looking at her.

He leaned over, brushed his lips across her cheek, and whispered, "I need someone like that in my life."

*He needs someone like me?* She shuddered with pleasure on more than one level. *Do I dare let myself believe that for even a moment?*

As if he sensed her inner conflict, he raised his head and said, "The machine won't let me put less than five dollars back on, but let's finish the game."

She nodded, still flushed and dazed from the nearness of him. The outcome of the game was the last thing on her mind.

He punched in a code that added five dollars in credit back to his machine, then brought her hand up to his mouth and kissed her knuckles. "For luck," he said.

They both hit the "Bet" button at the same time. She won two dollars. He won $800. She pulled her hand free and framed her face in amused outrage. "That is not right."

He turned toward her, leaned over, and gave her a brief, gentle kiss on the lips. "I'd say it is. With you, even when I lose, I win."

*See, that's where we're different. If I play, I could lose everything.*

His words echoed through her, and the feel of his lips lingered on hers. Had they been alone, she might have launched herself into his arms.

*I don't want this to end.*

*But where do we go from here?*

As he and Alisha strolled the deck after dinner, Brett marveled at how quickly the day had flown by. The sun was setting on the ocean horizon, and it saddened him to think they'd only have one more day together before they reached Grand Turk and he flew home.

*Unless I stay.*

When they stopped to lean on a railing and watch the sunset, his eyes were drawn to Alisha's smiling face instead. He put an arm around her as if to brace her from the wind, but he didn't try to hide the truth from himself. He enjoyed holding her. Being with her felt good. So damn good.

She rested her head on his shoulder and let out a contented sigh. He gladly would have stood there indefinitely.

A day of Ping-Pong, shuffleboard, and mai tais would normally have left him feeling restless, but it hadn't. Even when he traveled, he worked. Between his cell phone and his computer, he was usually able to keep up with everything at the company almost as well as if he were in his office.

He hadn't checked his e-mails all day, and he hadn't felt tempted to. His stomach churned—either at that thought or due to the variety of foods he'd ingested at dinner. When he'd told the chef he wanted the meal to be special, he hadn't anticipated hours of endless courses.

She glanced at Brett's face. "You look a little green. Are you seasick?"

"No, just too full. I should have paced myself."

She chuckled. "Everything was amazing. The chef obviously wanted to impress you. How many times did he say, 'It is my honor, Mr. Westerly'?"

He shrugged. "I get that a lot."

She hip-checked him. "Watch the ego, you're already bloated enough."

"Bloated?" He looked down at his still-flat abs. "I would offer to prove I'm not, but I'll let my stomach settle first."

Alisha laughed. "Charming. Is that a line you use with all the ladies?"

He thought about it and answered honestly, "No, but I don't need to impress you." When he saw confusion enter Alisha's eyes, he realized how what he'd said might be taken. He hadn't meant that he didn't care enough to try to impress her, he meant that she was the first woman he felt comfortable enough around to just be himself. With her, he wasn't Brett Westerly, wealthy businessman. He was just a man spending time with a woman he couldn't get enough of. He was about to attempt to rephrase his comment when a crew member approached them.

"Mr. Westerly?"

"Yes," he answered.

"I have a message for Miss Coventry."

"That's me," Alisha said. "Is something wrong?"

"No, no," he hastened to assure her. "Your name was drawn out of a raffle in our jewelry store. You may pick up your prize at your convenience."

"I didn't enter a raffle," Alisha said, then turned to Brett. "Did you?"

He shrugged. *Enter one? No. Had one created? I may be guilty of that.* On and off that day he'd thought about why she'd refused the bracelet. She wanted it, but accepting it from him made her feel like she was doing something wrong. The solution had come to him out of the blue and had been easy enough to arrange via his suite's butler. If all went the way he'd planned, she'd never know. "It's probably a promotion to bring you back."

"Like a coupon." She turned to the man who had given her the news. "Is the prize thirty percent off something that costs several hundred dollars? If so, I'm not interested."

The man deftly dodged her question by saying, "I'm sorry. I don't work in the sales department. I was simply asked to pass the message along to you." With that, he excused himself and walked away.

Alisha looked cautiously optimistic. "I guess it doesn't matter if it turns out to be a coupon. The prize doesn't matter. I won something. Do you want to come with me to see what it is?"

He agreed to. He couldn't wait to see her expression when she found out what the prize actually was.

# Chapter Nineteen

Alisha's enthusiasm grew as she and Brett entered the ship's jewelry store a few moments later. The woman who had shown her the bracelet earlier smiled and waved them over when she saw them.

"Miss Coventry. How exciting. We don't have too many raffles this big, but when we do, it's a reason to celebrate, yes?"

"I guess so," Alisha said with caution. She glanced at Brett, but his expression remained neutral. She turned back to the salesperson and tried to silence the pessimistic thoughts in her head. Was the celebration the catch to winning the prize? She'd get something, then have to star in a cruise commercial or promotional equivalent? She might normally have thought that was a fun possibility, but all she really wanted to do was enjoy her time with Brett.

"Would you like a glass of champagne?"

Before Alisha had a chance to accept or decline it, the glass was handed to her. Some of the other customers in the store stared. "Thank you," she said politely and took a nervous gulp. "I can't believe I won. I didn't even enter a raffle."

Without missing a beat, the salesperson answered, "Then you truly are lucky."

Alisha was about to ask if her name had been drawn from a list of all the ship's passengers when the woman took out a piece of paper and waved for them to follow her to one of the display cases.

The same display case that held the bracelet Brett had wanted to buy for her.

*He wouldn't have . . .*

*He couldn't have . . .*

*No.*

He was a man who played by his own rules, but arranging for her to win something she wouldn't let him buy her? *Just how much do I think this man actually likes me? Enough to spend the day with me? Yes. Enough to want to cheer me up with gifts when he knows I'm sad? Okay. Yes. But to arrange a whole raffle? Just for me? Now who has the bloated ego?*

The salesperson opened the back of the display and said, "You won a five-thousand-dollar voucher that is redeemable only in this store. Of course, you can have your pick of whatever you would like, but if I remember correctly, there is something here that you liked."

"Five thousand dollars?" Alisha's mouth dropped open. "What do I have to do to get it?"

"Nothing besides claiming it when you return to the United States."

"Just like that? I seriously won?"

"Yes," the woman said with a smile.

Alisha hopped up and down as the enormity of her prize sunk in. She turned and hugged Brett spontaneously. "I won five thousand dollars. *Thousand.*"

He returned the hug and her smile. "Now you can have the bracelet. That's fantastic."

Alisha tensed. *I can. I won enough to get exactly what I wanted.* Coincidences like that didn't happen. Did they? But what was the alternative? To believe that Brett had somehow arranged for her to win?

When the salesperson clasped the blue diamond bracelet on her wrist, Alisha wanted to believe good things could simply happen.

They didn't have to be part of a master plan. Brett wasn't trying to manipulate her.

*He won money. I won jewelry. Why couldn't that happen?* It was the most beautiful piece of jewelry she'd ever owned, and it would always remind her of this time with Brett. It would be like having a little piece of him with her always.

And the universe wanted her to have it. Why else would she win the amount needed to get it?

*Is this my consolation for holding on to my principles? I didn't take the easy way—this is a sign that I made the right choice.*

"I can't believe I won it. Everything about this cruise has been amazing so far. I don't wear much jewelry, but you were right, Brett, I'll wear it every day. It's perfect."

He kissed her forehead and hugged her closer. "I'm glad it worked out for you."

There was a part of her that wanted to ask him if he was in any way responsible for her winning it, but she didn't want to discover he was. *Don't overthink this. He had nothing to do with it. And I don't have anything to regret. I can wear it and still look Rachelle in the eye.* "Me, too." She rocked her wrist back and forth, admiring the sparkle of the deep-blue stones. "I don't know how the rest of the cruise will go, but it will be hard to top today."

The salesperson interrupted just long enough to say that the paperwork for the bracelet would be available on the last night of the cruise and that it would be brought to Mr. Westerly's suite.

"You mean, Miss Coventry's," Brett corrected firmly.

"Oh yes. Of course. All of the paperwork will be in her name." The woman looked momentarily flustered, then congratulated Alisha again. She rushed off and returned with a box and bag for the bracelet.

Alisha took it and met Brett's eye, noting the lack of guilt. The staff on board tended to go out of their way to please him as if they'd been given specific instructions to do so. "Do you know the owner of the ship?"

He smiled. "The CEO of the ship line."

*Am I wrong?*

*Stop. The best way to ruin anything is to dissect it.*

*Mom always said, "If you dig long enough, you'll always hit dirt."*

*Oh God, now I'm using her advice to justify my actions? I really am in trouble.*

Brett neither confirmed nor denied that his association with the cruise line had been the reason for her winning. "I hear they're showing a movie at the pool tonight. If we hurry, we can catch the start of it."

"I'd love that. Let's do it."

When they arrived on the deck just above the pool area, they were met by a man with a blanket. The usual reclining chairs had been replaced by round canopy daybeds. One of them had been reserved for them. None of the blogs about cruises that Alisha had read ever mentioned anything like this. "Did you arrange for them to change out the seating?" she asked.

His blue eyes held hers, but he didn't answer her question.

She watched the opening credits begin to roll on the screen below. "You knew this was my favorite movie. I remember telling you it was."

His expression remained carefully impossible to read. "You may have mentioned it."

"And I told you I'd always wanted to go to a drive-in."

A corner of his mouth curled in a sexy hint of a smile. "If you hate the idea of lying in my arms under the stars, we could go watch it below with that herd of children."

"Oh, you're good."

His smile widened. "That's what I've been told."

She rolled her eyes and laughed. "Are you sure there is enough room for me, you, and your ego on that daybed?"

He wiggled his eyebrows. "Only one way to find out."

◆ ◆ ◆

Brett hoped Alisha wasn't going to quiz him on the plot points of the movie, because with her curled up to his side, he sure as hell wasn't able to concentrate on anything. His senses were in lustful overdrive. He remembered once reading an article online about how postponing one's pleasure intensified it. He'd dismissed the article as a load of New Age crap, but he had to admit he was physically attuned to Alisha in a way he'd never experienced before. It wasn't just about wanting to have her calling out his name while he thrust his cock deeper and deeper into her. It had become about the pleasure of her breath caressing his neck when she turned to speak to him. He was aware of every place their bodies made contact, every beat of her heart against his chest, every time she adjusted and her hardened nipples brushed against his arm.

His body begged to roll over and take what it was painfully craving to plunder. Her mouth. Those amazing breasts of hers. It would take only a shift of his weight for him to be able to slide a hand under her skirt and sink a finger into her pussy. He didn't, though. When they came together, and there was no doubt in his mind that they would, there would be no reason for either of them to regret it. He'd make sure of that.

Alisha's hand was absently caressing his chest as she watched the movie. She turned her head so she could see his face. "Thank you for tonight. No one has ever gone out of their way to make me feel special the way you do."

He couldn't stop himself; he leaned in and kissed her lips gently, but forced himself to pull back before he lost control. If she knew the real him, not the vacation him, she wouldn't look at him with so much trust in her eyes. "I'm not a nice man."

Her hand stopped and splayed across his chest. "Really?" There was a beauty to her that affected him on so many levels. He wanted to have her, but he also wanted to protect her from any hurt that might come from being with someone like him. She deserved a man who believed in forever.

"I have impossibly high standards for everyone around me, as well as for myself."

"Okay."

"People fear me in the business world, and I've given them reason to. I've always won, no matter the collateral damage."

"And?"

"And I'm a fucking miserable bastard. Just like my father. Just like his father before him. I like you, but I wonder if I'm not a bull trying to carry a crystal vase. Is there any version of us where you don't end up hating me when it ends?"

She laid her head back on his shoulder without answering and hugged him. He blinked back an emotional response to the simplicity of her support.

When she spoke, her tone nearly broke his heart. "I have spent half of my life worrying that I'd become my mother and the other half hating that I didn't save her from my father. I know a bastard when I see one, and I don't see one in you."

His kissed the top of her head. "My family would debate that point."

She hugged him again. "Not if you showed them the side you've shown me. I've never met a more caring man. Since the first time I met you, even when your words were cutting to Spencer, I knew you wanted the best for him. You've stepped forward time and time again to take care of me, to keep me safe. Bring that approach to your brothers and sisters, and they'll adore you." She raised her head and met his eyes. "Unless you already have and they don't know it."

He tensed.

She continued, "Just before college I qualified for financial aid, but Rachelle was denied. We wanted to go to the same school, so we scrambled to find a place we could both afford. At the last minute a scholarship came through that made it possible for her to go to

Boston College with me. I remember thinking that when she or her family needed something, miracles abounded. Doors slammed shut for them just like the rest of us, but then they would open and everything would work out. I used to joke that their guardian angels worked overtime. Was that you? Did you watch out for them? Pay for their schooling?"

Brett didn't answer. He didn't want to lie, but he had never wanted to be applauded for taking care of his family. He remembered finding paperwork proving that his father had paid for the nurses who'd cared for Mark during the last months of his life. His father had never told a soul, nor had he. He cleared his throat. "My father was wrong about many things, but he got a few right. He always said that the best good deed is one that no one knows about."

"That's beautiful." She chewed her bottom lip. "It also explains why he let everyone think it was him and not your mother who cheated. So, he funded Rachelle's education?"

Brett met her gaze, but held his silence. It was probably better if she believed Dereck had been the guardian of the next generation of the family. He wasn't used to anyone considering him anything but a cold-blooded shark.

She shook her head. "No. It was you. But how much of it? Did you help Nicolette along the way? Tell me you didn't rig the contest she won. She's so proud of that."

"No, I didn't rig it. I don't believe in handing success to anyone. All I've ever done was make sure they had what they needed. They brought the talent. I merely removed obstacles."

"With Spencer, too?"

Brett didn't admit to it. He didn't need to. She knew.

She said, "He has no idea."

"Exactly."

"You need to tell him. All of them. They grew up thinking you didn't care about them. Imagine if this brought you all closer."

He loved that she believed the world worked that way, but he didn't want her to discover herself in hotter water with his family. "How would Spencer handle discovering I had anything to do with his success?"

She whistled. "He'd hate it." She sat straight up and turned to look down at him. "But they deserve to know. It might change everything."

He sat up as well and took her hand in his. "Things are already changing, but the last thing Spencer needs right now is another reason to doubt himself."

Her shoulders slumped. "Because of me. You're right, your family is still reeling from the last time I tried to help them. I need to learn to mind my own business."

He hated the sadness that had entered an evening he'd planned to make her happy. "You didn't make the mess my family is in."

She wiped a tear from the corner of her eye. "You didn't, either." After a quiet moment, she said, "Your family deserves to know how much you love them."

He held her eyes. "They will. Someone came into my office and made me see that they need more from me. I intend to be more visible in their lives now."

"Yeah, you're a real bastard," she said with a chuckle as she wiped another tear away.

"A miserable one," he added. *At least, I was before I met you.* He kept that last part to himself. He wasn't ready to verbalize how she made him feel.

The expression in her eyes changed. Desire replaced sadness, and he felt the power of it like a punch in the gut. One kiss was all it would take for him to put aside the reasons he was holding back. One kiss would likely be enough to topple her resolve.

And it would be so fucking good.

But then what?

*She loves my family. Genuinely, wholeheartedly loves them. And they love her.*

*Being with me could destroy that.*

"I'm ready to call it a night. Ready?" He edged off the daybed and held out a hand to her.

She took it and allowed him to help her to her feet. She searched his face, then nodded. "I've seen this movie a hundred times, anyway."

They stood there simply staring into each other's eyes. Her breathing was as shallow as his, and he could almost hear her questions. *She's wondering if I'll leave her at her door without a kiss or carry her to my bed.*

He turned and started walking. She fell into step beside him.

He let out a harsh breath.

*I'm asking myself the same damn thing.*

# Chapter Twenty

A few minutes later, with Brett beside her, Alisha took her key lanyard out but stopped before opening the door to her room. What had he asked? *"Is there any version of us where you don't end up hating me when it ends?"*

That didn't sound like a man who was using her to steal a win from his brother. In fact, nothing about him supported that fear.

He was honest with her, though, about not seeing what they had as something that would last. That should have been reason enough to not give in to temptation, but it wasn't.

No man she'd ever been with compared to him, and none ever would. He was cocky in his confidence, humble in his kindness, and sexy as hell. A woman could spend her life looking and never find a man who stepped up and did what needed to be done without complaint or expectation of gratitude.

*Is there any version of us where I don't end up hating myself? That's the better question.*

*I'm beginning to resent Rachelle.*

*I shouldn't have to choose.*

*But since when does life work out the way it should?*

*If it did, Brett's family would see him for the good man he is. They would pull together instead of apart when life throws shit at them.*

Blue diamonds flashed on her wrist, and she turned to him. "Did you create a raffle so I'd win the bracelet?" He opened his mouth to answer, but she placed her fingers across his lips. "It doesn't matter, does it? Either way, I'll never wear it without smiling and remembering this trip with you. You need to know, though, that if you did arrange it after I said I didn't want it—I'm not upset. I'm beginning to understand you, and I wish the world had more people like you in it." She lowered her hand.

He caught it and held it tightly. "I wish I were half the man you think I am."

She leaned forward, ready for the kiss he looked about to give her. His nostrils flared. Her eyes fluttered closed, and her body hummed in anticipation.

The kiss didn't come, though. Eventually, Alisha blushed and her eyes flew open. His expression was tight with the same hunger raging through her, but he let her hand go. "I enjoyed today."

"Me, too." Before she had time to think about how desperate she might sound, she asked, "Will I see you for breakfast?"

His lips pressed together for a moment, then he said, "I have e-mails piling up. Some can't wait."

"I understand." She didn't, though. He looked angry with her, but they hadn't argued. She actually felt like their day together had brought them closer in a way she'd never expected.

He groaned, raised a hand, and buried it in the hair on the back of her neck. "Alisha, I—"

"Yes?"

His hand dropped, and he turned away. "Good night."

He was at his door and gone before she had a chance to respond. To the empty hallway, she whispered, "Good night."

Alisha let herself into her room, threw her key on the shelf, and kicked off her shoes. Fully clothed, she let herself fall backward onto her bed. Sexual frustration warred with embarrassment. She'd all but offered herself to him, and he walked away.

*Which is for the best.*

She pulled a pillow over her head. *So why do I feel like I'm dying?*

Rolling onto her side, she punched the pillow. *I'm being an idiot. I spend half the day thinking he might be using me and the other half mooning over the perfection of him.*

*I tell him I don't want to be with him, then hate him for respecting my stance. He doesn't want to hurt me, doesn't want to hurt his family.*

*Asshole.*

She punched the pillow again. *Since when do I need a \man to be happy? I don't.*

*Definitely not someone like him.*

Flopping onto her back, she replayed the day in her mind. The more she reviewed, the worse she felt for trying to vilify him to console herself.

*Yeah, because who wants a gorgeous, sweet man who puts the welfare of his family first?*

She couldn't imagine anyone fearing him, not if they really knew him. She thought back to when Mark had wanted to die at home rather than in a hospital. The insurance had denied covering Stephanie's requests for visiting nurses in addition to hospice because Mark's illness had been long and expensive. Yet then they'd reversed their decision without explanation. At the time, Stephanie had been too grateful to question why, but Alisha wondered what she'd think if she knew it was Brett who had likely made that happen.

*He loves his family so much more than they know.*

*His family.*

*Not mine.*

' The last week had slapped Alisha with the painful realization that when push came to shove, she was not one of them. She could have been there for them, but instead she was on the outside, wondering if she would ever be close to them again.

Did Brett feel the same?

He'd said the summer had been a humbling series of realizations that there were things he couldn't fix. His family was one of them. She was sure. She wished there was some way she could help Rachelle and the others see what a good brother they actually had.

Brett was right, she couldn't tell them all he'd done, but surely there was something she could say. Rachelle wouldn't be happy when she found out that she and Brett had been on a cruise together. *I keep worrying about upsetting her more, but there's no avoiding that one.*

She raised her arm so she could see the diamond bracelet. *Which parts of this matter, and which are just bullshit? I should be able to accept a gift from anyone I want without Rachelle hating me for it. I should be able to acknowledge how I feel about Brett without feeling like a traitor.*

*None of that should change the fact that Brett has been a good brother, even if it was behind the scenes.*

She took out her phone to text Rachelle. There were things her friend needed to know, even if it ended their friendship.

Are you there?

Yes.

How is everyone?

As good as can be expected. I haven't seen much of anyone besides Mom and Nicolette. Everyone else is MIA. How are you?

Okay. Alisha took a deep breath. Brett is with me. You and I have never had secrets. I didn't know how to tell you, but I also don't want you to find out from someone else.

Rachelle didn't write a response.

Alisha continued, I know you're not happy about it, but there's something I need to say. Please, just listen for a moment. Alisha took Rachelle's lack of answer as permission to go on. With shaking hands, she typed: I didn't mean for anything to happen between us. Honestly, nothing really has, because neither of us wants to hurt you. You need to know that about your brother. He loves you so much. Your happiness is important to him. You may not see it, and he may not know how to show you, but he would do anything for you. I'm okay that you're angry with me, but don't be with him. This was my fault, not his.

All I asked was for you to not be with him now. Right now. While my family is falling apart.
I know. And that's why we haven't done anything. I swear we haven't. We've spent time as friends, but it hasn't gone further than that.
But you're on a cruise together now?

Yes. She could have defended herself. She could have explained that Brett had joined her on a cruise that she hadn't invited him on. But no. She refused to do that to Brett, and she wasn't all that certain that Rachelle deserved an explanation.

There was a long pause. Then Rachelle wrote: If you're looking for permission to fuck him, just do it. I don't care anymore.

Rachelle's harsh words cut through Alisha and tears filled her eyes. She dropped the phone beside her. Her gut reaction was to hit back, but that wouldn't make any of it better. Not for her, Rachelle, or Brett.

She picked up her phone and called Rachelle. If their friendship was about to come to an end, it wouldn't be because she hadn't fought for it. As soon as Rachelle picked up, Alisha said, "You do care. You're angry. This sucks. I know. Guess what, it sucks for me, too. Do you think you're the only one hurting right now? I love you, all of you. I'm sorry that Spencer found out about his father the way he did. I wish I could go back and not agree to the fake engagement. You have no idea how much I regret going to see your grandmother. But I don't regret Brett. He has been the only good in all this."

Rachelle's voice was thick with emotion. "You like him. I get it. But did you have to do this *right now*? No matter what Spencer says, he'll feel like he lost to Brett again."

"No, he hasn't. They're not in competition. Or they shouldn't be. They're brothers. And I'm not some prize that someone won or lost. Spencer and I were never really engaged. You know that. You came up with the idea."

"So now this is *my* fault."

Alisha shook her head. "It's no one's fault. Sometimes shit just happens." *Thank you, Brett, for helping me see that. I've been drowning in an ocean of guilt that I heap on myself. Not everything is my fault. Sometimes shit happens. You can let it hold you down, or you can fight it off and stand back up.* "I love you, Rachelle, but I deserve better than this. I'm not asking you for permission to do anything because I don't need it. I've always thought of you as my sister, which should mean that we support each other through the tough times. That's what friends do. Call me when you remember that."

Alisha hung up and covered her face with her hands. Maybe she'd made the situation better. Maybe she'd made it worse. But she was done hiding bruises—physical or emotional.


Brett paced the length of the suite's living room, hating how he'd left it with Alisha. One more look from her, one touch, and he would have kissed her with all the pent-up fire within him. Instead, he'd done what he'd never respected anyone for: he'd retreated.

He told himself it was for her, but it was also for himself. The way she made him feel scared him. It was too intense, too beyond his ability to control. If he gave it the power to, it might consume him.

*So I ran.*

Deciding that a shower might help clear his head, he removed his shirt and shorts, but continued to pace in his boxer briefs. He should just knock on her door. Fuck everyone else and how they felt. Whatever he and Alisha did was none of their business. It shouldn't stop them from doing what they both wanted to do.

*I feel that way, but Alisha doesn't. That's what matters.*

*That's why I'm here instead of there.*

He called his sister and was surprised when she picked up on the first ring. "We need to talk, Rachelle."

"About Alisha, I'm guessing," she said, then sniffed. "I know you're with her."

"I am." Something in her voice made him ask, "Are you okay?"

"Not really, but what did you call to say?"

"You can talk to me, Rachelle. It doesn't matter about what."

She made a sound like she was about to cry, then held it back. "It's nothing you don't already know, but it's hard. I just got off the phone with Alisha. But you probably already know that."

"No, I said good night to her a while ago. What happened?"

"We argued about you."

His gaze flew to the connecting door. Was Alisha as upset as Rachelle sounded? "Alisha didn't invite me here. In fact, she has told me on several occasions that she couldn't see me because it would upset you. I couldn't stay away from her. If you're angry with anyone, be angry with me."

Rachelle sniffed again. "The only one I'm angry with is myself. I just keep making mistake after mistake. Things are bad here, Brett, and every time I try to help, I seem to make it worse. Alisha and Spencer's engagement was my idea. Look how that turned out. Mom barely comes out of her room. Spencer said he's done with all of us. I've never seen them like this before. Nicolette came home drunk the other night. She told Mom she had no right to keep that kind of secret from all of us, and she wants a paternity test done because she won't believe anything Mom says from now on. I know none of this was Alisha's fault. I told her to stay away from you only because I was afraid if Spencer found out you were with her, things would get worse. I'm not sure they can, though."

"Alisha is a loyal friend to you."

"I know that." She let out a shaky sigh. "I don't know what to do, Brett—about any of this."

"Do you want me to come home?"

"No. A week won't make a difference. But maybe you could come see Mom when you return? I can't reach her."

Brett wasn't sure he could either, but he'd try. "It's all going to be okay, Rachelle. Families survive worse than this all the time."

"Do they?"

He had no fucking idea, but he said what he knew she needed to hear. "Absolutely. I'll come see you when I return, but right now you need to call Alisha back. She thinks she can lose you over this."

"She won't. She's my best friend. I love her. I'll always love her."

"I'm not the one you need to say that to." He hung up, walked over to the connecting door, and laid his hand flat on it. He couldn't force his sister to do the right thing, but he hoped she did. Either way, he wanted to be there for Alisha. He raised his hand to knock on the door but lowered it when he heard her phone ring. Normally, he couldn't hear her in her room, but standing at the door, he could. He told himself to walk away, but stayed where he was.

"Hi."

A short pause. He couldn't hear the other side of the conversation, but that didn't stop him from hanging on Alisha's every word.

"I'm sorry, too."

A long pause.

"Oh, I'm so sorry to hear that. Of course I understand."

Silence.

"I love you, too."

Pause.

"I promise. I'll call as soon as I get home."

Her voice rose in surprise when she said, "He did? What did he say?"

Brett held his breath.

"I know I said I didn't need your permission, but I won't do anything if you think it'll hurt you or Spencer. You're my family."

Nothing could have dragged Brett away from the door just then.

"Are you sure? I don't even know if he's still interested. I've turned him down so many times."

*Would knocking on the door and yelling, "I sure as hell am!" be wrong?*

"I'll tell you how it goes. Yes, I'll keep those details to myself, but do you think I should wait until tomorrow to talk to him? He said he had work to do."

*No e-mails here. Not a single one I care enough to read.*

"I can't just knock on the door and tell him that you're okay with us being together."

*Yes, you can. In fact, saying it naked would be even better.*

"You're funny. Yes, I'll call you tomorrow to give you the G-rated version of what happens. Love you."

Brett looked down at the prominent tent in his boxer briefs and smiled. *If she even needs to ask—will this suffice as my answer?*

# Chapter Twenty-One

Alisha walked over to the door that connected her room to Brett's and laid a hand on it. Once she knocked, everything between them would change. Was she ready for it?

Images of him flashed through her mind. She saw him sitting beside her on the dock, barefoot in his suit, there simply because he wanted to make sure she was all right. She remembered how gently he'd taken care of her when she was sick, how thoughtful each of his gifts had been.

It wasn't a competition. She didn't know what it was, but she had a feeling that if she walked away from him now, she would spend the rest of her life regretting it. A week. A month. A year of him was better than a lifetime without him.

*I'm a survivor. If he breaks my heart, I'll pick myself up and go on.*

She unlocked her side of the door and knocked softly once, then more firmly.

"Come in," he said as if he were directly on the other side of the door.

She opened the door. A huge smile spread across her face at the sight of him. There he was in all his glory, like some half-dressed gladiator. Her breath caught in her throat at the muscular perfection of his bare chest and broad shoulders. Her gaze slid lower, across his flat stomach to his dark-blue briefs that did nothing to conceal his enormous erection.

Her thighs quivered as warmth spread through her. She raised her eyes to his. Any feeling of embarrassment was far overshadowed by the hunger in his eyes. She gulped, then said, "So I talked to Rachelle and—"

He stepped forward and dug his hands into the hair behind her ears. As he lowered toward her, she whispered, "I'll tell you about it later."

His mouth plundered hers. There was no hesitation, no gentleness. She met his kiss with a matching hunger, opening her mouth wider for him. His tongue darted around hers, tasting, luring. It demanded all of her, and she gave herself over gladly, finally.

His lips were hot and wet as he kissed his way across her cheek. "I want you so fucking much," he growled into her ear.

"Oh yes," she whispered back. *God, yes.*

He lifted her shirt over her head and unsnapped the back of her bra with professional speed. With a groan, he lifted one of her breasts to his mouth. He licked across it once, an act that sent a shiver of pleasure through her, then took it deeply into his mouth. The way he suckled, then flicked his tongue back and forth over her nipple had her whimpering and begging him not to stop. He did, but only to give her other breast the same attention.

Her hand sought his manhood, but he said harshly, "No, I'm already too fucking turned on. Your tits are heaven, but I want to taste you." He unzipped her skirt and slid it down, along with her panties, for her to step out of.

His hand sought her sex, and he slid a finger between her lower lips. "You're so wet I could fuck you right now, but I want you to come for me first."

He lifted her, carried her to the couch, and sat her on the arm of it. Her feet dangled above the floor, so she steadied herself with an arm along the back of the couch. He left her there for a moment, then returned with a condom box that he dropped on the floor between her spread legs. He removed his briefs, releasing his long, thick cock.

She licked her lips, drawing his attention back to her mouth. He stepped between her legs and bent to kiss her again. The tip of his cock rasped against her leg. Her hand wrapped around it, loving the promise of its size and hardness. "You feel so good," she said.

He groaned, and as he moved to kiss his way down her chest again, his cock slipped out of her hand. "So do you." He nipped at her rib cage. "So fucking good." His lips burned a path across her stomach to just above her mound. Instead of diving in, he pushed her thighs farther apart and kissed his way from her knee to just before her sex and then repeated that action on the other side.

Alisha was clenching the back of the couch with one hand and steadying herself with her other. She felt off-balance and completely at his mercy, but joyfully so. She realized something very important in that moment: she trusted him in a way she'd never trusted a man before, and that allowed her to give herself fully over to how good he made her feel.

His talented tongue darted across her lower lips, and she adjusted her seat so she was spread open for him. He groaned in approval and thrust his tongue deeply inside her. She shuddered at the power of the act. He found her clit with his thumb and began to move back and forth across it in a thrilling rhythm. His tongue plunged in and out of her, deeper with each stroke. She put a leg over one of his shoulders and pulled him closer with it, urging him to continue.

The man had been blessed with a tongue of fantasies. Strong. Relentless. When she thought it couldn't get better, he moved his talent to her clit. She clasped her legs around his head, and he chuckled. "Easy there."

"Sorry," she said, but she had already forgotten what for. As he flicked his tongue over her clit, he sank one of his fingers deeply inside her, then a second, hitting the spot she'd given up on a man ever finding.

That was all her body needed for her orgasm to explode. She shook and grasped at him as wave after wave of fire seared through her. His touch turned gentle, and he kissed his way across one of her thighs again. "I love the sounds you make when you come," he said.

*What sounds?* Alisha wasn't aware of having made a single noise. It had been that good.

While Alisha came slowly back to earth, he stood and rolled a condom on. As if she were one of those skinny women she'd always envied, he lifted her into his arms and settled her legs around his hips. Had she been capable of speech, she would have told him she was too heavy, but the feel of his cock teasing her entrance robbed her of all coherent thought. All that remained was the raw, primal need to feel him inside her.

The wall behind the couch felt cold on her shoulder blades, but his breath was hot as he kissed her neck. She ran her hands over every inch of him that she could reach, from his strong back to his amazing ass.

He dipped the tip of his cock into her, then withdrew it. She rocked against him, trying to take him deeper. He held her hips with his hands and thrust upward into her. Alisha clung to his shoulders and clenched herself around his cock each time he entered her. He started his rhythm slowly, each time filling her more. She writhed in his arms, loving how perfectly they fit.

"I'm trying to be gentle, but you feel too good," he growled.

She realized then that, although she'd given herself over to their lovemaking, he was still trying to protect her. She bit his bottom lip and said, "Don't hold back. Fuck me, Brett. Oh God. Do it."

His back muscles flexed beneath her hands, and he took a step so she was pressed more fully against the wall. His breathing changed, and he pounded into her more powerfully with each stroke. Due to his size, it was a painful pleasure, but one that brought another wave of orgasm. She met him thrust for thrust, whimpering for him to plunge harder. He rocked her with a glorious, wild ride that brought tears to her eyes.

She cried out his name as she came. He grunted and shook against her as he followed her lead.

For a while afterward, they stood there, both gasping for air in the aftermath. He kissed her lips softly, then withdrew and lowered her to her feet. "Is that what you wanted when you knocked?"

His lusty, pleased smile brought an answer to her lips. "How embarrassing if it wasn't."

He stepped away for a moment, to remove the condom, then returned and lifted her up into his arms. He sat on the couch and positioned her so she was on his lap, facing him, with her sex spread open above his already hardening cock. He took one of her hands in his, lacing his fingers with hers. His other hand came up to cup and caress her bare breasts. "Please don't be embarrassed with me."

Their connection seemed natural. "I'm not."

He absently circled one of her nipples with his thumb. "Good, because I like you naked. You're perfect."

She'd never felt that way, but she didn't need to be every man's ideal as long as she was his. "You're not so bad, yourself."

He grinned. "I know."

She rolled her eyes, but her sarcastic retort died on her lips when the tip of his shaft dipped into her. "Do you have another condom?"

He reached over to pick one off the arm of the chair and gave her a cocky smile. "Why, is there something you want?"

She rose onto her knees, moved her breasts across his chest, and whispered into his ear, "Only if you have what it takes to fuck me again."

He chuckled. "You have a dirty mouth for a kindergarten teacher."

"You have no idea," she teased, loving how he flushed at her forwardness. She swirled a hand coquettishly across his chest. "I can control it, though, if you don't like it."

He ran his hands down her back and gripped her bare ass. "Don't you dare." He slid her back onto his legs so that his cock stood upright between them. "Although I can imagine better uses for your mouth than swearing."

Alisha eased herself onto the floor and pushed his legs apart before crawling to kneel between them. "Really? I can't."

He wound his hand through her hair, tugged her face closer, and demanded, "Take me as deep as you can. I want to feel those lips of yours wrapped around my cock."

She flicked the end of it with her tongue. "Like this?"

It might have been a dangerous game with another man, but this was Brett. Even if she drove him to lose control, he would take care of her. That's who he was. He hauled her closer still and ran the tip of his cock across her lips in a circular motion. "Open your mouth for me."

She did, and he thrust himself deeply in. She had to stretch her mouth wide to accommodate the size of him, but it was worth it. His eyes half closed, and he groaned. She bobbed her head up and down, taking him as deep as she could. His pleasure was her pleasure. She ran her hands over his thighs hungrily, then brought one to cup his balls.

"Touch yourself," he said huskily. "I want to see you make yourself come."

She did what she was told and began to stimulate herself as she loved him with her mouth. Her own hot wetness felt good on her fingers. She stroked herself faster and faster while nearly gagging herself on the length of him. It didn't matter. His desire matched hers.

Heat began to build within her to a level that could not be contained. She moaned with him in her mouth as she thrust her own fingers into herself and pumped them in and out.

"I'm close," he said and pulled out of her mouth just in time to come all over her chest. She continued at a frenzied pace to come right after him.

"Fuck, you're amazing," he said.

After she caught her breath, she looked up and smiled. *Wow.* She stood on shaking legs, went to the bathroom to clean up, then crawled back onto the couch. This time she laid her head in his lap. She'd had what she considered good sex before, but never anything like what they'd just shared.

"Not so bad yourself."

A while later, Brett lay awake in his bed with Alisha, still naked, cuddled to his side. He said the first thing that came to mind. "I never let women sleep over." He hadn't meant to say it, but the revelation of how tempting it was to have her in his arms all night surprised him.

He didn't know what to expect as a reaction, but her indulgent smile radiated warmth. "That's good to know." She cuddled closer to him.

The intensity of his feelings for her confused him. He didn't want her to leave any more than she seemed to want to. Still, that didn't mean he'd feel the same way the next morning. He didn't believe in letting a woman sleep over. One night would lead to a left toothbrush, then a few outfits appearing in the closet. Before he'd know it, he would be living with someone he'd never officially asked to move in. Brett had seen it happen to more than one of his colleagues, but had never let it happen to him. He didn't give women the keys to his apartment, so he never had to ask for them back. It kept things simple.

Still, Alisha felt good beside him. He kissed her temple. "I'm not saying you have to leave, but I don't want you to think—" He stopped because he didn't know what the hell he'd been about to say. *That we're a couple? What's worse? If we are? Or aren't?* She raised herself up onto an elbow, and the beauty of her bare breasts temporarily made him lose his train of thought. When he finally raised his eyes to hers, the serious expression on her face brought him back to the moment.

"You don't have to worry. We talked about this, remember? I don't believe in forever any more than you do."

Brett hadn't liked that marriage conversation, and the updated version wasn't sitting well with him, either. "Because you don't need a man in your life to have the children, house, and dog you dream of."

Her nose wrinkled, then relaxed. "Are you upset with me?"

"No," he said almost angrily. When he heard himself, he said, "No," in a neutral voice. *What am I doing? I should be relieved instead of arguing the point with her.*

She sat up, looking confused. "You meant it about not letting people stay over, didn't you? I thought you were joking."

*Now I not only am an ass but look and sound like one, too.* "I was."

She smiled in relief. "Sometimes I can't tell."

He pulled her back down into his arms. "Come here." The kiss he gave her was that of a sated lover. "Go to sleep. We'll both make more sense in the morning."

She gave his side a light tweak. "Hey, I'm making perfect sense."

He closed his eyes. "Sleep."

She settled against him again and sighed contently. He waited for her breathing to deepen before he slid out of bed, put on lounge pants, and made himself a stiff drink.

He should be in a great mood. He'd wanted her, and he'd had her. The sex had been phenomenal. There was no reason to believe they couldn't have more of the same, and according to her, she was fine with agreeing that it was temporary.

He opened a glass door and went onto the deck. The sound of the ship breaking through the waves added to the calming effect of the scotch. He sat in one of the lounge chairs and soaked in the peace of the setting. He couldn't remember the last time he'd sat quietly to enjoy anything. His mind was always racing with the challenges of a present project or a strategy for the next one. He'd never given himself time to question if he wanted what he was fighting so hard to keep.

Until Alisha.

She was slowly changing how he looked at everything. In the past, hearing a woman say she didn't believe in marriage or forever would have been just fine with him. With Alisha, he wanted to prove to her that some things did last.

*Too bad I don't believe they do.*

He took a long gulp of the scotch.

*People don't change.*

*I may want to.*

*The afterglow of a mind-blowing fuck might have me convinced I could, but how long would it take for me to disappoint Alisha? Work has always come first for me. What makes me think I'd be a better husband than my father was?*

Two hands began to massage his shoulders. He laid his hand on top of one of them. "I thought you were asleep."

Dressed in one of his T-shirts, she walked to the side of the chair. With a simple flick of her chin, she asked if she could join him. He placed his drink down and shifted his legs so there was space for her between them. The wind blew, giving him a teasing look at her bare bottom as she turned to sit in front of him before she leaned back against his chest. He wrapped his arms around her, just below her breasts, and gave himself a moment to feel.

She laid her arms over his. "I was, but I rolled over and you were gone. It's so peaceful out here at night. I hope you don't mind if I join you."

He nuzzled her hair. Being near her was always a turn-on, but this time that feeling came second to the desire to hold her. Her bracelet twinkled under the light of the moon. He ran a finger over it. "Not at all. I was out here thinking about us."

He felt her light chuckle against his chest. "And it drove you to drink?"

He kissed her neck. "A little. This would be a hell of a lot easier if you were like every other woman I've dated."

She took a deep breath. "I'm going to take that as a compliment because I think you meant it as one."

"I did. I really enjoy being with you. You're intelligent, funny, gorgeous as sin, and I admire your integrity. I can't think of another person I can say all that about."

She smiled up at him. "What was that middle part again?"

He knew what she was referring to, but decided to have a little fun with it. "Intelligent?"

"After that."

"Funny?"

"One more."

He hugged her. "You know you're beautiful."

She sighed happily. "You make me feel like I am. I was never cheerleader or prom queen material."

He ran a hand up and down her arm. "Is that how you measure your beauty? If a bunch of horny teenage boys think you measure up to some Photoshopped model? Your beauty is deeper than that." She nodded, but didn't look as if she believed him, so he continued, "I love your curves. I know too many women who live on carrot sticks and define themselves by how many 'likes' their photos get on social media. They want me to pose with them so they can say they've been with me. That kind of self-obsession makes a woman ugly to me. Your beauty is natural. Steady. It doesn't come off when your makeup does. Your face and body would make any man stop and take a second look, but it's who you are on the inside that pulls me back to you."

She blinked back tears. Then, with a completely straight face, she asked, "Is now a bad time to admit that for me it *is* your ass? You were right. You do have a nice one."

Her reference to his earlier joke took him off guard, and he let out a deep laugh that broke the silence of the night. "Just as I suspected."

They laughed in unison, then quieted. Some women might have robbed the peace from the setting, but Alisha added to it. She seemed to crave the calm as much as he did. Was this what she found at her lake house retreat? Why she went there when she was upset?

He wanted to be her sanctuary.

*But how realistic is that?*

"Do you enjoy your job?" he asked. He wasn't sure why the answer to that question felt so important to him now. He knew which parts of her life were in disarray. He wanted to know about the parts that weren't.

"I do. Don't get me wrong: there are good days and bad days. I age a little every time a parent picks up a child from school and doesn't tell anyone. There is nothing worse than realizing a child is gone and not knowing where they went."

"Does that happen? Aren't there safeguards against that?" With how often schools were in the news, he wouldn't have thought something like that could happen.

She didn't seem offended by his question. "Oh, there are rules. Schools are all about rules and procedures now, but the human element always finds a way around those. It could be a parent who sees their child in line and calls to them. Or a parent who volunteers for a field trip and leaves with their child without telling anyone. It doesn't happen often, but enough that it's my favorite before-school-starts nightmare."

He ran a hand through her hair. "Would you still want to work if you didn't have to?"

She tensed. "You mean if I won the lottery?"

"Or married someone who made it unnecessary for you to work." He could have kicked himself for that comment. He wasn't ready to promise her anything, but that didn't mean he didn't want to hear the answer, not that he completely understood the reason why.

She was quiet long enough that he wasn't sure if she was going to answer, then she said, "Those are two totally different scenarios. If I won the lottery, I don't know what I would do. I'd like to think I'd donate a good portion of it. I wouldn't leave teaching, though, unless another job came along that I enjoyed as much. What I do gives me a good deal of satisfaction. I know I make a difference." She wagged a finger in the air. "I definitely wouldn't leave teaching for a man, not even one I married. I would never want to be on an allowance or give anyone that amount of control over my life."

He opened his mouth to say something, but she cut him off.

"I'm not judging women who choose that life. There are plenty of people who do it and are happy, but it requires more trust than I've ever had in anyone."

He understood her thinking, but it made him sad. Alisha needed to be in control because she knew what it was like to suffer at the hands of someone else. Her childhood had made her strong, but it had also left her wary. He hated that someone so protective of those around her had trouble believing anyone would stand with her just as steadfastly.

*It would be so easy to say I'll be there for her.*

*Why can't I?*

*Because I don't want to be the next person to disappoint her.*

"I was planning to fly back when we reach port," he said.

"And now?"

"I want to stay, but we need to be clear about what we're doing."

She sat up and turned so she could face him. "Clear. Okay. What *are* we doing?"

She didn't look angry or upset. It might have been easier if she had been. At least then he would have known what to say. "Enjoying a vacation together."

She cocked her head to one side. "Are you saying you want this to end when we get home?"

Although part of him thought that's what he wanted, he didn't answer immediately because that definitely *wasn't* what he was saying. His thoughts became scrambled each time she looked at him.

A sad smile lifted one side of her mouth, and she spoke before he had a chance to. "That's probably for the best. I haven't even told people at work that I'm no longer engaged to Spencer. I don't really want to go back and explain how I ended up with his brother."

The ease with which she accepted a time limit he hadn't even verbalized, grated. He wasn't okay with things ending as soon as they returned home.

She patted his thigh. "It doesn't have to be awkward between us when we go back. I tend to stay friends with men I've slept with."

*What the hell? I'm not okay with* that, *either.*

*Friends?*

*To look but never be able to touch? Hell no.*

*And who are these ex-lovers she's friends with? No man sticks around a woman he's had sex with unless he thinks there is a possibility of another chance.*

She gave him a funny look. "Are you seasick again? You don't look so good all of a sudden."

He stood up and growled, "I don't get seasick."

She put her hands up in mock surrender as she followed suit. "Whatever you say."

He was done talking. The more he tried to verbalize how he was feeling, the worse he was making things. He decided to return to when things were going well. "I'll take you up on that." He advanced on her.

She laughed. "Oh, will you?"

"I will, and you'll like it." He ran his hands up the back of her legs and forcibly grasped her bare ass, pulling her roughly against his instantly hard cock. "I'll make sure you do."

Her eyes half closed, and she purred, "Is that a promise?"

"It is."

He might still be untangling his feelings for her, but he wasn't at all confused about this. He wanted to fuck her until she was calling out his name as she came, until she couldn't remember anyone before him. He picked her up, slung her over his shoulder, and carried her through the suite and up the stairs. He tossed her onto the bed and stood over her. He'd never seen anything more beautiful than her on his bed, smiling in his shirt, with her wet pussy naked and ready for him.

# Chapter Twenty-Two

The next morning, after eating breakfast in their suite and sharing a leisurely shower together, Alisha and Brett chose a morning walk instead of a run. Even if the ship hadn't been moving back and forth more than it had the day before, Alisha wasn't in the mood for a workout. She was thoroughly, happily relaxed.

Every once in while a question born from old insecurities would pop into her head, but she was far too de-stressed to worry about much of anything. The sky was dark gray, but on the inside she was all sunshine and daisies. She knew she was sporting a perma-smile, but it was Brett's fault. A night of orgasms had left her in a sexually sated daze.

They walked hand in hand, talking about nothing in particular. The topic didn't matter. His deep voice was a caress of its own. She asked him questions about his life simply to hear him speak.

During the walk, they passed a woman alone, leaning over the railing, with tears running down her cheeks. It took a moment for Alisha to downshift into reality. "I know her," she whispered to Brett. "I met her my first day on board. She's here with her husband and family for a vow renewal. They do it every year."

Brett pressed his lips in a flat line before answering. "Do you want to see how she is?"

Alisha bit her lip. "She looks pretty upset." She and Brett came to a stop a few feet away. They had a choice of walking by and stopping to ask her how she was, or turning around and going the other way. "I should at least see if she's okay."

Brett kissed her briefly. "I agree. If she needs to talk, I'll grab a coffee and meet you at a table over there."

Raising a hand to his cheek, Alisha said, "You're a good man."

He smiled, then walked toward the coffee bar.

As she approached, Alisha asked, "Nadine?"

Nadine straightened and quickly brushed away her tears before turning to face her. "Oh, hi."

When she didn't say her name, Alisha provided it. "Alisha. We met at the buffet on the first day. I gave Ethan a ride to your table."

A smile spread across Nadine's face, and she sniffed. "I remember. Sorry I didn't recognize you at first. I have a lot on my mind right now."

Alisha joined her by the railing. "Are you okay?"

Tears filled Nadine's eyes again. "I will be. I just didn't want to lay this on anyone I'm traveling with. Everyone is having a great vacation."

"Except you."

"I was, then—" She sniffed. "You don't want to hear this."

"I wouldn't be standing here if I didn't care."

Nadine nodded and wiped the corner of her eye. "I received some news today that I just need to process. I was hoping to cry it out before anyone woke up."

Moved by the woman's pain, Alisha laid a hand on her arm. "Is there anything I can do?"

"Are you a psychologist?" the woman asked with a sad laugh.

"Kindergarten teacher, remember?" Alisha joked gently. "Practically the same thing. If you need an ear, I'm here."

"I just have to get out of the funk I'm in and pull myself together before I talk to my family."

Alisha nodded in quiet encouragement.

Nadine turned back toward the railing. "This trip is not only to celebrate our ten-year wedding anniversary, but it's also my five-year anniversary of being cancer-free. Josh and I were dating when I was first diagnosed. He married me knowing that and stayed by my side through all of my treatments. I beat it five years ago. They say the longer it's gone, the less likely it is to come back. I was told I might not be able to have children, though Ethan had other plans. After all the medicine I had taken, we worried he wouldn't be healthy, but he's my little miracle baby. I am grateful every single day. Grateful to have Josh, my family, and now a son. Our vow renewals are more about saying thank you than needing to promise forever to each other again." She covered her eyes with one hand. "It should be enough that my family is here to celebrate this with us, but we had planned our renewal for tomorrow in Grand Turk. The captain announced bad weather might mean that we skip that port. The wedding coordinator doesn't know if she can get our deposits back from the venue before we arrive in Nassau. We put all of our money into helping our family afford this trip. We can't swing paying for another place."

"I'm so sorry," Alisha said, fighting back tears of her own. Nadine's story was beautiful and touching at the same time.

Nadine shrugged one shoulder. "It's not about the venue. It's just that every other renewal went without a hitch. We never had one fall apart like this one is. It scares me. I know it doesn't mean anything, but I can't help but worry that it's a sign. Maybe I've reached the end of my luck." Her shoulders shook as she wiped away fresh tears.

"It's not. Things like this happen. They mean nothing. I'm sure the coordinator will figure something out before we reach Nassau. It's a glitch, that's all."

Finding her composure again, the woman smiled sadly. "My head knows that, but I have so much to live for now. I get scared. I'm so sorry to burden you with this. I just don't want to say this to Josh. He's been so good to me. There is no reason for me to make a big deal out of not having a venue for the renewal. If I can't afford another venue, we'll do something on the ship. Like you said, it means nothing. Right?"

"Right."

Nadine turned and gently squeezed Alisha's hand before dropping it. "It's too bad it didn't work out. I was going to invite you to it if I saw you. I pointed you out to my cousin Henry, and he thought you were beautiful. He's single again. Or almost single. I could find out more about his situation if you're interested."

"Oh, thank you, but not necessary."

"He's a good guy, who would be on his best behavior because his parents are on the trip."

"Wow, I appreciate the offer, but I met someone."

Her eyes perked up, and she smiled. "You did? That's fantastic. And you're sure he's not married?"

"I am."

"Do you know anyone who knows him? Sorry. I worry. I can't help myself. You said you just broke off an engagement. I don't want to see anyone take advantage of your fragile state."

Her concern was genuine, which made it impossible not to like Nadine. "It's all good. I know him."

"Oh my God. Imagine the coincidence of that. You come on a cruise by yourself and you meet a single man you know. It was meant to be."

Feeling a little uncomfortable with where the conversation was going, Alisha said, "I should get going. He's waiting for me."

Nadine scanned the area. "Is that him? Oh my, he's a hottie. Don't waste another moment with me. I wouldn't if he were waiting for me."

Alisha chuckled as her eyes met Brett's across the open pool area. "He is pretty amazing."

"Well, get back to him, then."

Alisha studied Nadine's expression. "It's not a sign."

Nadine smiled, even though her eyes still looked glassy from emotion. "I know. Thank you for stopping to talk to me. I feel better already."

Giving in to an impulse, Alisha leaned forward and hugged her.

Nadine returned the hug with force, then let go. "If I find a place, do you want an invite?"

Day one, Alisha would have said no, but a vow renewal focused on simply being grateful sounded like a celebration she didn't want to miss. She told Nadine her room number and said she would love to go.

As soon as Brett saw her walking toward him, he stood and met her halfway. "That looked like an emotional conversation."

Alisha linked arms with him. "It was. Funny how impressions of people can change when you learn more about them. I thought she was one of those brides who couldn't let go of their wedding day. Now, more than anything else, I wish there were a way to help her have her vow renewal."

They fell into step, continuing their walk around the ship. "Tell me about her."

Alisha told him how she'd met Ethan first. Then Nadine, her husband Josh, Brandi, and a group of their family. She laughed as she recounted her fear that they'd changed her dinner seat to be with them. Then she told Brett what Nadine had said. She was dabbing the tears from her eyes when she finished. "I understand her fear. She can't control the cancer, and it has the power to take her away from everything she loves."

Brett stopped and pulled Alisha into his arms. He tucked her beneath his chin and held her. Against her hair, he murmured, "Have I mentioned that I'm filthy rich?"

She raised her head and arched an eyebrow at him.

"Money can be its own burden, but there are perks to having a lot of it. Would you like to get that venue for her? Anonymously, of course."

"You would do that?"

"No. *We* would."

It was right then that Alisha knew that despite what she'd told herself and him, Brett already owned her heart. He was a very complex man, and she loved every new layer she uncovered. Loving him didn't mean he'd stay with her. Love couldn't stop whatever was meant to happen. Nadine might face cancer again, although Alisha prayed that if she did, it was only when her son was much, much older. She wasn't ready yet to articulate her feelings, and she didn't think he was ready to hear them, so she simply hugged him tighter. "Yes, Brett. Yes, please."

"Then let's go find that wedding coordinator."

Later that night, Brett told Alisha he needed to make a few phone calls before dinner. She went to her room to shower and change, and he took a moment to reflect on the day. He was both pleased with how quickly the coordinator had been able to find a perfect beach location for Nadine, and surprised at how right it felt. Alisha had the potential of being a true partner. He could imagine her talking him into and out of all sorts of escapades. He wouldn't be able to say no to her because her heart was in the right place. Her caring wasn't confined to what would also benefit her. Like him, the people she loved would always come first. *Even virtual strangers roused her unreserved thoughtfulness.*

He didn't want to be slotted into a friendship role when the cruise ended, because he didn't want their romance to end. Not when they got back. Not ever.

He was a man who trusted his instincts, and they were telling him that Alisha was the one, even though he'd ardently refused the notion that there would be a one. No other woman had stolen his heart the way she had. It was no longer a matter of figuring out how he felt, but what the hell to do now that he knew.

He called the person he knew would be most affected by it. Spencer answered in the impatient tone Brett had expected.

"What do you want, Brett?"

"How are you holding up?"

Spencer angrily expelled a breath. "You didn't call to see how I'm doing. You want to tell me something. What is it? Is Mom not my biological mother? If so, I have to say I'm not sure I give a shit. And before you tell me not to be angry, put yourself in my fucking shoes. I don't know who I can trust anymore. Did you know about Mark?"

"I didn't. I would have told you if I did. You had a right to know." Spencer's confusion was understandable. He'd been lied to for a long time. That was another reason Brett knew he needed to hear about Alisha from him. "We need to talk about Alisha."

"You like her. I know. You told me."

Brett gripped the phone tighter and plowed forward. "I love her, and I'm reasonably certain she loves me. She's afraid you'll be hurt by this. Rachelle is, too. I know you won't be, not if you remove this from everything else that's going on. Your engagement was fake. She agreed to it because she wanted to help you. Don't stand in the way of her having a chance at something real."

Spencer snorted. "Wouldn't you like that? Then you can sleep with her guilt-free."

"I'm serious about her."

The line was quiet while Spencer processed that. "What does that mean?"

"I don't know, but I want her by my side while I figure it out."

"And you want my blessing? You're not going to get it. I can't imagine a worse person for her. She's all about family and you're—"

Brett's temper rose, but he kept it under control. "Not as different as you think, but I don't expect you to see that yet. If you can't be happy for me, be happy for her. She has been a good friend to you. Be one to her."

Spencer didn't answer at first, then he said, "If you hurt her, I'll kill you."

Good enough. "Understood, but that won't be necessary. I'm a better man because she came into my life, hopefully a better brother as well. When we get back, I'll prove it to you."

"Where are you?"

"With Alisha." Brett walked to the glass door of his suite and looked out over the water. "You're my brother, and I've always been here for you. I may not have done it the way you would have liked, but I've always cared about you and always will."

"Did you tell Mom about Alisha yet?" Spencer asked.

"No, but that's my next phone call."

"Rachelle probably already told her the truth about us, but it's not like she has a right to judge anyone. Honestly, I can't stand to talk to any of them right now."

Brett sighed. He could tell Spencer what might have contributed to their mother's infidelity, but it was a topic for another time. "I understand your anger, but Mom loves you. You should call her."

"I have nothing left to say to her."

"She's hurting, too."

"If that's all, I have to go. I have a big meeting in the morning."

"With?"

"Good night, Brett. Tell Alisha I'm fine with this."

"I will."

Spencer hung up then, and Brett called his mother. After greeting each other and spending a moment pretending everything hadn't changed since the last time they'd spoken, Brett asked, "How are you, Mom?"

She sighed sadly. "I've been better. Spencer hates me."

"He doesn't. He's angry, and he has a right to be."

Her tone became thick with emotion. "I've made a lot of mistakes, but I never meant to hurt him. I thought it would be easier for him if Dereck was his father."

*For him? She's either lying to me or herself.* "Did Mark know?"

"No. He may have suspected. I almost told him in the end, but . . ." His mother made a sound like she was crying. "Have you ever done so much wrong that doing the right thing seems like it would make things worse?"

*Yes, but I didn't let it stop me.* "Spencer deserved to know his real father."

"He did. Mark loved him."

Brett could have argued how it wasn't the same, or enough, but he didn't. His mother needed to have that conversation with Spencer, not him. He could have asked about Nicolette and the truth about her paternity, but he had something else to discuss with her. "You were right. Spencer's engagement to Alisha wasn't real."

"Rachelle told me."

"Did she also mention that I'm with Alisha now and it's serious?"

Stephanie made a pained sound. "Something about the two of you being on a cruise together? I don't know what to say or what to think. I just hope you both know what you're doing. She's not like the women you normally date, Brett."

*Interesting.* "How would you know?"

"A mother pays attention. You like flashy women, people who fit into your world. Are you sure this is about Alisha and not some kind of competition with your brother?"

*If she thinks that, she doesn't know me as well as she thinks she does.* "I don't know how to play the piano. Rachelle, Spencer, and Nicolette do. I don't. Eric doesn't." Putting how he felt into words was difficult. In the past he wouldn't have attempted it, but it felt like a step he needed to take if he wanted to be with Alisha.

"I don't understand. Why are we talking about playing the piano?"

"Why was it important for the others to learn it?"

"My father loved to play. I loved to. I wanted my children—" Brett tensed as his mother seemed to come to a surprised stop at her own words. Her breathing became ragged. "I don't know what you want me to say. I was wrong about more than I can ever apologize for. I guess that makes me a horrible mother, but I tried. I did what I thought was best for all of you. You weren't neglected, Brett. Your father gave you everything."

There was nowhere good that conversation could go. According to Rachelle, their mother was already full of regret and hiding in her room. *Focus on what you can do something about.* "Alisha loves you. Whatever you think of us being together, don't let it change how good you are to her. She needs you. And from what I can see, we all need her just as much."

"You really do have feelings for her."

"I love her, Mom." *I love her.* The declaration was easier each time he made it. He'd gladly spend the rest of his life telling everyone he came across that Alisha Coventry was the woman for him. "And if she says yes, I'm going to marry her. If she says no, I'll ask again and again because I can't imagine my life without her in it."

"Be good to her, Brett. Treasure her every day."

"I will." His mother wept, and his heart ached for her. Most people didn't fall into categories of good or bad. Instead, they were a complex mix of both. He couldn't understand the choices she'd made, but he also hated to see her hurting. "It'll be okay, Mom. This will all work out, you'll see."

# Chapter Twenty-Three

There was a bittersweet feeling through the next couple of days. Alisha and Rachelle were speaking again—mostly about how things were back home, but also about Brett. It took Rachelle a little bit to warm to the idea, but once she did, she kept gushing about how good Alisha was for Brett.

To Alisha's utter shock, Stephanie called her and said she couldn't imagine a better daughter-in-law. Even Spencer chimed in with a text: Spoke to Brett. Know you're with him now. Want to hate you, but you're too damn nice of a person. He is lucky. Be happy, Alisha. You deserve it.

At first Alisha was surprised that Brett had called his family about them, especially because he didn't want their relationship to continue past the cruise. The more she thought about it, the more she was convinced he'd done it to smooth things over for her back home. She resented him a little for that.

He had no right to ask her question after question about her past as if he couldn't learn enough about her. He shouldn't make the sex between them so good that she could cry, then tuck her against his side as if she belonged there. The kiss he woke her with each morning made her sad.

*When it's not meant to last, it shouldn't be this good.*

She studied the way he ate, hoping to catch him doing something disgusting, but his manners were impeccable. Once or twice she tested his patience and argued with him just to see what he would do. He never lost his temper. He listened, debated, left her feeling like he valued her opinion even if he didn't agree with it.

*I know I said I'd be okay with us ending, but I lied.*

*I'm not okay at all.*

On Friday, she went back to her room to prepare for Nadine's Bahamian beach wedding. After planning the event with Alisha, Brett had used his connections on the ship to make sure the wedding would not only happen but also be perfect. To Nadine it would look as if everything were coming together last-minute, but in the background a machine was set in motion to ensure that it all went smoothly without the couple ever knowing anyone had helped them out.

Brett had done all that—*the selfish bastard.*

*How did it take me so long to realize that I love him?*

*How can he not see I'm in love with him?*

*I tell myself I don't need anyone. I'm a survivor.*

*But if he doesn't start acting like an asshole soon, I may not survive this one. This one may very well break me. He might break me.*

She slipped on the dress Brett had bought for her and smiled sadly at her reflection. *If you can't stay, Brett, I'm going to at least make it damn hard to forget me.*

A little while later, dressed in a tux, Brett sat beside Alisha in a white fold-up chair on a sunny beach. She was easily the best-looking woman on the beach. The last two days had been perfection, but he hadn't found the right time to tell her how he felt. The joy on her face as she watched the ceremony unfold before them made him want to profess his love right there and then.

"Isn't it beautiful?" Alisha asked.

Brett spared a brief look at Nadine, who smiled ear to ear as she stood beneath an arch of white orchids with her young son at her side and her husband across from her. "It is."

Alisha's hand was holding his, but her focus was on the ceremony happening before them. Then she glanced at him and his breath caught in his throat when she mouthed, "Thank you."

He brought her hand up to his lips. He leaned down and whispered in her ear. "No, thank you. I'm glad we did this. You've changed me, do you know that?"

"You're wrong. I didn't." Her eyes misted with tears. In a soft voice only he could hear, she said, "You were already an amazing man. All that good was already in you."

He didn't believe that for a second, but he loved that she did. She saw the good in everyone, and he was grateful she'd seen it in him, too. The idea of spending a lifetime at her side, keeping her safe, making her smile . . . simply loving her . . . suddenly felt not only doable but fated. He wasn't a man who believed in destiny, but she was meant to be his. Some part of him had known that since the very first day when she'd poked a finger into his chest and told him to treat Spencer better. "I love you."

Her gaze flew to his, and her jaw dropped open. "Did you . . . did you just say what I think you said?"

He kissed her sweet lips. "I did."

In the background, the minister said, "This couple represents marriage at its best. To hear their story is to be reminded of both the fragility of life and the strength of love. May we all come together many more times to celebrate another year of their commitment to each other and the beauty that love brings to our lives. Do you, Josh, vow again to spend the rest of your life loving this woman, in good times and in bad, in sickness and in health? Will you stand by her side, remove any spider that enters your home, cheer her when she's sad, and help her find her keys when she loses them?"

The crowd watching the ceremony laughed. "I do," Josh said.

*Me, too,* Brett thought. *I want all that.* To Alisha, he said softly, "I can't promise that things will be easy when we get home. My family is still a mess."

A funny expression entered her eyes. He cursed himself for bringing up the issues that waited for them back home. "I used to think of them as mine, but lately I've felt like an outsider."

He saw her pain and understood it too well. He knew exactly how it felt to love them, but not feel like one of them. He hugged her to his side and sought the words to comfort her. He thought about his grandfather, who had been a good husband, despite giving in to his weakness in the end. His mother had created a loving home and a refuge for Alisha, but had chosen a path that left half her children either behind or in the dark as to who they really were. He struggled with the complexity of family and what it meant to all of them. "They love you. Don't give up on them. Things will work out."

"I need to believe that." She laid her head on his shoulder. After a moment, she looked up at him in wonder. "You really love me?"

"I do." He smiled and added with gentle humor, "And you feel the same about me. The idea of a day without me nearly destroys you."

Her laughter rang out. The couple in front of them turned around and gave them a disapproving look. Alisha looked as unbothered by it as he was. Her smile was as bright as the sequins on the bride's gown. "You're right."

"Say it," he commanded softly.

"That you're right?" she asked innocently.

"You know what I want."

Her eyes danced with mischief and desire. "More of last night?"

*That, too.* It was the first time he'd ever had a boner at a wedding, but he had a feeling it wouldn't be the last, not with her in his life. "Say you love me," he growled into her ear.

The minister continued, "Do you, Nadine, vow again to spend the rest of your life loving this man, in good times and bad, in sickness and in health? Will you stand by his side, keep trying to master his mother's lasagna recipe, support his Monday night football addiction and forgive him, and keep letting him pretend he's in charge even though everyone knows he isn't?"

Alisha's eyes never left Brett's. "Trust is hard for me, but I trust you." She raised a hand to caress his cheek. "You're strong and gentle at the same time. You make me feel loved in a way I thought wasn't possible. I didn't think I needed anyone to protect me, but if you're applying for the job, I should tell you that I love you, too."

*Thank God.*

In the background, the minister said, "Then by the power vested in me by the Commonwealth of the Bahamas, I declare you happily married. You may kiss your wife."

Brett kissed Alisha, then murmured, "Marry me, Alisha."

He'd imagined her throwing her arms around his neck, but she hesitated. "Just like that?"

"Yes."

"I know they say they're okay with us being together, but what if . . ."

Although her concern for others was part of what he loved about her, she deserved happiness, too. They both did. He refused to be pushed into choosing her or his family. "You want a family? Be mine. Then, together, we'll make it right with them."

Tears spilled down her cheeks. "Together." She wiped at her tears, smiled, and whispered, "Yes." She threw her arms around his neck and kissed him soundly.

The crowd stood to watch Nadine, Josh, and Ethan walk down the aisle together. Brett broke off the kiss in time to see them stopping to speak to each row of guests. When the couple came to where Brett and Alisha were, Nadine winked at them. "You don't have to stay for the reception, but I'm glad you came."

Brett shook Josh's hand. "We were glad to hear it worked out for you."

Nadine looked at Alisha. "This place came out of nowhere, and the money came through from the other venue just in time. Like a sign."

"A really good one," Alisha said and hugged Brett.

Ethan said something, but Brett didn't hear him, so he bent closer to the boy. Ethan snatched Brett's sunglasses off his face and put them on. Nadine said, "Give those back, Ethan."

Ethan shook his head.

Brett held out his hand.

Ethan's face scrunched up. Brett kept his hand out while the boy refused.

Josh leaned down and talked to his son. "Give them back." Ethan refused. Josh looked at Brett apologetically. "Watch your hand, he bites sometimes."

But Brett leaned in closer to Ethan and in a firm voice said, "Men don't bite men, do they?"

With big round eyes, the little boy shook his head.

"I'll take the glasses now, Ethan. Thank you for holding them for me."

Ethan handed them back.

"I like your suit. You look like a big boy," Brett said in the tone of voice his father had often used with him.

Ethan smiled. "Big boy. Big boy." He jumped happily and ran off toward something else that had caught his attention.

The guests slowly followed Nadine and Josh toward the reception area. Brett hung back with Alisha.

She was watching him with a keen expression. "You're going to be a good father."

He pulled her into his arms. "God, I hope so. My father did his best, and look at us."

She framed his face with her hands. "Yes, look at you. Strong. Kind. Loyal. He didn't fail."

They kissed deeply.

When Brett raised his head, he said, "I found your father in Connecticut. You won't hear from him again."

Alisha's smile fell away, and she tensed in his arms. "What did you do?"

"I didn't have to do anything. He overdosed six months ago. I didn't know how to tell you, but I wasn't going to keep it from you. My father lost my mother because he closed her out. I won't ever do that to you." Brett waited, barely breathing. Would she hate him for being the bearer of bad news? Had he tarnished their moment? He didn't believe that secrets made things better. They certainly hadn't for his family. He had to believe that telling her was the right thing.

A series of emotions showed on her face. Fear. Sadness. "Thank you." Then relief.

"Part of me was always afraid he'd come back. Does that make me a bad person?"

"You? Bad? Never." He hugged her closer and kissed her forehead. "You're safe now. No one will ever hurt you again, not while I have a breath left in me."

Her smile returned. "I feel sorry for anyone who comes for you, because they'll have to deal with me."

The look in her eyes was one he'd seen the first time he met her when she'd been protecting Spencer. The memory didn't make him jealous; instead, it filled him with intense gratitude. Forever would never be enough time with a woman like her.

The sound of a man clearing his throat behind them was enough for them both to look up. The minister stood a few feet away from them with a smile on his face. Like two children caught doing something wrong, he and Alisha laughed and scooted away.

They were walking back to the ship when Alisha stopped. She frowned and swatted his chest with the back of her hand. "I was dying imagining us ending."

He could have apologized or said something sweet, but he knew another way to make her smile. "I completely understand. I'm quite a catch." He laughed and backed away as she swatted at him again.

They were both laughing when he picked her up and swung her around. "What am I going to do with you?" she asked.

He lowered her to her feet and wiggled his eyebrows. "Still not sure? I guess I'll have to show you again."

She blushed, but desire lit up her eyes. "I guess you will."

"Race you to the room." They ran toward the ship, laughing the whole way. People stopped and stared, but he didn't care. She'd said yes.

*Alisha Coventry said yes to marrying me. We are getting married.*

Forever was looking pretty fucking fantastic.

*Even better if it starts off naked.*

# Epilogue

Alessandro returned his teacup to its saucer with a clatter that turned the heads of several ladies in the upscale Back Bay tearoom. "It's just as I said, 'Love is always the answer.'"

"If so, I'm not certain we asked the right question." Delinda narrowed her eyes at the curious fellow patrons, and they hastily looked away. Her debutante years may have been long gone, but her place in the upper crust of Boston society remained solid.

Alessandro picked up a custard canapé and studied it before popping it into his mouth. He spoke louder than he should, laughed with the boisterousness of a man who'd had one too many drinks even when he'd not had a drop, and looked completely out of place. No one would think of mentioning it to him, though. Although he was a first-generation American, he'd made his name both in New York and Boston. When it came to refined Old World class, the Westerlys had never been surpassed. The Andrades had a more tumultuous relationship with wealth. It had come and gone over the generations with them, and fighting their way back to the top had given them an equally formidable reputation.

Delinda had always thought of herself as someone who could give the Queen of England a tip or two on etiquette. As she watched Alessandro chomping his way through his fifth finger sandwich, she wondered if he was truly as happy as he appeared. If so, what did that mean in terms of what she'd always been told was essential?

*Strip away my money and status, and who am I?*

She glanced around the room briefly, noting how she held the attention of the other women and how they still looked away out of respect. *This used to be important to me, but what does their opinion of me matter?*

*I would trade all of this if it eased Spencer's pain.*

"In trying to make things better, I made them worse, Alessandro. Yes, Brett is engaged, but at what cost? I doubt Spencer will ever forgive me for being the one who told him the truth about his father. I'll never forgive myself." She used her napkin to dab at the corners of her eyes. "Perhaps it's best if I rescind the marriage clause and simply give everyone their inheritance now. If I do so, Spencer might see that he may not be my blood relative, but he has always been my grandchild."

After wiping his mouth with his napkin, Alessandro shrugged and said, "Your heart is in the right place with this, but money won't help Spencer cope with what he's learned. It won't bring him back to you, or prove his place in your heart. Only you can do that."

"I tried. I don't know how to reach him."

"But you know someone who does. Someone who probably feels just as awful about the choices she made as you do."

"Stephanie?" Delinda scoffed. "Why would she ever help me?"

"Because no matter how different you two are, you have something very important in common: you both love her children. That's why I invited her to join us."

Delinda looked up as Stephanie approached their table. Alessandro stood and greeted her with a kiss. Delinda felt the eyes of everyone in the room watching for her reaction to her ex-daughter-in-law's arrival. Delinda had never hidden her dislike of Stephanie, but maybe, just maybe she'd been wrong to do so. Her son had once loved this woman. Her grandchildren still did. Even Alisha, who wasn't related to her, loved Stephanie.

Perhaps Alessandro was right. Perhaps she'd been the stumbling block all this time. What had he said? *If you want a rose garden, don't plant weeds.* Had she really been planting weeds? If so, that had to stop. *I don't want to die alone, and I do want my family to find happiness.*

Delinda rose to her feet and held out a hand in greeting. "So good of you to join us." It was only when she held Stephanie's hand in her own that she noticed the dark circles beneath her eyes.

"Although I appreciate your invitation, Delinda, I should warn you that I can't seem to hold it together this week. I already had a good cry this morning and intend to have another this afternoon. I know how you hate public displays of emotion . . ."

Delinda met Alessandro's eyes, and she felt the wall around her heart begin to crumble. *Pride or family?* She knew what Alessandro would choose. *It's time I follow his lead.* "I made quite a mess of everything, didn't I?"

Stephanie's hand trembled in hers. "I'm the one who left Dereck and kept the truth about Mark from my children. I'd say the mess is mine."

An answer came to Delinda with such clarity that she swayed on her feet. "We both made mistakes that hurt the ones we love. Perhaps together we can find a way to make amends."

Stephanie brought her other hand up to wipe a stray tear from her cheek. "Do you mean that?"

Alessandro bent and kissed Delinda's cheek. "I'll leave you two ladies to sort out the details, but remember—with love there is always a way."

Delinda retook her seat, smiled, and waved him off. "Go on, now. We'll be fine." She motioned for Stephanie to sit across from her. A waiter quickly cleared away Alessandro's dishware and replaced it with a new set.

Stephanie was nervously unfolding and folding the napkin on her plate. In the past, Delinda would have reprimanded her for it, but she held her tongue. *I feel as upset as she looks. Had my first nanny not been as quick to crack my knuckles with a ruler, I would be doing the same.* Years fell away, and Delinda remembered Stephanie looking just as nervous the first time Dereck had left the two of them alone. *How sad that we never progressed past that. I could have been kinder to her.* Delinda reached out and placed her hand gently on Stephanie's. "I know I wasn't the mother-in-law you'd hoped for."

"I'm sure I wasn't the daughter-in-law you'd imagined for Dereck."

"We were poorly matched, but it's time we move past that. My heart is breaking for Spencer. There has to be something we can do."

Stephanie covered her face briefly with her hands, then said, "If you've come to me for ideas, I'm all out. Rachelle and Nicolette look at me with disappointment I've never wanted to see in my children's eyes. And Spencer, he won't answer my calls anymore, and I don't blame him. I should have told him about Mark."

"I was sure you had. Why didn't you?"

Looking away, Stephanie scoffed, "You wouldn't believe me."

"You might be surprised at what I'm willing to believe lately."

Stephanie met her eyes. "I didn't want to take him from Dereck in that way, too. Dereck knew Spencer wasn't his. He knew it before Spencer was even born, but we gave our marriage another try. Nicolette was the result. I wasn't happy in the marriage, though. I felt more alone in it than I've ever felt out of it. That doesn't mean I didn't feel guilty. Leaving split our family in two. I didn't want to separate them further or hurt Dereck. I never wanted that."

Delinda had seen a similar sad expression in her son's eyes when she asked about Stephanie, and suddenly she understood. "And you never told Mark because you still love my son."

"Yes," Stephanie answered softly. "Mark was a good man who loved my children and me. He ate dinner with us each night. He was our cheerleader, our inspiration, and often our voice of reason. I never understood how he so easily took three children into his heart. He lavished them with love and support. *He deserved more from me,* and I hate that I couldn't love him the way he loved us." Stephanie's story would have been harder to accept if Delinda hadn't also loved a man so completely that nothing and no one could ever fill the void he left when he died. They had more in common than Delinda had ever realized.

"All any of us can do is follow our hearts. I tried to improve my relationship with my grandchildren by offering them their inheritance early. It didn't work out as I'd planned."

"I told them it was your love for them that prompted the offer, but I don't understand the stipulation that they marry."

Delinda sighed. "It worked for Alessandro's family. The lack of attendance at my eightieth birthday party was a wake-up call. Alessandro's daughter had a theory that falling in love healed old wounds. I was desperate. By the way, how are you and Brett?"

Stephanie raised a shoulder in resigned agreement. "Good, I think. Alisha makes Brett happier than I've ever seen him."

"And you and Brett are getting along now?"

"It's like we were given a second chance to get it right."

Delinda was typically cynical, and almost cautioned Stephanie, but held her first response back instead. Brett's words returned to her: *They're nicer than we are. They say supportive things to each other. Leave each other feeling good about themselves.* "I'm so glad to hear that."

*Love always finds a way.* Falling in love with Alisha had somehow helped Brett and his mother reconnect. Delinda questioned if she might be giving up too early on an idea that was beginning to show merit. "I like Alisha. She not only has spunk but heart as well. She's good for him."

"Yes. I couldn't agree more."

"Then let's help Spencer. You and I. If we worked together, I bet we could find the perfect woman for him. Someone strong, loyal, loving. Someone who would make him as happy as Brett is."

Stephanie chewed her bottom lip. "I don't know if that's a good idea."

"Do you have a better one?"

"No."

"Then we're in agreement. The only way to fix this is to find Spencer a wife. Now, who do you know?"

# About the Author

Ruth Cardello was born the youngest of eleven children in a small city in northern Rhode Island. She's lived in Boston, Paris, Orlando, New York, and Rhode Island again before moving to Massachusetts, where she now lives with her husband and three children. Before turning her attention to writing, Ruth was an educator for two decades, including eleven years as a kindergarten teacher. She is a *New York Times* bestselling author who loves writing about rich alpha men and the strong women who tame them. *In the Heir* is the first book in her Westerly Billionaire series. Learn about Ruth's new releases by signing up for her newsletter at www.RuthCardello.com.